GHOST MOUNTAIN

AJ BAILEY ADVENTURE SERIES - BOOK 4

NICHOLAS HARVEY

DEDICATION

*This book is dedicated to my Mum, Jan Harvey.
Her love and caring have been unwavering, her spirit for adventure
infectious, and her bravery since August 1ˢᵗ, 2019 inspirational.*

1

SUNDAY

Carlina Arias slowly became aware she was dreaming. Well, more likely a nightmare, she figured, as her hazy mind fought to focus. The last clear memory she had was of that son-of-a-bitch Raposa apologising, after he had forced her onto the small boat. Then the lights went out. Now she felt someone pulling on her ankle and her lungs were starved for air. Water surrounded her, cloaking her naked body. That bastard took her clothes off? With a rush of panic her mind cleared further and she realised the nightmare was for real, and she couldn't breathe. The world surrounding her was dark and blurry. Her hands shot out and clawed at the warm, salty water. She looked up and could see a dim light above her, though her eyes stung and wouldn't focus. Who was pulling on her ankle? She swung an arm down and found a rope where she expected a person to be. The pressure on her lungs was overwhelming – she desperately needed air.

Thoughts bounced through her mind like antelope leaping across the plains. Nothing would stay in consciousness. It felt like her brain was reading notes fluttering down around her. How had she ended up here? She'd put in her time and had been heading to the airport, cashier's cheque and plane ticket in hand. She had done everything they'd asked. Her English was damn near perfect, she was popular with all the guests, she'd never breached their stupid rules. Not even a single call home to the Dominican Republic. Some of the other girls sneaked a call in once in a while to someone back home, secretly using a guest's mobile phone, but she never did. Of course, 'back home', what a joke. She had no one there to call anyway.

Her fingers grabbed the rope tied around her slender ankle and violently wrenched the knot, to no avail. Pointing her toes, she pushed on the rope looped around her leg but it was held fast by her heel. Reaching down with her other hand she forced the loop as hard as she could. The fibres of the tether scratched and dug into her flesh, but she kept shoving and bravely resisted the urge to scream. The pain of skin being dragged from her heel, and instep, was excruciating, but she had to free herself from whatever the rope was attached to, pulling her towards the sea floor. Carlina gritted her teeth against the agony, and pushed with all her might. Lubricated by the blood escaping from the wounds, the rope finally gave and slipped away, freeing her.

The surge of elation soon gave way to another wave of panic as she kicked towards the light. It seemed dimmer and much farther away than a few moments ago. Now, the primordial need for air consumed her. Could this be it? The notion floated by like the other thoughts invading and leaving her. Not quite eighteen years. Was that all she'd get? It felt so unfair. Her birthday was only a few weeks away. She was just about to start a life that was worth living, and here she was, drowning before it could start. Eighteen years filled with poverty, abuse and servitude. She'd given the last year in trade for a future with hope, promise and freedom from men and women who saw her as nothing more than a sexual object. From the first time her father had laid his disgusting hands on her when she was barely thirteen, to her final guest last night. All they wanted was her body. Well damn it, they'd taken everything a woman's body had to give, and now it was her time to live, on her terms, not theirs.

Carlina kicked and reached and pulled at the water with every-thing she had. The pressure felt like clamps around her lungs, burning and searing. Despite her swimming towards the surface, the darkness was closing in. The dream began to consume her as her mind lost its meagre grip on the conscious world. She struck out with each limb, and each motion stole a little more oxygen from her body. She had to make the surface, she had to live. To have the life she had sacrificed and given herself for, all she'd been through, both at home and here on the island. Another note wafted by but this one stopped and stung her heart. How could Cristal let this happen? She had been the mother Carlina had never known. The woman had nurtured her, patiently taught and instructed her. She'd been firm, but always fair, and even held her when things seemed too much. The only person Carlina had ever known to hold her with no other intention than to comfort and love. Oh how she yearned for those arms around her now. To bury her face in the woman's neck and hide from everything foul and evil the world had shown her. Hide from the darkness consuming her now. How could Cristal let this happen?

Carlina's arms could reach no more. Her legs had lost all strength to kick. The urge to open her throat against the throttling constriction was all consuming. The world closed around her like an opaque blanket and against her will her lungs finally gasped for air, and found only water. The fingers of her right hand were tickled by the cool breeze brushing over the waves but Carlina never knew it. The young girl's body reached the surface, but her soul would never see eighteen.

2

MONDAY

Annabelle Jayne Bailey's thirty-six-foot Newton dive boat gently rolled and pitched in the Caribbean Sea as she, and her local Caymanian employee Thomas Bodden, helped the last diver back on the boat. The group of eight were together on a diving trip to Grand Cayman, and had chartered AJ's Mermaid Divers boat for the week. Jack Benson ran a dive shop in North Carolina, and each year he offered the trip to his customers, staying at a rented condo on the famed Seven Mile Beach, and diving every day with Mermaid Divers. Jack, a likable man in his fifties with thinning hair and a soft, southern American accent, had become a good friend to AJ over the years, and always brought an amiable and competent group of divers with him.

"So, how did you like Ghost Mountain?" AJ asked in her region-less English accent, as she and Thomas finished stowing the divers' gear, and pulled the ladder at the stern of the boat.

She was answered with enthusiastic comments from all, which always made her smile.

"That was a real treat. Thank you for getting us on that site," Jack added. "I know it's a bit out of the way, but boy, it was a treat."

AJ climbed the steep steps to the fly-bridge, and shouted back down to the deck, "Happy to do it. We were lucky with the current being light. Usually it's too strong off the point here."

She fired up the diesel motor and Thomas released the line tying them into the mooring buoy on the dive site. After letting the engine idle for a few moments, she swung the wheel hard to port, and eased the throttle forward. Making a half circle she pointed the boat east, running parallel to the shallow reef that framed the outside of the North Sound. She felt the intensity of the early spring, mid-morning sun, and grabbed her long-sleeved tee-shirt from the dash, slipping it on over her swimsuit. She spent her days on the ocean, so she did her best to protect her skin, and her full-sleeve tattoos, from the UV rays.

AJ enjoyed this week each year. Jack surrounded himself with people he enjoyed being around which made for a fun group that loved diving, and their time on the island. This year he had two other couples along with his wife and two single guys. All were experienced divers, but most were all too familiar with the quarry back home they regularly dived and trained in. For them, the warm, gin-clear waters of Grand Cayman were a slice of heaven. She slipped a baseball cap on to keep her shoulder-length, purple-streaked, blonde hair from blowing in her face, and turned it backwards so the wind wouldn't catch the bill. She kept the motor at just above idle – they were in no hurry to get to their second dive site. The first dive had been deep and they would spend at least forty-five minutes letting their bodies dissipate the excess nitrogen they had absorbed, a by-product of breathing compressed air at depth.

Jack and his wife, Sherry, joined AJ on the fly-bridge, leaning against the sturdy frame supporting the hard-top shading them from the sun.

"You mentioned the currents are usually strong at Ghost Mountain?" Jack asked in his slow, easy manner.

"That, and vis can be poor there," AJ replied. "Wave action from the west and the north converge at the corner which makes it tricky. It's also a gathering point for the Green Monster." AJ grinned at them both.

"Green Monster?" Sherry asked, looking concerned.

AJ laughed. "Yeah, that's the name we call the mangrove waters that drain out of the North Sound when the tides drop. They're nutrient rich but full of particulates and run-off from the mangroves and they're pulled out into the sea before being carried by the currents to the open water. With the waves and currents heading to the point they often cause poor vis over there."

"Guess we were lucky then, vis was easily more than a hundred feet today," Sherry said, clearly relieved there were no real monsters involved.

"Any requests for the second dive?" AJ asked.

Jack smiled. "Anywhere wet and full of fish," he replied. "You never disappoint us, wherever you think we'd like."

AJ thought for a moment and eyed the waters ahead to see which dive buoys were open, as the other dive operations moved their boats between dives.

"I was thinking Princess Penny's if no one else is on it. I don't think we dived Penny's when you were here last year, did we?"

"It's been a few years I believe," Sherry replied. "I remember liking that dive a lot though."

AJ nodded. "Alright, let's head that way and see."

Thomas glanced over his shoulder from the bow where he'd remained after freeing them from the mooring. AJ caught his eye and shouted down. "Penny's sound good?"

Thomas beamed back with his infectious smile and gave them the okay sign. Turning back to the water ahead he continued carefully scanning the surface in their path.

"What's he looking for?" Sherry asked.

"Sea turtles," Jack answered. "Right?"

"Yup," AJ confirmed. "It's easy to forget they breathe air; they have to come up and grab a gulp every once in a while. Biggest hazard to turtles used to be man taking them for meat and their shells; now they're protected from hunters, their foe is still man, but now it's boat strikes that kill them. They're hard to see as they bob on the surface, especially between swells, so when we can we watch for them."

"Thomas has been with you a while now, hasn't he?" Jack asked warmly.

AJ grinned. "Three years. He was my first, and still my only, full-time employee. I can't imagine being without him; he's as much a part of Mermaid Divers as I am."

"Are any more locals getting involved in diving? I know you've said before he's a rarity – not many islanders work in the dive industry," Sherry asked, looking at the lanky, brown-skinned young man.

"There's a few. Suzy Soto started a scholarship program to train young Caymanians in diving to encourage them to pursue the career. Many of the dive operations have contributed."

AJ thought for a moment before continuing. "It's funny, when Suzy's husband, Bob, started the first dive operation on Cayman, it was all locals involved. When the industry grew, the locals seemed to lose interest, and ex-pats took over. But they've historically made their living from the seas, fishing, catching turtles and freediving for conch – it's in their nature to be on the water, but for some reason scuba diving hasn't captured their interest. I think the local involvement with Soto had more to do with Bob than it did with diving. He was a charismatic and adventurous guy who people enjoyed being around."

Their attention quickly turned back to Thomas at the bow who waved a hand frantically in the air then pointed to the water ahead, slightly to starboard. AJ eased the throttle back to idle and turned to port. She stood up from the pilot seat and tried to spot the turtle. Thomas lowered his hand and stared at the spot he'd been pointing at. He turned to look up at AJ; all trace of his smile was gone.

"That ain't a turtle, boss," he shouted, his voice shaking. "You better call the marine police."

AJ stared at the water as they coasted closer. "Oh no..."

The naked body, of what appeared to be a light brown-skinned female, floated face down in the clear blue water above the reef.

3

MONDAY

Cristal Sombrio sat at her desk overlooking Salt Creek at the north end of Seven Mile Corridor, the narrow stretch of island sandwiched between Seven Mile Beach and the North Sound. Her office was furnished with a modern, minimalist flavour, carefully devoid of any personal touches, indications or mementos. The neutral blue-grey paint was offset by the floor-to-ceiling windows revealing the small, man-made bay and mangroves beyond, which allowed bright sunshine to reflect off the water and bathe the room. She idly swung back and forth in her black Arper designer chair, deep in thought. She absentmindedly drummed her fingers on the glass desk, skipping a beat where the missing pinkie of her left hand would have tapped. For years after the Brazilian cartel had removed the digit with a knife, she would sense the absence with every void in the rhythm or shortened grip. But after twelve years, the scar had become a strength, another weapon in her arsenal along with her stunning good looks and her bold, fearless presence.

She rose from her chair and wandered to the window, glancing at the two-storey villas to each side of the central building her office sat atop. Three villas either side mirrored each other, all facing the water at an angle to maximise the view, and their privacy. Carefully placed screening walls and windows only to the creek meant the deck and interior of each unit couldn't be seen from anywhere except the mangroves across the bay. The birds and iguanas were the only creatures that could spy on the small, exclusive resort known as the International Fellowship of Lions.

Cristal lit a cigarette and surveyed the waterfront. A concrete sea wall ran the length of the property with a small 20' centre console the only boat tied up. Further down, four jet-skis rested on floating docks, tethered to the sea wall. A knock came from her door and she told the person to enter in Portuguese without turning around. An athletically built man in his thirties entered the office, carefully closed the door, and took a few paces into the room. Raposa had a confident manner, his head high, firm shoulders pulled back giving an appearance taller than his 5' 9" frame.

"Any problems last night?" Cristal asked without turning, her voice sharp.

"None. She has left the island," he replied in a relaxed tone.

"We need to think about recruitment again," she said, finally turning and exhaling a stream of cigarette smoke. "Three more will be leaving the island over the next few weeks, six in total in the months to come. We should line up replacements." She stubbed her cigarette out in an ashtray on her desk and returned to her seat.

"I'll reach out to my contacts and see what they have available. Any preferences?" Raposa asked with a grin.

Cristal clicked a few keys on her laptop and a series of pictures appeared with notes below them. Each photo was of a pretty, young girl, all looking happy and posed in nice clothing and expertly applied make-up.

"Focus on darker toned, we need a better range. We have Hispanic, so stay away from Dominican and Venezuelan. We could use one more white girl too, but that's lower priority, and no Russians. They're too cold and aggressive." She spoke in an even voice as though ordering take-out for lunch. "Get three black girls – I need two, we can choose the best from the three."

Raposa nodded, "I'll work on it. If I leave on Cova do Leão in a week or so I can return within ten days at the outside. Peter is bringing her in this afternoon for supplies. I'll talk to him and have him start preparing the boat. The two girls on board will be ready to come ashore then anyway, so the timing is good."

Cristal stared at her screen and replied, "Okay."

Raposa knew her well enough to recognise his signal to leave, and eased quietly out the door.

She scrolled through the pictures and added a note or two. She paused on a photo of a gorgeous girl with a broad smile and blue eyes that shone brightly. Beneath the picture was her name: Carlina Arias. Cristal typed below her name in red letters, 'Contract expired, March 2020'.

She leaned back and lit another cigarette, slowly exhaling a long stream of smoke. Cristal felt a vague, distant pang of sympathy for the girl. Or perhaps it was just irritation that she now needed to find a replacement to satisfy guests at the resort. Irritated sat better in her mind, retaining her steely resolve. Cristal had always been an even-tempered woman, a trait passed down and reinforced by her father. Marco Sombrio had been a cell boss for the Comando Vermelho, Rio's major cartel, until he was gunned down outside a restaurant by the rival Terceiro Comando gang. Three gunmen on the back of motorcycles tore the man's body to shreds with automatic weapon fire. Several other innocent diners were caught in the barrage, as the windows shattered and bodies fell. Cristal's mother and younger brother had been one step ahead of Marco. Many of the bullets that killed the man passed through his wife and son before hitting him. Cristal had stepped back inside to retrieve her forgotten coat. Unscathed, she rushed outside to stand and stare at her family in a river of their own blood, flowing across the pavement. On that day, fifteen years ago, at age twenty-five, her life was forever changed. No hysterics, no tears, she absorbed every detail of the massacre. Every shred of torn flesh, every gaping wound and disfigurement cemented her hatred for the men who took her family from her. It also instilled a numbness for the value of a life. So many lives came and went each day on the streets of Rio de

Janeiro. One day she had a happy, wealthy family and the next she was alone. Cristal headed the hunt for the killers, supported by Comando Vermelho. Each gunman was found. None died quickly. Two of them were made to watch their wives die in front of them. The single man endured his parents' death before his own lengthy demise began.

Given leadership of her father's cell she soon expanded business and increased revenue for the cartel. No one dared cross her. Her legend soon outgrew truth and she became unstoppable, pushing the Terceiro Comando completely from her section of the city. Even Cristal began to believe her own myth, as the years went by. She felt bigger than the cartel itself and tired of handing them the largest portion of the profits from drug sales, prostitution and gambling. Brought back to earth with the wrath of the other bosses, and the loss of her little finger, she took her small fortune and left Brazil, more determined than ever.

With a fleeting glance at Carlina's picture, she closed her laptop and stubbed out her cigarette.

4

———

MONDAY

AJ impatiently waited for an answer on her mobile phone. They'd pulled alongside the body and Thomas had gingerly felt for a pulse. Finding none, and feeling the body was stone cold, they'd left her in the water, knowing revival attempts were futile. Thomas gently tipped her head to see her face, relieved he didn't recognise her. They had left the poor girl floating, to avoid contaminating any evidence, and called the marine police on the VHF radio.

The ringing finally ceased on AJ's mobile and a man's voice answered in a Caymanian accent.

"This can't be good. You never call to wish me a happy birthday or merry Christmas. How can I help you today, AJ?"

"I'm sorry Detective Whittaker, happy birthday whenever your birthday is," she replied tentatively. "But yes, I'm afraid it's bad news. I already called the marine police but I thought you'd want to know too. We've come across a body floating off the north wall."

After a short pause the detective responded, his voice switching to a sterner tone. "I see. I assume you're sure there's no sign of life?"

"I'm afraid not, I'd say she's been in the water a little while, body's cold. We haven't moved her except to check for a pulse. Wanted to ask you before we did anything else," AJ explained.

"Good, okay, I'll round up my SOCO and head out there. Is the marine unit there yet?" Whittaker asked.

AJ looked towards the cut in the North Sound reef. "Clearing the cut now, about three or four minutes away."

"I'll be there in twenty." Whittaker finished and hung up.

AJ took a deep breath. Seeing the body brought back a flood of memories from the year before, when a woman she'd become close to was murdered on AJ's other boat. It had been over four months since the incident and she was finally reconciling the loss in her mind.

"What should we do with everyone?" Thomas whispered, nodding towards their group of divers patiently waiting under the cover of the fly-bridge, out of the way.

"Yeah..." AJ mumbled, snapping back to the moment. "Let me call Reg and see if he can spare a divemaster or someone to stay on the boat and you can take them for the next dive. I'll stay with the police until Whittaker clears me."

She quickly dialled Reg Moore, her mentor and fellow dive operator who she shared a dock in West Bay with. His gruff London voice quickly answered.

"Morning girl, what's up?"

AJ spoke quietly into her mobile, "Bloody hell Reg, you'll never believe this, we found a girl's body floating out here on the north."

"Really? Think it's from a refugee boat?" Reg asked. The islands had seen occasional boats with fleeing Cubans passing by their waters and their craft were always meagre and poorly equipped for the open seas.

"Looks like a girl or a young woman. She's dark skinned and, Reg, she's naked. I dread to think what happened to her." AJ's voice wavered as the thoughts and memories raced through her mind.

The powerful Joint Marine Unit police boat's motors burbled

and rumbled as they carefully pulled alongside and Thomas helped them tie to the Newton.

"Marine unit's here, I'd better go. Do you have anyone out north who could help Thomas if I send him off with my group, Reg? I need to stay here with the police."

"Where's he heading?" Reg asked.

"We were going to Princess Penny's," AJ replied as two policemen stepped aboard her boat.

"Alright, tell him to head there and I'll get someone over to help him."

AJ quickly thanked Reg and hung up, extending a hand to the first policeman.

"Hi, I'm AJ, we haven't touched the body except to check for vitals, and Detective Whittaker said he's on his way."

The policeman, a tall, square-shouldered local, smiled at AJ.

"We've met, but I don't expect you to remember. You'd just swum out of a sinking ship at the time."

Another moment she'd like to forget, she thought, "Oh, okay, well, this time we just stumbled across this unfortunate person."

They both looked at the body bobbing gently in the calm ocean. With the engines shut down the only sound was the water slapping against the hulls and the creaking of the bumpers sandwiched between the two craft. If it wasn't for the tragedy of someone's death, the moment was tranquil and serene. They stared in silence and AJ's demons began creeping back in. Visions of Hazel's body and her own hands covered in her friend's blood refused to stay away, despite her best efforts to think of pleasant times. It felt like her mind was a separate entity in constant battle with her brain, playing tug-of-war with her thoughts and emotions.

The VHF radio on the police boat crackled before a voice reported that Detective Whittaker was en route with an ETA of fifteen minutes.

Relieved by the break in silence, AJ asked, "If I stay with you officer, can Thomas here take our group on their way? I can give

Whittaker all the information from our end and Thomas will be available later if he's needed."

The policeman looked at his compatriot, who shrugged his shoulders. He looked down at AJ, who was almost a foot shorter. "Sure, that should be okay."

AJ and the two policemen moved over to the police boat, helped Thomas release the ties and pulled the bumpers. Thomas climbed the ladder to the fly-bridge, started the diesel motor and put the boat in drive.

AJ shouted up to him, "Reg is sending someone to meet you at Penny's. I'll figure out how to meet you after we're done here."

Thomas gave her an okay sign and the stunned group of divers watched the police boat shrink in the distance as they pulled away.

"Are you okay miss?" the first policeman asked.

AJ looked up at him. "Not really," she answered honestly. "I wouldn't choose to be here looking at this poor woman, about the same as I'd guess she didn't choose to be floating naked and dead in front of me." She instantly felt bad – the man was just being nice. "That came out a little harsh, I'm sorry."

He smiled and shook his head. "That's okay. Fortunately, we don't have to deal with dead bodies too often on the island, but I dare say we see more than you do. It's still a shock."

"Thank goodness for you guys, I couldn't do your job. I'm not cut out for everything you have to deal with," AJ said quietly, unable to take her eyes off the body.

The sound of an engine running hard reached them and they both looked to the horizon and could see another marine police boat approaching from the cut. The pilot eased the throttles back a few hundred yards out and dropped the boat out of plane to coast towards them, lessening the wake following them in. They didn't tie alongside but instead carefully manoeuvred close to the body, rotating the craft around until their narrow swim step allowed them to reach the girl.

Detective Whittaker, a slim man in his fifties dressed in slacks and a white button-down shirt, waved to AJ.

"Morning, Miss Bailey."

"Hey, Detective Whittaker. Sorry we keep meeting like this," AJ greeted him sympathetically.

He scratched his head and nodded. "Does seem unfortunate. Might as well call me Roy as we do spend some time together it seems."

AJ managed a smile as the boat she was on carefully pulled alongside and was tied to the second patrol boat. Whittaker met her at the railing and shook her hand across the gap between the two craft.

"This is our scene-of-crime officer, Rasha; she'll take some pictures and help remove the body."

Rasha, a woman in her mid-thirties, waved back at AJ, who nodded a greeting.

"Morning," Rasha said in an English accent as she began taking photographs of the body in the water.

Maybe it was television and movies, but she expected the SOCO woman to be super intense and nerdy. She was surprisingly normal-looking. AJ couldn't help but watch as Rasha knelt on the swim step and examined the corpse. After a minute and what seemed like a hundred photographs, Rasha carefully rolled the body over in the water. It indeed appeared to be a girl, no more than eighteen at AJ's best guess, maybe younger. Her light brown skin had a strange greyish hue. When AJ looked at the poor girl's face she quickly turned away. The fish had begun their job of breaking down the body, starting with the eyes and the lips.

"Where did you first spot the body, Miss Bailey?" Whittaker asked, deliberately drawing AJ's attention away from the corpse.

"She hasn't floated far from where we first saw her," AJ replied, looking around at references on the shoreline. "Thomas was watching for turtle as we moved from Ghost Mountain towards Princess Penny's. He spotted her."

The detective scratched a few words in a notepad he produced from his pocket. "Did you move the body at all, turn it over, anything like that?"

AJ shook her head. "No, as I said, Thomas checked her for vitals and he said she was cool to the touch, colder than she should be at least. We found her face down. Left her alone and called you." She shielded her eyes from the piercing sun getting high in the sky as the morning rolled on. "Anyone reported missing lately?"

Whittaker flipped his notepad closed. "Not that I recall, no."

"Refugee perhaps?"

The detective scratched his head as he turned and watched Rasha wrestling into a wetsuit. She'd set her slacks and shirt aside, wearing a one-piece swimsuit underneath. She smoothly dropped into the water and the policeman who'd piloted the boat handed her a large mesh body bag. Whittaker studied the dead girl a moment before turning back to face AJ on the other boat.

"Maybe, certainly looks mixed race, black and Hispanic, could be Cuban. Doubt it though."

Rasha looked up from slipping the bag under the girl's body, "Agree. Nails are too nice."

Whittaker turned back to Rasha. "And no tan-lines. This girl has maintained a careful and well-groomed appearance, too careful for a refugee."

AJ looked out across the vast ocean to the north, and then back towards the island. She wondered where on earth this girl could have come from to end up floating out here.

"There's signs of foam around her mouth and nostrils, Roy; likely she drowned," Rasha said, her gloved hand holding the girl's jaw.

"Maybe she fell off a boat," Whittaker said, not very convincingly.

Rasha looked up. "I'd say she came off a boat, but she may have had help."

Whittaker looked at her quizzically. "Oh?"

"Got a pretty good welt on the back of her head," Rasha commented as she began zipping the closure on the body bag.

"Could that be from a fall? Banged her head on the way in?" Whittaker wondered aloud.

"Could be," Rasha agreed, "but this girl had something tied around her ankle." She pointed to the raw wound around the girl's heel and ankle. "I think you'd better order up a forensic pathologist."

"Oh," Whittaker mumbled to himself. "It appears I should."

5

——————

MONDAY

Raposa stood on the dock in front of the resort and watched the 80′ Hatteras motor yacht ease in stern first, coming to a stop against the bumpers hung over the side. With a whirring sound and stirring of water towards the bow, the pilot expertly used the bow thruster to nestle the big boat neatly against the dock. Across the stern the Portuguese words 'Cova do Leão' could be seen, and below it in smaller letters, 'Bahamas' identified the boat's country of registration. Raposa tied the Hatteras to the dock cleats, securing the bow line first, before repeating the exercise at the stern. He stepped aboard as the pilot shut down the big twin diesels. Swiftly climbing the stairs to the enclosed fly-bridge he opened the rear door and greeted the captain, speaking in English.

"Peter, welcome back ashore."

Captain Peter Van Heerden was a weathered-looking man in his fifties with an imposing, broad-shouldered physique. His salt and pepper beard was full, but trimmed perfectly and his uniform neatly pressed. He touched the brim of his cap in greeting and spoke with a South African accent in a low booming voice.

"Mr. Raposa, good evening. Shouldn't need to be here long, supply run and we'll be off again. Anything new I need to know?"

The man asked, while shutting down the extensive electronics on the boat's helm.

Raposa sat on the couch behind the twin pilot chairs. "She'd like us to take a recruiting run. Soon. I'm waiting to hear back from a couple of my contacts, but I suspect we'll hit Jamaica, so won't be gone long."

Van Heerden nodded, "I'll start looking at weather and preparing the boat. How soon would you guess?"

Raposa leaned back and looked at the ceiling, thinking a moment. "I'd say within the week. If they have at least two candidates we'll leave. How are the two aboard? Any trouble?"

Van Heerden glanced at the Brazilian. "They're about ready I'd say, or as ready as we can get them. One has struggled with her manners – she's a street kid, never sat in a real restaurant in her life." He raised an eyebrow. "But she's a keen one in other ways, believe me, she'll be popular even if she doesn't know a soup ladle from a teaspoon."

Raposa laughed. "I'll look forward to seeing what you mean in her final review."

Van Heerden came close to smiling, a rarity for the stern man, then quickly returned to business. "We'll need to plan ahead for the engine service I mentioned to you. Needs to be done in Miami; there's no one here on the island with the expertise for the big cats. Besides the service, one of the generators needs attention and the desalination system has been playing up."

"No problem," Raposa said, waving a hand as though it was nothing, "but it will need to be when no girls are aboard. Too risky to take any of these young ladies to the States."

"Agreed." Van Heerden replied, finishing up at the helm. "After the training for the next group then?"

Raposa shrugged his shoulders. "That should be fine. Let's say five weeks from now."

Van Heerden walked towards the rear door that led to the exterior steps down to the main level. "I'll make the arrangements." He opened the door and held it for Raposa, who rose from the couch, and the two men left the fly-bridge, Van Heerden locking the door behind him.

The salon resembled more of a luxury hotel room than anything you'd imagine on a boat. Immediately on the right, three stools sat in front of an exotic wood, curved bar, opposite a long couch on the left. Ahead, a polished teak dining table was surrounded by six upholstered chairs and polished wood cabinetry lined the walls forward of the long side windows. Sitting on the couch were two young women both wearing colourful summer dresses and looking expectantly towards the two men.

"Good evening, ladies," Raposa said, smiling.

"Good evening, sir," both girls said in unison.

Abigay was barely seventeen. A Haitian girl with a curvy figure and deep bronze skin that shone in the low evening sunlight pouring through the starboard windows, she diverted her eyes to the carpet. Raposa walked over and gently lifted her chin with his hand.

"Eye contact, my dear. Regardless how nervous you may feel, maintain eye contact. Gives you strength, shows confidence, even when you may not feel that way." He smiled and the young woman looked up, managing to return the smile and keep her eyes on his.

Zoe had no such fear and ran a hand suggestively up Raposa's thigh. She was lighter toned, slender with sharper facial features, belying her mixed racial heritage. Raised on the Lesser Antilles island of Martinique, her father was a visiting Belgian tourist and her mother a local maid in the hotel where the man had stayed. Her mother had no way to find the father of her child without enquiring of the hotel management and losing her job in the process, so she raised Zoe alone and the boisterous girl soon became a handful. At fourteen Zoe ran away, island-hopping on any boat she could negotiate transport aboard until she was arrested in the Bahamas for stealing from a market stand. Raposa's contact bailed her out in exchange for joining Raposa on the yacht bound for the Cayman Islands. Now, at not quite sixteen years old, she was eager to please her boss and enjoy the spoils offered, regardless of the cost.

Raposa took the girl's hand from his thigh. "Remember Zoe, allow the client to choose his preference; they must always be made comfortable, never pressured."

Zoe grinned, "They'll always choose me," she said in her French accent, "don't you think?"

Van Heerden shook his head. "Told you."

Raposa laughed. "Many will," he said and turned back to Abigay who seemed to shrink in the presence of the bolder girl, despite being the older of the two. "And some will prefer the shy girl."

Abigay smiled, her soft features looking even younger.

"Joining us for dinner, Mr. Raposa?" A female voice came from the front of the salon where an opening led to the galley. Raposa turned and nodded to a uniformed white woman in her forties with hair pulled back in a tidy ponytail.

"Hello Marguerite." He glanced at his watch. "Why not, I'll rarely pass up one of your fantastic meals."

The woman bowed her head. "We'll set the table for six then." She looked up and beckoned the two girls. "Come on ladies, let's show Mr. Raposa how well you're doing."

The men watched the two pretty young women walk across the salon in their skimpy summer dresses and bare feet. Raposa took a deep breath and looked around at the splendour of the boat's interior. Long way from the streets of Rio, he thought, a very long way.

6

MONDAY

AJ finished rolling up the water hose and stowed it in the storage bin at the front of their dock in the Yacht Club marina. The sun was nearing the horizon in the west and the rich orange and yellow tones bathed the boats, casting long shadows over the water. She looked around the deck of the Newton to see if she'd forgotten anything in preparation for the next day's trip. Satisfied all was ready, she stepped over the gunwale and walked across the rear deck to retrieve her rucksack. She looked up and saw Thomas returning from taking gear to the van. He paused at the storage bin and curled up the air tank fill line, dropping it in the bin. The marina had a compressor with lines running to the top of each slip for the dive boats to refill their scuba tanks each day. Following Thomas was Reg, a soft cooler bag slung over his shoulder. They both stepped down to the boat and Reg paused to look AJ over, his eyes soft and sympathetic in contrast to his rough, seafaring face and mop of greying hair.

"So, how was the rest of your day? Hope it improved," he said, setting the cooler down and pulling out three Strongbow cider bottles.

AJ rolled her eyes, "Well, we didn't find any more dead bodies, so I guess it was good."

They all sat on the cushioned benches under the shade of the fly-bridge and passed around the bottle opener. Reg stroked his scraggly beard and muttered, "Not something you really get used to, seeing things like that. Shouldn't get used to it anyway. Sorry you both had to deal with that."

"Could have been worse, right?" Thomas said quietly, looking at the other two. "That poor girl had a much worse time of it than we did."

They all nodded sullenly. AJ felt sad for the girl, sad for the two of them having to be that close to death, again. But seeing Thomas so deeply affected really hit home. Her employee and friend was always so happy and vibrantly full of life it was shocking to see him so glum. He was serious when he needed to be but his broad smile and carefree laugh was never too far away; but not today. She worried how badly he seemed to be taking this.

"Thomas dealt with it more than me: he spotted her and was down on the deck when we got to the body," she said, directed to Reg, but hoping she could draw Thomas into talking about it. "I just had to stick around and talk to Whittaker a while."

She really wasn't sure exactly what aspect of the tragedy had impacted Thomas so strongly, but maybe she could help him if she understood it better.

"That couldn't have been easy, Thomas?" Reg added, seeming to sense where AJ had been leading. "The sea isn't kind to a body."

Thomas rubbed his forehead a moment but finally spoke. "Wasn't too bad, she'd been on top so the crabs hadn't taken their turn yet. Little fish had got to her some. Not too bad, but I'm not really the squeamish type anyway."

They all took a few sips of cider and AJ thought about how else to approach the problem when Thomas surprised her by speaking again.

"Just glad I didn't know her, you know? I got a lot of family on the island, Boddens go back to the early settlers here. I got family I don't even know I got. But she didn't look Caymanian. Just relieved it wasn't my kin."

Once the investigator had said the girl appeared Hispanic, AJ had assumed she wasn't from Cayman, and had been trying to figure out how she may have ended up off the north wall. It hadn't occurred to her that Thomas would have been worried about knowing the girl. The Boddens indeed went back to 1658, when records indicated a Welshman named Watler was accompanied by a man named Bodden on a visit to the islands. His grandson, Isaac Bodden, was born on Grand Cayman around 1700 and is considered the first recorded permanent inhabitant of the Cayman Islands. Thomas's family had over 300 years of history in the Caymans. AJ had been to family gatherings and it was impressive how many people turned out. He undoubtedly had distant relatives he didn't even know.

"Whittaker have any idea who the girl might be?" Reg asked.

"No, he didn't," AJ responded sadly. "Said she didn't fit any missing person description he knew of. Interesting though, he and the investigator lady both noticed the girl had nice nails, and ruled out her being from a boat escaping Cuba. Maybe a tourist who fell overboard, but nothing has been reported, they said. Oh, and she'd been whacked on the back of the head; the lady noticed that too."

"Could have banged her head falling overboard I guess," Reg said.

"Yeah, maybe, but naked?" AJ commented.

"Hey, I'm sure that's not that uncommon on some of these boats. Cruising around, drinking, having a good time," Reg said. "Or a cruise ship?"

"Pretty sure no cruise ships pass by the north, do they?" she countered and Reg and Thomas both shook their heads.

"But the other thing was she had a mark around one ankle – the SOCO lady seemed concerned over that. Whittaker too," AJ added. "Not sure what's sadder, thinking she died accidentally or if she was murdered."

"Hate to think of a murder here on Cayman," Reg said, shaking his head, "Been a safe place to live for a long time. Wasn't too many years ago we'd think nothing of leaving the house unlocked all day. Like everything else in this world, times are changing I suppose."

"I wish we could blame the growing crime on visitors, or the influx of more Jamaicans after hurricane Ivan, but it's the local kids most of the time." Thomas said, clearly unhappy.

"Why d'you reckon that is?" Reg asked.

Thomas shrugged his shoulders. "Tough to know for sure. My guess is same as everywhere else in the world, the Internet and TV opens places up to see what goes on everywhere. Was a time a young Caymanian would grow up and do whatever his father done, fishing most likely, but maybe building boats or sewing nets, farming, whatever. Now, they see all the wealth around and all the athletes and movie stars, and they want something more, make a name for themselves, get some of that wealth. They get restless on our little island and start making trouble. It's only a few but that's all it takes in a small place like this, just a few."

"That's true enough," AJ agreed. "On an island that sees only a couple of murders a year and has one of the lowest crime rates in the world, it doesn't take much to move the statistics."

"Guess today saw that number jump, if that unlucky kid was murdered," Reg said thoughtfully.

7

TUESDAY

AJ checked behind her as she angled down the sandy-floored crevasse between two coral heads, making her way deeper to where the north wall fell away abruptly. Grand Cayman was nothing more than the peak of an undersea mountain, barely breaking the surface of the Caribbean Sea. The coastline gave way to the water in gently sloped coral reefs and sand flats before meeting the edge of the mountain, and plummeting to depths of several thousand feet. The group were scattered at various depths but were all following her and accounted for. Several of Jack's group were amateur underwater photographers. They tended to lag behind when they found picture-worthy critters or corals, but they were all excellent divers and navigation was easy in the 120'-plus visibility of the clear water. She finned her way to the drop-off and the vast sea opened up before her between the refracting sun at the surface and the inky black of the deep water below. The large expanse of reef they'd just swum across quickly felt minuscule compared to the vastness of the open ocean they faced. AJ led the group away from the wall and, turning, pointed down to a magnificent coral encrusted natural archway below them. Deeper than recreational divers should go, the arch was an inviting swim-through, but they satisfied themselves with the impressive view from above.

AJ hung at a depth of a hundred feet while all the divers caught up and had the opportunity to take in the 'Hole in the Wall' the site was named for. Looking to the east she made out movement in the deep blue water, and gently tapped a few times on her tank with the stainless-steel carabiner she carried. Pointing in that direction she drew the divers' attention to the eagle rays gracefully swooping towards them. Four of the giant fish cruised effortlessly along the face of the wall, ducking to deeper water past the divers, their slight change of depth the only indication they had noticed their observers. Cameras flashed but the group knew to remain calm and not chase the rays. Sudden movement would have them flap their majestic, spotted wings and disappear even faster.

Back aboard the boat, AJ and Thomas helped the divers shed their gear and began to switch tanks in preparation for the second dive. The group slipped their wetsuits down to their waists and huddled around the photographers' cameras, excitedly admiring the pictures. Sherry put a hand on AJ's shoulder and gave her a big smile. "That was really special, thank you."

AJ grinned as she finished buckling Sherry's buoyancy control device, or BCD, into her fresh tank. "That was quite a sight, huh? Really lucky to catch four in a group like that."

Sherry was forty-something, as was her husband, and was a plain woman by most people's standards. But her smile lit up a conversation, and AJ found her presence uplifting. Something they all needed after yesterday's alarming discovery of the body.

"Here, here, look." One of the photographers offered the screen of his digital camera with a great shot of the eagle rays passing below with the sun from 130 feet above illuminating their speckled backs in contrast to the darkness of the drop-off.

"Great shot," AJ said, waving Thomas over to look.

"They were just close enough for my strobe to add enough to the sunlight to light them up like that. That's a once-in-a-lifetime shot right there," the photographer enthused.

Once all the gear had been switched, AJ headed up the ladder to the fly-bridge, and started the diesel motor. Thomas freed them from the mooring and, dropping the drive in forward, AJ eased the boat away, idling towards shallower water. After a few minutes Thomas joined her and leaned against the hard-top framework, handing her her stainless-steel water bottle. She looked up and thanked him. He was far more chipper today, but she could tell he still wasn't quite himself. He was looking back towards the west where they'd found the girl.

"Hard to stop thinking about her, huh?" she said quietly.

Thomas shrugged his shoulders. "I guess. Probably not something we should forget easily, right?"

AJ slipped her baseball cap on to keep her wet hair contained and nodded. "True. You had any thoughts on where she may have come from?"

"Had to be off a boat I suppose," he answered slowly. "Couldn't have come from far as she hadn't been in the water long enough, and anyone drowning near the shore would stay near the shore."

AJ took a long drink of the cold water and took her time replying.

"I double checked the tides from Sunday night. Low tide was 2:50am so the water would have been drawing out of the sound until then. High tide was 9:55am Monday morning, about the time we found her."

Thomas frowned and looked up at the North Sound ahead of them off the starboard side, "You think she came out of the sound on the Green Monster?"

AJ shook her head. "I really doubt it. It would be a one-in-a-million chance for her body to make it through the cut. Much more likely she'd have been dragged over the reef, in which case the body would have been cut to ribbons. Didn't look like there was a mark on her."

"Apart from the bang to the head, and her ankle," Thomas reminded her.

"Yeah. Apart from that," AJ said softly. "They weren't scrapes though, I don't think they were from the reef. So, adding all that up, my best guess is she started in the water farther out beyond the wall. Probably beyond where the Green Monster reaches. Then she was pushed in towards the island when the waves and currents were strongest between low and high tide."

"Must have gone in east of where we found her then." Thomas pointed to the ocean off the port side. "The waves would have moved her to the west towards the point."

AJ followed Thomas's lead. "That puts her in the water north-east of where we are now, right?"

"That's my guess," Thomas said looking back and forth from the point to the open water, "If we hadn't found her, she would likely have been pushed off the north west corner around midday, when the tide drew out again."

AJ looked at the reef line that marked the edge of the North Sound. The sound was a vast, shallow, sandy-bottomed bay with a line of coral marking its outer edge between Rum Point on the east side, and the north-west tip of Barkers National Park to the west. The reef barely broke the surface at low tide and lay menacingly a foot or two below at high tide. Several cuts had been made through the reef years ago to allow boats to travel safely through the eight-mile barrier. Outside the sound the reef quickly sloped to thirty feet, then gently continued deeper to around a hundred feet, where the wall plummeted to thousands of feet at the base of the under-water mountain that formed the island.

"That lines up with the cut a little too perfectly," she said, frowning. "A boat came out the North Sound, headed straight for deep water, and threw her overboard."

Thomas stared at the open ocean to the north and touched a finger to his forehead, chest then each shoulder, making the sign of a cross. "Dear Lord, I hope you're wrong."

He looked at AJ sullenly. "But I'm pretty sure you're not."

8

———————

TUESDAY

Raposa laid cash inside the bill folder the waiter had left, and finished his cappuccino. He always paid cash. Leave no trace, no breadcrumbs that can be followed. Few people knew his real name. He'd self-promoted his nickname while a teenager in Brazil and over the years it had saved him many times. Stealthy, like a fox. The view across the harbour and open water from the deck at Casanova's restaurant was delightful, as was the Italian food they served. Everything in Casanova's was extremely Italian, from the menu, to the waiting staff, to the owners. Pictures of the owners with special guests and celebrities lined the entrance hall, candles dripping wax down Chianti bottles adorned the tables, and mandolin-infused traditional music softly accompanied the diners. At the weekend, in the evenings, a violinist swanned amongst the tables and red roses were readily available for purchase. The whole scene would be kitsch and tacky if it wasn't sold with complete commitment. Raposa felt like he'd made a short visit to Naples or Venice every time he dined there, although he had nothing accurate to compare with, as he'd never set foot in Italy.

He left the restaurant and stepped to the pavement, where a steady stream of cruise ship tourists ambled by in search of things they readily find at home. Apparently they had a Burger King in their sights as the Hard Rock Cafe and Margaritaville were in the other direction. Raposa shook his head and turned right towards the town centre by the harbour. He'd had his eye on a Breitling Superocean Heritage B20 in black and gold with a steel strap. The jewellery store in town had the exact model he wanted and he'd been working on the salesman to get the price down. Raposa didn't pay retail. In times gone by he'd have simply taken it. Waited for some unsuspecting tourist to make the purchase then mugged them around the corner. But these days, especially on the small island, he couldn't draw attention. Besides, he relished the feeling of being able to buy it after so many years of poverty. He dodged tourists on the narrow pavement until he paused at the main cross-walk at Harbour and Cardinal. A policeman directed traffic despite the functioning light, much to the tourists' delight. The man spun, twirled and enthusiastically blew his whistle in his pristinely pressed black-and-white uniform. Sweat careened down his brow as the man guided, waved, danced and thoroughly entertained. Traffic moved more slowly with the distraction, but traffic was pretty much gridlocked in the tiny streets when the ships were in town anyway.

As Raposa waited for the white gloved hand to beckon him across the street, he noticed someone trying to remain unnoticed. The girl was far too pretty to avoid detection but she seemed to manage handily amongst the untrained eyes of the visitors. She had the face of a girl but the lean, developed body of a woman. She wore a simple blue floral sun dress, sandals, and her long black hair was neatly held in a ponytail. She leaned against a wall under the overhang of the store fronts, looking down, yet her eyes saw every-thing. Everyone. Mesmerising eyes, that glowed a golden amber. She might well look down; anyone staring into those captivating eyes could never forget them, he thought. With a blur of motion the girl turned and gently bumped against a woman carrying a plastic bag of souvenirs in one hand and her handbag over her shoulder closest to the buildings. Raposa watched the handbag swing and the young girl turn away as quickly as she'd moved in. The woman continued down the pavement completely unaware.

A whistle blew loudly and the policeman's hand whirled like a windmill, alerting Raposa it was safe to cross the road. He mingled with the other people crossing, keeping his eye on the girl who was walking his way down Harbour. She passed by the crosswalk and turned on Cardinal so he waited a moment on the pavement before turning the corner and following her. For a moment he lost sight. The crowd thinned on Cardinal but she'd disappeared somewhere. He picked her up again across the street turning down Albert Panton. She's good, he thought, she moves quickly when needed, but without any drama or fuss; she was invisible in the town she clearly knew well. He followed at a distance and watched her sift through the purse she'd pulled from the handbag. Passing a city rubbish bin she dumped the purse and pocketed the credit cards and cash. Turning left down the driveway between two buildings she glanced back down the street. It was the first time Raposa had actually seen her check behind but he knew she'd probably noticed him several times now. He stopped and turned, confident the girl would circle back to the busy waterfront. He didn't want to raise her suspicion.

Raposa knew all these moves. He'd started picking pockets in Rio when he was nine years old. By fourteen he was the best in town and by sixteen he'd moved on to work for the cartel. For nearly twenty years he'd worked for Cristal or her father. He owed them everything. Certainly the ability to buy a Breitling watch and not think twice about it. He had money that would make him a king back in Brazil; maybe he'd retire there one day. Or maybe he'd settle in Miami where a large Brazilian population enjoyed the excesses of America without the dangerous streets of home.

He made his way back to Harbour and nonchalantly headed east towards the jewellery store. He knew she was back on the street somewhere and would be wary of him, having seen him already; he needed to appear oblivious. He entered the store front with a careful glance back down the street through the shop window as he entered. Sure enough he caught sight of her. Well, he spotted a hint of her blue dress between the pedestrians, but he knew it was her. Because that's what he would have done. Follow the suspicious person until you're sure they're not following you. The salesman greeted Raposa enthusiastically, shaking his hand and steering him straight to the cabinet containing the watch.

"It's your lucky day Mr. Ramirez, a gentleman was just here admiring this very watch, he said he'd be back with his wife later today so I'm glad you've beaten him to it. This watch is destined to be on your wrist."

The man removed the watch from display case and laid it alluringly on a velvet pad on the glass counter. Raposa chuckled to himself; the salesman had dutifully remembered the false name he'd used. He looked at the watch and glanced over at the shop window, wondering where the young woman was now. He'd been obsessing over this watch for a month now but the girl had him even more distracted. She might be perfect except for one thing. Cristal had a strict rule: no local girls. Too much fuss if they were noticed missing, too easy for the girls to have a change of heart and simply walk home, too risky. But Raposa had a feeling in his bones about this one. She seemed independent, a loner, and she was stunningly gorgeous. Sure, she looked plain and muted to blend with the crowd but he had an eye for potential, developed over the two years since Cristal had planned, organised and built the resort. He could see the girl with a subtle touch of make-up, her hair conditioned and styled, an elegant designer evening gown and a few pieces of jewellery that would sparkle off her milk chocolate skin.

"This watch retails for over six thousand US, Mr. Ramirez, but I can sell it to you today for fifty-two hundred."

Raposa looked at the salesman sternly. "You told me five thousand the other day."

The man didn't miss a beat. "Then five thousand it is, sir," he replied with a broad smile. "Cash or card?"

He swooped the watch up and retrieved the box from the display, ready to ring up the sale.

"Thirty-eight hundred CI, cash," Raposa responded, with one eye still on the street outside.

The salesman put the watch back down, quickly pulled his mobile phone from his pocket, and tapped the numbers into the calculator app. He proceeded to put on an Oscar-winning performance of head-shaking and furrowed brow.

"That's below my cost, Mr. Ramirez. I mean, I really want you to have this watch but my boss would never let me take a loss like this. We're friends so I would gladly do it but he won't let me, you understand."

Raposa laid thirty-eight one hundred Cayman dollar bills on the glass top and looked at the man.

"Thirty-eight hundred. There it is, it's all I brought, so I'm either buying the watch for that or I'm picking it back up and leaving now." His hand moved back towards the cash and the salesman finally gave in.

"Okay, okay, because we're friends. But you can't tell anyone I gave you this price, you'll put us out of business."

Raposa smiled and thought about cutting the man's throat for even suggesting they were friends.

It took the salesman a frustratingly long time to ring up the sale and write out the receipt to an Oswaldo Ramirez of Miami Beach, Florida. He droned on about warranties and yearly services, none of which Raposa cared about. If something went wrong with his beautiful new watch, he'd pin the man against a wall behind the store and beat him until he replaced it. Deep down he hoped something would go awry and give him an excuse.

Back on Harbour he scanned the pavement in both directions looking for the girl. She was nowhere to be seen. He turned right as that's where he'd first spotted her, and his car was parked that way. Back at the corner of Cardinal the policeman must have been on his break as he was absent, and the traffic flowed a little better. Raposa looked around as though deciding where to shop next, but carefully took in the shadows and movements in the crowd. He saw a flash of blue dress and a tourist stumbled and turned, holding up a hand in apology. Raposa laughed; the girl was really good. The man would be standing in line to return to his cruise ship before he realised his wallet was gone. He followed the girl at a distance. She took a different route this time, another indication she was well versed in her trade. She disposed of the wallet in a bin on Fort Street and continued into the back of downtown. Raposa kept well back and almost lost her several times as she ducked and weaved through car parks and small streets. At Rock Hole Road the office buildings quickly gave way to small cottages and shacks. The wealth of downtown becoming a stark contrast to the run-down homes and dirt-floored dwellings that had been there for fifty years or more.

The girl unlocked a padlock and slipped through the doorway of a tiny dwelling with a corrugated steel roof and bars for windows. Raposa grinned. Maybe the kid had some family in there, but by the lack of any toys outside, there were no children. The hut was no bigger than a 10′ by 10′ shed. No power lines led to the structure. He now knew where the girl with the golden eyes lived. He'd be back.

9

TUESDAY

AJ hurried through the front door at the Greenhouse Cafe off North Church Street in George Town. Her friend Jen waved to her from behind the register at the back of the dining area as she walked through the busy tables of locals and cruise shippers.

"Hey girl, didn't think I'd see you all week; everyone's diving north, aren't they?" Jen asked as she rang up a customer's bill.

"We're not going out this afternoon – got a night dive instead, so I have the afternoon free." AJ replied. "Well, when I say free, I mean I'm getting lunch, heading to the bank, grabbing some supplies for the boat, getting Nitrox tanks filled and then heading back to go on a night dive."

"That doesn't sound like an afternoon off." Jen laughed.

AJ shrugged. "Oh well, fun group on the boat, so work doesn't feel much like work. How's your day?"

"Crazy busy, but that's good too. What can I get you?" Jen asked, as she retrieved a pastry from the display next to the register and put it on a small plate on the counter.

AJ laughed. "One of those apparently, and I'll have a Forest Range panini please."

"Believe me, you'll like the scone," Jen said. "Save it for later. Drink?"

"Oh yeah." AJ looked at the menu board. "A Cowardly Lion smoothie please."

Jen rang up the order and, after paying, AJ turned to look for a place to sit. In the corner she noticed Detective Whittaker alone at a table for two. He looked up and caught her eye and she waved hello. He pointed to the empty chair and she made her way between the other tables to join him.

"Are you sure you don't mind, Detective? I don't want to disturb your lunch."

He smiled. "Please, call me Roy, and I'd enjoy the company." He stood politely while she took her seat.

Whittaker was in his fifties, a veteran of the Royal Cayman Islands Police Service, with salt-and-pepper hair buzzed short, glasses and a slender build. He had two personality modes; friendly, relaxed and disarming, or all business. Not a man that ruffled easily, he prided himself on following logical and lawful pursuits of his cases.

"Thank you, Roy," AJ responded. "And I insist you call me AJ. Miss Bailey sounds like a schoolteacher." She chuckled.

The detective took a bite of his sandwich and chewed slowly, looking at AJ, who fussed with her place setting and flipped her phone face down and put it on silent. When he finished the bite he grinned.

"Go ahead," he said, amused.

AJ looked at him with a puzzled expression, "I'm sorry?"

"You're itching to ask me something – go ahead and ask," he replied before taking another bite.

AJ blushed a little, but was not surprised the man was good at reading people; after all, he was a detective.

"The girl? What have you learnt about her? I can't get her off my mind," she said quietly, aware they were in public surroundings.

He finished chewing and dabbed his mouth with a napkin, "It's still early days, so not much I'm afraid. No match to any missing persons, but if she's from Cuba, Haiti, South America or many other places, they don't report most, or any, of their missing persons. She died around midnight, we know that much, and we believe she drowned. The wound to her head appears non-fatal, but with that, and the injury to her ankle, consistent with a restraint, we're proceeding with a murder inquiry."

AJ was surprised Whittaker was so forthcoming, and felt a lump in her throat when he confirmed they suspected foul play.

"Bloody hell, Roy, she looked so young, just a girl."

"We think between seventeen and nineteen years old," he replied softly. "Indeed, very sad."

AJ's food arrived, but as hungry as she'd been when she arrived, her appetite had subsided with her thoughts of the drowned girl. She took a sip of the smoothie and the detective finished his sandwich.

"We were thinking about the tides this morning, Thomas and I – we were out north again today," AJ started tentatively. Whittaker nodded as he chewed, so she continued, "Based on low and high tide times and the way the waves run off the north, I think a boat may have come straight out of the Main Channel cut and thrown her overboard in deeper water."

The detective's expression didn't change at all and AJ wondered if the man ever played poker. His tone became serious as he switched from conversationalist to detective.

"That's useful information, and consistent with the conclusion our marine police came up with," he finally said, taking a few thoughtful moments to continue, "Which means she was on island."

AJ hadn't thought about it from that perspective; she'd been caught up in the idea of a boat and what had taken place in the water. Of course, if she'd been taken out there on a boat from the North Sound then she'd most likely been on the island and hadn't come from a passing vessel.

"Can you match her to records of arrivals, or work permits or something?"

He nodded slowly. "We'll run facial recognition against all our records, but first our artist has to work on the picture we have of her."

AJ shuddered as she recalled the poor girl's face, partially disfigured from the marine life. "Of course. That's awful to think about. That can't be a fun job for anyone to do."

"Nothing about a case like this is fun, I'm afraid. But, unfortunately necessary, so we'll do our jobs as best we can and see where it leads us," he responded, shifting back to an easier tone.

"Well, I hope you're able to find who did this. Let me know if there's anything more I can help with," AJ offered.

Whittaker grinned, peering over his glasses at her. "There's no crashed aeroplanes or villainous Nazis around you're aware of, I assume?"

AJ blushed as he referred to a couple of past events where their paths had crossed – the downed plane from Cuba being a particular sore point, as she and Reg had withheld that information from the police for a while. It had been for innocent reasons, but they had been fortunate it all worked out okay and the detective hadn't made anything more of it.

"No, I promise, I've told you everything I know, which isn't very much."

He rose from his seat and smiled. "Well, thank you for the company, and thank you for confirming our thoughts on the movement of the waters. Have a good afternoon."

Whittaker left and AJ tried a bite from her sandwich. It was tasty, as Jen's concoctions always were, and she found her appetite returning. It was still hard to shake her thoughts of the young girl. The more she learnt, the more personal it felt. She had no idea if the girl had been caught up in something illegal, or for that matter, whether she was a good or bad person. But having seen her frail, delicate body devoid of life, it was hard not to imagine her as an innocent teenager.

Jen made her jump when she sat down clumsily in the seat vacated by the detective.

"I need a damn drink," she exclaimed rather loudly to a few chuckles from neighbouring tables. She glanced at her watch.

"Gotta be five o'clock in England, right?" Her expressive features were as questioning as her words.

AJ laughed. "You forget you're American, Jen."

Jen's face contorted into a look of shock. "You're right, I do forget sometimes, and then there's times I wish I could do a better English accent."

"Or New Zealand," AJ countered, "Everybody loves Kiwis. Have you ever heard anyone say they don't like a Kiwi?"

"Every Australian?" Jen said, with a deadpan look.

AJ laughed again. "Oh, that's right, I forgot they hate each other."

She collected herself and smiled at her friend. "Thanks Jen, I needed a laugh."

Jen smiled back. "I heard, rumours have been going around already; really sorry you and Thomas had to be the ones to find the body."

AJ nodded. "Yeah." She thought about what else to say, but couldn't think of anything worth saying.

10

TUESDAY

Raposa waited by the kerb outside Island Air, the private jet terminal at Owen Roberts International airport. The security guard had checked by to see who he was but seemed to understand anyone driving a white Chevy Suburban with blacked-out windows was probably there to pick up someone important. The vehicle was ridiculously big and uneconomic for the small island, but extravagance was what the guests expected. He loved the big Suburban but hated driving the left-hand drive American vehicle on the right side of the British Overseas Territory streets. Fortunately, the Range Rover Evoques, provided with each villa for the guests' use while they stayed at the resort, were right-hand drive. Cristal had thought of just about everything when she planned the International Fellowship of Lions and the place ran like a finely tuned timepiece. Quite important for a venture this size that operated with a small crew, and an element on the wrong side of the law.

The sliding doors opened, and a teenage girl appeared with three gentlemen in tow. She was laughing as she guided the men towards the Suburban and a porter followed them pushing a rolling cart stacked with suitcases. Raposa got out and opened the back door to the vehicle, having already pressed the button on the remote to raise the lift gate.

"Here we are gentlemen," the girl said in accented English. "You remember Raposa, of course," she added, and stepped aside as the men all shook hands.

"Good to see you again," Raposa greeted two men, who spoke with New York accents. "And this must be your friend, Mr. Symanski?"

A slight man with the appearance of a forty-year-old professor nodded and shook Raposa's hand.

"Good to meet you," the man replied nervously, nudging his glasses up the bridge of his nose.

"Please, make yourselves comfortable and we'll head straight for the resort." Raposa closed the back door and tipped the porter before getting back in the driver's seat. He glanced over at the tall, thin blonde as she buckled herself in. He'd happened across Nora on a recruitment trip to the Bahamas. The Norwegian runaway had ingeniously made her way across the world on her own to the Caribbean, quite a feat for a sixteen-year-old. She'd been with the resort for over ten months now. He didn't look forward to the day she finished her contract in a few weeks' time. She flashed her bright blue eyes at him, and he managed a smile as he pulled away.

"How was your flight?" Raposa asked.

"Easy," Al Jacobs replied, a portly man with an arrogant air about him. "Bill's Lear 75 is stupid fast, it took, what guys?" He looked at the other two.

"Three hours," Bill Russo responded nonchalantly. "Be a little less going home." Russo was taller with slicked-back hair that had to be dyed to be that dark black at age fifty-four.

"Yeah, three hours," Jacobs echoed.

Russo was quieter than Jacobs but took in everything around him, and from the background checks, Raposa knew he was mob connected in New York. Not a man to mess with.

"Hey," Jacobs started. "So how's this work with Joe here?" He shook his thumb in Symanski's direction. "He get his own villa or what?"

Raposa took a breath; the man's grating manner was not what the Brazilian was used to, but he remained polite.

"Miss Sombrio is waiting for us at the resort and she'll meet with Mr. Symanski. All the background work has been done so it's up to Mr. Symanski if he'd like to become a member or not. He would be our fiftieth and final member, so we're all excited at the prospect." Raposa glanced in the rear-view mirror at the new visitor, who seemed to be transfixed on Nora. He's hooked before we even get there, he thought.

"Joe does accounting work for both me and Al – we vouch for him," Russo said in an authoritative tone.

"Yes sir," Raposa replied quickly. "I believe the choice is with Mr. Symanski, sir."

In the mirror Raposa saw Russo nod approvingly. Symanski continued to stare at Nora's long blonde hair.

"We want to go diving this trip. You know, that scuba stuff. We snorkelled before, but we want to go under this time. You know, with a tank and the shit you breathe through." Jacobs declared loudly.

"Are you gentleman certified divers?" Raposa asked politely.

"Certified what?" Jacobs shouted.

"He means are you trained to dive – you have to take a course to do it, right?" Russo added in a calmer voice.

"That's correct sir, but we can accommodate you, there's guided diving you can do without taking the full certification course. They'll give you some basic safety instruction, then take you on the dive. The instructor is with you at all times. What day would you like to go out?"

"I don't want to sit in a classroom for hours, I just want to go underwater," Jacobs snapped back.

Russo laughed – apparently, he found his friend to be amusing; Raposa on the other hand wanted to let the man have his wish and go underwater; without any breathing apparatus.

Raposa glanced at Nora but she seemed to be ignoring it all, casually watching the world go by out the window. He didn't know how the girls could do it sometimes. Pretend to like these foul men. He understood the money part, and knew too well most of them had come from much harsher conditions, but still. He wanted to kill Jacobs with his bare hands and all he had to do was ride around with him in the Suburban. He reminded himself the girls also rarely left the resort, so just driving to the airport and back was something of a treat. They accompanied the guests to dinner prepared in the villa but not if they ate at restaurants outside the resort. The girls weren't allowed any phones, computers, social media or outside contact during their contract, for security reasons. Anyone violating the rules had their contracts instantly terminated and forfeited all the money they'd been accruing. Fortunately, this had only happened one time so far in the eleven months the resort had been open to clients.

"It's all done from the boat, Mr. Jacobs, there's no actual classroom time. Usually there's one dive, but if you'd like, we can arrange for several. Did you have a day in mind?"

Jacobs stared out the window as they approached the resort, so Russo replied. "We fly back late Saturday, so let's do the diving on Friday."

"I'll arrange it," Raposa replied as he slowed the Suburban, allowing the ornate steel gates to part after he pressed the remote opener. An eight-foot wall extended from both sides of the gates to the edge of the property where it turned ninety degrees and continued to the water's edge, thus securing the grounds on all sides by wall or water. Along the top of the wall ran a metal strip that could be electrified when deemed necessary. Security cameras covered the property in overlapping patterns and sophisticated surveillance software operated the system without human interaction. The business was designed to run with the minimum number of people. Every added person was an added expense and an added security risk. Number one priority was security, number two was customer service. Without security, the resort wouldn't exist to provide customer service. That was Cristal's theory. Raposa was in charge of security, as well as many other responsibilities.

Parking the Suburban in front of the main three-storey building, Raposa guided the guests through the tall, tinted glass doors into the reception lounge, where six comfortable chairs were arranged around a glass top coffee table. The walls held paintings of various scenes from the island both above and below water, and a side table housed a coffee machine that spouted various fancy drinks with the press of a button.

Raposa invited the men to take a seat while he and Nora exited through a door at the back of the room where Cristal stood waiting in the hallway at the base of a stairwell. She smiled at Nora and touched a hand to the girl's cheek.

"That'll be all for now my dear, why don't you run along. I'm sure you'll be invited to dinner later."

Nora passed by Cristal and started up the stairs to the next floor which housed the girls' dormitories. Cristal turned back to Raposa.

"They bring their guest?"

Raposa chuckled quietly. "Oh yes, the guy is their accountant or something – probably count the times he's been laid on one hand. He'll sign anything you put in front of him if it gets him a girl. He couldn't stop staring at Nora. Super creepy."

"A problem, you think?" she asked cautiously.

"Nah, even the girls could handle him if he plays up; he's never lifted anything heavier than a pencil in his life," Raposa replied with disdain.

"Good, I'll take him aside now then while he's still foaming at the mouth." Cristal smiled.

11

TUESDAY

Thomas carefully piloted the Newton through Main Channel cut in the North Sound reef. The swells were minimal, but currents could often surprise the unwary, and drag a boat towards the coral lurking just below the surface on either side. On the horizon off the port side, the sun was low in the sky and began its magical colour display of deep oranges, scarlets and yellows. Once clear of the cut, with twenty feet of water under the keel, Thomas turned east and spotted the mooring buoy they'd discussed. AJ stood beside Thomas, sipping her coffee from her stainless-steel travel mug. They'd been quiet on the ride out, apart from choosing the dive site. She'd told Thomas about her lunch with Whittaker when they were waiting for the group to arrive at the dock, and they'd both fallen back into a melancholy funk. She surveyed the open water and broke the silence.

"Looks like it's just us out here tonight," she said quietly, seeing no other boats beyond the sound.

"That's good, hopefully more critters will be out as it's nice and quiet," Thomas replied. "Want me to take this one?"

AJ rested a hand on his shoulder. "Nah, I got this one, I need a little time in my happy place."

He nodded his understanding and she headed down the ladder to prepare the line to tie into the mooring.

Once they were set on the mooring AJ gathered the group for a quick briefing. All the divers had multiple night dives in their logbooks, so she focused on the site itself, and the dive plan. Glancing at her watch she began.

"Okay everyone, we're on Lemon Reef, which is a great shallow site for a night dive. As you can see the sun has set and we have about an hour before the moon rises. We're a couple of days past full moon so it's a waning moon, but should be pretty full and bright. The idea will be to splash towards the end of twilight, so we have a little ambient light to get orientated, then it'll get really dark, and we'll finish under a rising moon. Moonrise is 7:50pm so let's aim to get in shortly after seven, in about fifteen minutes' time. Make sure each buddy pair has at least one spare torch, or flashlight as you call it in America. If anyone needs a spare, I have a few extras.

This is a shallow reef, around thirty feet, so we'll easily be down for an hour and should see plenty of fun critters that only come out, or behave differently, at night. You guys all know the drill for night diving; just remember to avoid disturbing the parrotfish, they'll be readying their mucus sleeping bags when we get in at dusk, and be fully enclosed and asleep by dark. It's a big stress on them to wake them. Don't shine your torches in each other's eyes, especially mine." She chuckled. "And make circles on the sea floor with your beam if you want to attract anyone's attention."

AJ checked around for any questions.

"Can you find us an octopus?" Sherry asked with a big grin.

"I promise you there's several octopus down there... and I'll try my best to find you one! Okay, ten-minute warning, gang."

AJ waited for the last of the group to giant-stride off the swim step before quickly donning her gear and preparing to follow them. Thomas stood by with a hand on her tank to help steady her. Boats rock and dive tanks are heavy so even the most experienced divers can slip on a wet deck occasionally. She smiled at him before pulling her mask down. He still looked concerned and she knew the girl in the water was weighing on his mind. She gave him a friendly punch on the arm and stepped off the back of the boat.

Gathering the group at the mooring point, AJ took a good look around and reminded herself of the terrain and familiar landmarks. The reef was a series of fingers and ridges of coral that sloped deeper towards the drop-off. They'd be staying away from the wall, so she checked for signs of current before choosing which direction to head. The sea fans were barely sweeping back and forth from the surface swell and she sensed no current pulling her or bending the soft corals in a particular direction. They were an hour or two from high tide so the outward flow from the sound was slowing and being negated by the incoming waves. Perfect conditions. She decided to head east, away from the cut, and turned her torch on as the last of the sun's refractions gave way to the cloak of night-time.

She had handed out chemical glow sticks to the group, which everyone had tied to the tops of their tanks. The clients' were green, and AJ had her own, which was yellow. As she turned and checked her chicks following her like a mother hen, it made it easier to count them. As always, the photographers had their camera rigs so she made sure to cruise slowly and give them time to line up their shots. Every few minutes the water lit up with the glow from their flashes. The lobsters were starting to come out of their crevices and hidey-holes, the prehistoric-looking crustaceans walking on ten spindly legs and scanning the waters with their long antennae.

AJ eased over a coral head, carefully going around a yellow sea whip fluttering its long, soft branches, and couldn't believe her luck. Catching movement from the hard coral below her, she shone her light to the side, so the outer edges of the beam illuminated the reef, without blasting it with bright light. Wrapped around the coral, with its body changing colour to match its surrounding, a reef octopus tried its best to camouflage itself. AJ made a wide circling pattern off to the side with her torch on the sea floor, and the divers soon gathered to see what she'd found. Sherry's eyes grew wide in her mask as her turn came to view the discovery and she reached a hand up to high five with AJ. Leaving the photographers to linger over the octopus, AJ finned her way slowly forward, noting several sleeping parrotfish, and carefully keeping her torch light away from them.

The undersea world was now completely black, apart from their narrow beams of light, and small fish flitted and darted through the illumination. It was easy to become paranoid and nervous in the strange world so full of life, knowing so many critters were buzzing around the divers unseen, but AJ loved the reef at night. For her there couldn't be a farther place from the everyday than right here. The busy, hidden world brought her calm and she revelled in the feeling of being in a place that felt so distant from the troubles and stresses of life above the sea. But thoughts of the girl still crept in, and once they started it was hard to fight them off. AJ had been alone in the water before, at night. She'd been close to drowning in the inky darkness, far from shore. A vision of herself morphed with the memory of the dead girl, face down with that strange grey hue to her skin tone. But for the intervention of luck, she might have been found floating face down herself. It was not a pleasant feeling and she wondered what the young girl had endured two nights ago. How alone she must have felt in the last moments. The first time AJ had come close to drowning, she'd been alone, and the fear, panic and helplessness had been awful right up to the moment she thought it was the end. A wave of peacefulness had washed over her at that moment. All she could hope for the floating girl was that her last memories of this world were peaceful too.

12

WEDNESDAY

Hallie stood in the shadow of one of the large, colourful posts supporting the deck of Margaritaville restaurant. She nonchalantly read the *Cayman Compass* newspaper while keeping an eye on the crowded pavement. She made a point of perusing the local paper to keep up with the latest island news, and to improve her reading and vocabulary. The crowd milled by sipping exotic cocktails from tall plastic glasses, with even taller plastic straws, and swinging plastic bags brimming with brightly coloured souvenirs. Hallie appeared to be part of the harbour front scene of George Town, a touch of local flavour in a sea of visitors. Picking pockets had been easier when she started two years ago. She was fourteen when her mother discovered crack and slowly descended into the darkness her addiction brought on. School became unnecessary for survival; money for food took priority, and Hallie taught herself to work the streets. At first, she was clumsy and only her swift feet saved her from being caught, but soon she developed her skills and became proficient at relieving people of their money, without them noticing. Her slight build, diminutive height and girlish features helped her stay invisible back then. Now, her body had developed, she'd shot up to 5′ 6″ tall, and all the men, from teenage boys to old timers, noticed her and took their time lingering over the view. She tied her hair back in a plain ponytail, wore loose-fitting dresses in muted tones and kept her head down as best she could. It was hard to hide her pretty features and impossible to shake the looks if they saw her golden amber eyes. She usually wore sunglasses, but she'd broken the last pair, and sunglasses were surprisingly hard to steal in a sunny Caribbean town. People wore them on their faces and didn't leave them in their bags. She could easily lift a pair from one of the shops, but she had an unspoken relationship with the shop owners; she worked the visitors and left the locals alone and in return they let her be.

Picking out a plump, sunburned lady in spandex pants and a tank top several sizes too small, she followed the woman's progress towards the restaurant front. She had a purse slung over her shoulder with the top zipper open. Her other hand clutched a Hard Rock Cafe bag. As the woman approached, Hallie dropped the newspaper, turned and slowly walked in the same direction, a few steps ahead. Once the woman came alongside on the congested pavement, it was simple to reach into the open handbag. Hallie felt a mobile phone which she pinned to her palm with her thumb while her fingers explored further. As soon as she felt the wallet she removed both items and clutched them to her chest. She hid the mobile and wallet beneath her hands and kept her elbows tight to her sides, as though she was making herself smaller to slip through the busy crowd. Spotting the first opening in the swarm of people going the other direction, she turned and mingled, once again lost in the blur of humanity. The whole event took less than five seconds. The wallet was thick, so she hoped for a good haul. The mobile and credit cards she'd sell to a fence she knew, and the cash kept her fed and clothed. If she didn't feed herself, no one else would.

She missed her mother sometimes. She missed the mother who had raised her alone and cared for her as best she could. That woman had loved her daughter, her only child. She didn't miss the drug-addicted ghost of a parent who stole from her daughter, and anyone else she could get close to, desperate to feed her habit. That unrecognisable person had left this world the year before. Hallie never knew whether her mother had overdosed, starved to death, or was taken another way. She had found her cold, dead body slumped against the fence, a hundred yards up the road from where the dirt path led to their shack.

Hallie glanced up as the crowd thinned past the restaurant entrance, and saw the man she'd spotted the day before. He was carefully looking away from her, but the stranger had been present too many times now to be ignored. He didn't look like a copper, certainly not with the Caymanian police. He was Hispanic looking, taller than her, very athletic and ruggedly handsome. She moved the stolen goods to the two large pockets on the hips of her dress and reversed direction again, sliding in front of a tall man to shield herself. After a few steps she heard shouting ahead and the crowd checked up, peering and shuffling to see what the fuss was about. Hallie instinctively edged towards the building, squeezing between a couple and their two kids. A woman's voice shrieked loudly, "Police! Police! I've been robbed!"

The urge to panic and run welled up inside but Hallie quickly suppressed the fear and took a few deep breaths. She had to decide which direction was the least threatening. She had no idea what this man was about, but she knew better than to throw it away as coincidence, having seen him again. Ahead was a hysterical woman calling the police, who would not be far away; several patrolmen lingered downtown and the dancing policeman was at the crosswalk. Across the road meant into the open, and she couldn't go into the jewellery store or the restaurant, as that would break their unspoken code. The crowd were stirring and clutching their valuables, as if a spirit was circulating amongst them, stealing at will. The movement gave her spaces and gaps to quietly edge between and deftly dodge through the crowd, past the screaming woman with no wallet or mobile phone, and off through the car park and alleyway between the buildings. As the ruckus faded behind her, Hallie breathed a sigh of relief. Emerging on Albert Panton she turned left, then crossed the street to duck between buildings again, and cross Edwards Street on the other side. Sticking to the car parks and alleys she quickly made her way north to Rock Hole Road, breaking into an occasional skip, the sixteen-year-old child still emerging when she had something to be happy about. She dumped the wallet, along with the debit and member-ship cards she had no use for. It was a good haul. One hundred and forty US dollars in cash, four credit cards and an iPhone 8. She'd get ten a piece for the cards and fifty for the phone; pretty good payday, she thought.

Hallie stopped in her tracks as she rounded the corner off Rock Hole Road onto the dirt path. Standing in the narrow walkway was the man she'd seen. He had a neatly trimmed beard and curly black hair, cut short and styled nicely. He wore cargo shorts, an expen-sive-looking short-sleeved button-down shirt and, more impor-tantly, a smart pair of Adidas trainers. The last part being the most important, because she was about to try and outrun the man who looked like he was fast and nimble on his feet. She set her feet and quickly thought about the best route to lose him once he made his move. Then he spoke.

"Please, I'm not the police and I mean you no harm at all," he said in accented but fluent English.

She cocked her head and eyed him carefully, still working on her escape map.

"I want nothing from you, I just want to talk."

Right, she thought. She was yet to meet anyone, especially a man, who didn't want anything from her. She instinctively kept her eyes low, but it was too late for that. Clearly, he'd been watching her, he knew where she lived. She wondered how she'd missed seeing him more, he'd obviously followed her farther than she realised, and she prided herself on her stealth and observation. She felt disappointed in herself.

"My name is Raposa," he continued, smiling warmly.

She noticed he had perfect teeth. The man looked like a professional football player, or even an actor; he was distractingly good looking. He made no move towards her and appeared completely relaxed. She wondered if he even intended to give chase.

"What do you want?" she finally asked, her curiosity winning over her instinct to run.

"Simply to talk," he said with a shrug, still smiling.

"Talk about what?" she asked suspiciously, her mind whirring with possibilities of what this stranger wanted to discuss with a petty thief.

He smirked and gestured back and forth between them with his hands. "I think we may have some business we can discuss, you and I."

She laughed quietly but her frown showed no humour. "I'm not a prostitute if that's your business, mister."

Her mother had brought men back to their shack and pleasured them in exchange for money, or drugs. As she'd slipped further into the darkness, her looks paid the price, so drugs became the only barter her body could buy. The men were less and less desirable types as her mother's sickness spiralled. In the beginning Hallie was sent away for an hour, but near the end her mother was oblivious to her presence. One man offered her mother more drugs to have his way with her daughter. Hallie ran away terrified and broken hearted when her mother agreed.

The man held his hands up. "No, no, you completely misunderstand me. I didn't think you're a prostitute and I'm not trying to buy you in any way. I run a business and we employ young ladies with intelligence and determination, like yourself. If you'll let me buy you a coffee or lunch, anywhere you feel comfortable, I'll explain everything. If you're not interested, then you'll have a free meal and be on your way. But I think you'll be interested. I can show you a way to leave your current life behind you, and never look back."

Hallie weighed up the risk. She was baffled as to what he could possibly have in mind that would set a destitute street girl up for the rest of her life, but the idea sure sounded appealing. She'd stay out of arm's reach and walk wherever they were going; no way was she getting in a vehicle with him. They could eat at the food truck that parked on Eastern Avenue – that was only a few minutes' walk.

"Okay," she finally relented.

13

WEDNESDAY

Thomas started the diesel motor and let it idle while AJ released the mooring line. They'd had two good dives that morning, one off the north wall, and then back to Lemon Reef to see it in daylight. He wasn't sure what they had in mind for the afternoon, but they had lunch in the cooler for everyone, so he knew they planned to stay on the water for their break. He heard AJ down on deck asking Jack.

"You mentioned you had early dinner reservations, right?"

"We do, 6:30pm at Ragazzi's, so we shouldn't be too late back," he heard Jack respond.

Thomas had only been to Ragazzi's a couple of times, both when Reg, and his wife Pearl, had taken AJ there and invited Thomas to join them. It was one of the best Italian restaurants on the island and the food had been incredible. The bill had to have been pretty incredible too.

"Ooh, Ragazzi's, my favourite," came AJ's mouth-watering reply, and then he heard her feet coming up the ladder. He stood and turned to face her.

"What you thinking, boss?"

"Maybe a longer lunch break to give them a good surface

interval and one deep dive instead of squeezing two shallow dives in? They're a bit pressed for time," AJ suggested.

Thomas thought about it for a moment. He'd been chatting earlier with a couple of the photographers and they were keen to get some more shots of eagle rays and a shark if possible.

"How about Eagle Ray Pass? I know it's right out from the cut, and everyone goes there, but it'll probably be open after lunch when the other boats stay shallow. The camera guys were talking about seeing more big stuff."

AJ nodded and started back down the ladder. "Good idea, I'll run it by Jack. Start heading that way."

Thomas dropped the boat in forward drive and gently eased more throttle, spinning the wheel to turn them east. He was always conscious of being smooth on the controls; the seas could knock the customers about enough without the pilot compounding their discomfort. Fortunately, most days in Cayman waters were like this day, even off the north side, flat calm with less than a one-foot swell. They dived off the west side the majority of the year, which was the lee side of the island, and best conditions year round. North was rarely dived in winter as the seas kicked up, but they tried to bring clients there for at least a portion of their visit spring through autumn. The days a nor'wester blew out the west and north dives, they moved south, which meant moving boats around to the South Sound and leaving from the public pier there. Those days were fun to dive somewhere different but chaotic as every dive operation was forced there by the weather, swarming the small car park and pier with people and boats. Thomas enjoyed diving north the best. The wall dropped off so dramatically and the corals were kept healthy by the constant flow of nutrients from both the open ocean and the Green Monster. And then there were the big fish. Eagle rays and sharks were seen less on the west side but far more common north, where they cruised the sheer drop-off. Reef and nurse sharks were customary but occasionally lemons, tigers and silkies showed up. The biggest treat was the infrequent sighting of hammerheads.

Eagle Ray Pass mooring was indeed open, and Thomas coasted the Newton up to the buoy, selecting reverse drive to bring the boat to a stop, allowing AJ to gaff the line. Once secured he shut down the motor and joined the group on the deck. AJ had already opened the cooler and started to hand out sandwiches, so Thomas helped her, and then set the Tupperware containers of fresh fruit on the centre table. He'd joined AJ nearly three years ago after working as an intern for Reg. She needed full-time help and he had grown up on boats, so handling the rigid inflatable boat, her only vessel at the time, was easy for him. He had only been diving a year but AJ quickly put him through the divemaster course so he could guide customers, taking some burden off of her having to lead every dive. This past winter he'd gone through his instructor training so now he could also teach certification courses to new divers. After nearly three years working together, the two of them operated like a well-oiled machine. Thomas couldn't imagine working for someone else. AJ treated him like a partner rather than an employee, and made him feel respected and appreciated.

Growing up the son of a fisherman in a lower income household, Thomas's main interaction had been with the local community in West Bay. The foreign workers were on the island to cater to the foreign tourists and that wasn't a world he was part of. He knew the restaurants bought his father's catch, and the tourists went to the restaurants, so they were essential to his family's livelihood, but their paths rarely crossed. His parents thought he was crazy when he told them he wanted to scuba dive and see if he could work for one of the dive operations. He was just out of school, where he'd been above average in most classes, but they expected him to join his father, fishing, as he'd done in his spare time since he was a little kid. His parents may have been traditional islanders, but they weren't short-sighted people, and to his surprise they encouraged him to give it a try. The one caveat they added was that after six months, if he wasn't making a living, then he would join his father. Thomas's older sister, Sydney, had excelled in school and received a partial scholarship to attend the University of

Miami in Florida. The family were all chipping in their part to pay for the balance of the expenses, and he was committed to do his share. He readily agreed to their request and set about finding a job. One of the first people he approached was Reg Moore. The imposing man operated from his own pier next to West Bay public dock, and seemed to have the most organised operation. Thomas didn't consider himself shy, but he was nervous when he approached Reg. The guy had a permanent frown and a deep, gruff voice that seem to make the ground tremble. On an island with a history riddled with pirate adventures, he pictured Reg as a swash-buckling tyrant, which didn't help him summon up the courage to talk to the man. When he finally approached him, he was pleas-antly surprised that despite the stern stare he was received politely, and Reg said he'd consider it. After striking out at several other dive operators, most suspicious of a local lad talking about diving, as it wasn't common, he checked back with Reg.

Starting at low pay he was given a month to prove himself. If he made himself useful, Reg told him, he'd teach him to dive and put him through the certification course at no cost. If he survived all that, without incurring the man's wrath, then he'd increase his pay and keep him on. Thomas was ecstatic. His father had raised him to work, and work hard, and he put that ethos to good use. Arriving early each day he tried to think ahead and anticipate what the crew needed every day to make their lives easier. As he quickly began to understand the workings of the operation, and earned the trust of the other employees, he made himself an integral part of the day-to-day routine. Unlike so many young men his age, he had no interest in appearing cool or nonchalant; he hustled and found work to do even when things were quiet. Thomas held his breath when Reg said his one-month probation was up, and the surly Londoner made him sweat for a few minutes, going on about how times were hard and money was tight. Finally, with a childish grin, Reg told him his diving classes started the next day.

AJ's laugh brought Thomas back to the moment, and he looked around the boat with a smile. Earlier that morning he'd guided the deep dive. It had marked his one thousandth dive since the first time he'd donned scuba gear, under Reg's watchful eye, and descended below the surface. He'd quietly mentioned it to AJ, who in turn gathered Jack's group and announced the milestone. Thomas had blushed with embarrassment. And beamed with pride.

14

WEDNESDAY

Hallie made Raposa order from the food truck while she sat on a low wall around the side, out of sight. About a year ago she'd been starving and had stolen a grilled chicken when the cook turned his back for a moment. She had regretted it ever since as the man had recognised her and now refused her service, even if she had the money. She loved the wraps and the traditional Cayman soup he made. She'd made the man, who called himself Raposa, walk ahead of her all the way. She was impressed: he seemed at ease, and didn't keep looking back to see if she had run off. He was a confident sort. He had talked about growing up in Brazil and living on the streets when he was young. She knew he was trying to relate to her, or more accurately get her to relate to him and form a basis of trust, so she was cautious to believe him. Although, if he was making it all up then he was well practised, as he certainly made it believable.

Raposa reappeared with an armful of food and a couple of bottles of soda. He placed the feast down on the concrete wall between the two of them, and handed her one of the drinks. She eyed him carefully while she took a long gulp from the bottle. She rarely indulged in sodas as water was free, and the cool, sugar-laced drink tasted sweet and refreshing. She sat it down and cautiously unwrapped one of the foil sheets, releasing steam and an array of aromas from the hot pulled pork sandwich. She took an enthusiastic bite whilst keeping an eye on the man. He was smiling at her as he ate his sandwich. She chewed the mouthful before speaking.

"What? Why are you smiling like that?"

He wiped his mouth with a napkin. "My apologies, I didn't mean to stare. I'm guessing you didn't always live where you do now, am I correct?"

Hallie paused and considered the question, her suspicious nature looking for the angle behind every word and action thrown her way. "No, when I was young we lived in a real house – why do you say that?"

He held up a hand defensively. "I'm not judging, just observing, okay?"

She nodded, and taking another bite of her sandwich she let him continue.

"You're clearly smart, and you're well mannered," he said pleasantly.

She took another drink from her soda bottle and didn't say anything. She had learnt over time to say little and listen carefully. When she was younger it amazed her what adults would say when they forgot the child was in the room. Staying quiet and being invisible had become a way of life. But now, approaching seventeen years old, her appearance was sabotaging her stealth. This man finding her being the latest case in point.

"Street kids miss out on learning some of the basic manners and graces," he continued when it became clear she wasn't going to respond. "You carry yourself well."

He pointed at her without menace. "Put you in a nice dress, a little attention to your hair and some subtle make-up, and you could pass in any banquet hall, fancy restaurant or movie premiere."

"I've never even been to a movie theatre, never mind a movie premiere." She laughed. "By the time the cinema opened at Camana Bay, we couldn't afford a ticket."

"That's too bad, but we can change that," he said, looking her squarely in the eyes, which made her uncomfortable. She was too used to avoiding eye contact. He's tricking me, she thought, with all this friendly chatter.

"So, what is it you think we can do business over? You should know, I work alone. I'm not beholden to anyone, and don't plan to be."

The man sat back and wiped his fingers on a paper napkin, "That's fine, I understand, I can see you're independent and seem to be getting by okay on your own. Your parents?" he asked carefully.

She stared at him blankly, trying to read his intentions. If she said she was completely alone he may take that as meaning defenceless. Unsure, she simply shook her head.

"Okay, so what ties do you have to the island here?" he asked.

"I have family here," she replied, a little too quickly. If he intended to whisk her away to do who knows what to her he needed to know she'd be missed. Of course, she knew that was a lie. Her mother had alienated the family and although several relatives had reached out to Hallie after her mother's death, she'd spurned them all. Her mother had repeatedly told her the family had turned their back on the two of them. None of them knew where she lived or what she was up to these days.

His voice was calm and soft. "What I mean is, if you had the opportunity to leave the island, to pursue a new life somewhere else, would you consider it?"

She finished chewing the last of the second sandwich she'd eaten and looked at the man. "You said lunch and you'd tell me whatever it is you think I'd be interested in. I've finished lunch and you're yet to tell me anything that makes sense. So, thank you mister, but I've got places to be."

He chuckled as she rose from the wall ready to leave. Humour was not really the reaction she expected, and she turned and scowled at him.

"Places to be?" he said, smiling at her.

She wanted to be angry, but something about this man was pleasantly disarming. She'd never been romantically involved with anyone, but she was sixteen after all, and well, she pondered, he's kinda sexy for an older guy.

A smile broke across her face. "Yeah, I have places to be. Maybe I was on my way to a movie premiere."

They both laughed and it was the first time in as long as she could remember that she truly laughed unguardedly. She sat back down.

"Thank you," he said gently. He took his mobile phone from his pocket and scrolled through pictures until he found what he was looking for. He held the screen in front of her so she could see.

"This is the yacht we own." He thumbed through several pictures showing the streamlined shape of the outside, and then the plush interior.

Hallie had seen pictures of boats like this in fancy magazines the tourist board used to promote the island. People left the glossy publications lying around as they were free at the airport and in the hotels. Raposa showed her more pictures of what looked like a hotel, and again thumbed through different views.

"This is our resort, it's here on Grand Cayman," he said. "We are a private club of sorts; only rich men, and a few women, from around the world can afford to be members, and we have strict rules for those who join."

"My house looks like that on the inside," Hallie chuckled, and they both laughed openly again. The images captivated her, and being close to this friendly and handsome man was a welcome escape from the life she was leading, the only life she really knew.

"We take young women, like yourself, and coach you to work as hosts at our resort. The training takes place mainly on the yacht before you'd move into the resort, and then you'd begin your one-year contract with us, working as a host."

"A host?" she asked. "What is a host? You mean I'd cook and clean the hotel?" Her mother had once worked as a cleaner at one of the smaller hotels, until she was fired for stealing toilet paper and shampoo.

"No, no, we have staff who service the rooms, and professional chefs who prepare all the meals. You would be like a guest in the resort, you mingle with the millionaires who stay with us, and spend time with them."

Hallie wondered what mingle meant. She knew what the word meant, but she was certain in this case something more than casually walking amongst them was required. She was sixteen, but she wasn't naive.

"You want me to have sex with these men?"

Raposa held up a hand. "Not necessarily. But sometimes that happens." The frown returned to her face and he quickly continued, "The guests' desires vary greatly, and different girls prefer different roles, but here's the part you need to know. We coach you, we house you, we feed you, we provide your wardrobe and all your hair and make-up needs. We take care of all your medical and we pay you ten thousand dollars a month for the length of the contract."

Hallie's frown melted from her forehead and her eyes grew bigger; her gorgeous golden amber irises sparkled. She was always careful not to let her imagination run wild when she turned the glossy pages of the magazines. The expensive homes, luxurious boats and beautiful clothes the rich people enjoyed, just minutes away from her dirt-floored shack. It was right in front of her, but it was not in her destiny and she had accepted that. But here was a man offering her the key to that world, an escape from never knowing where the next meal would come from, or the fear of finally being caught by the police. So what if it meant having sex with a millionaire? She looked at Raposa and pictured herself in his arms, on a yacht, with waiters hovering with glasses of champagne. As her imagination was finally unleashed, unabated, she heard him softly say, "After that, you're free to go wherever you dream of, live the life you deserve, with all the money you'll need to start over."

15

WEDNESDAY

Raposa pulled through the front gate in one of the Range Rover Evoques he'd taken into town. His mobile phone had been blowing up with messages from Cristal; she was mad about something and wanted to see him right away. He'd replied after leaving Hallie that he'd be back in an hour, to which she'd responded 'Now!' He parked the car in front of its villa and quickly hustled to the main building, making his way up the stairs to Cristal's office on the third floor. The whole way he tried to figure out what she could be so wound up about. She was ruthless, no doubt, but she was generally calm and even tempered, regardless of the situation. He nervously entered her office after knocking and hearing her snap back, "About time."

"What's the emergency?" he asked as he walked towards her desk.

She flung a copy of the *Cayman Compass* newspaper across the glass top and he read the headline before it stopped, sliding into his hand. 'Body found off north coast.'

Shit, he thought, how the hell did her body surface?

"She's left the island, isn't that what you told me?" Cristal said, menacingly calm now he was in front of her. "Well, she's back on the island now, isn't she?"

He preferred her yelling, he decided, at least he knew where he stood; this venomously controlled placidity hid the extent of her real intentions. He'd worked with and for this woman for a long time, but never did he underestimate her ability to turn on him, given a reason. He hoped this was not the reason. He quickly scoured the article and saw it had almost zero detail or information. It also, thankfully, did not have a picture of Carlina or an identification.

"Man, I'm sorry Cristal. I tied a shit load of weight..."

"Stop talking," Cristal blurted, interrupting him. "I don't want to know the details, that's the deal, remember?"

"Yeah, sorry," he said meekly. "I must have screwed up somehow. I'm really sorry, but at least they don't know anything, and there's no way she can be traced back to here."

Cristal stared at him blankly as she lit a cigarette. "The paper doesn't know shit – that doesn't mean the police don't know anything."

"The main thing is she can't be traced here, there's not a stitch of paperwork that leads her to us. She came here on the Cova do Leão, so they never knew she was on the island, I destroyed her student papers we had made, and she's never been reported missing from the Dominican," he said convincingly, but she still bit back.

"Are you sure you destroyed the papers?" Cristal sneered at him.

Raposa rolled his eyes. "Come on Cristal, you know me better than that. I know this is a screw-up, but I made one mistake and this was the first time we've done this. Well, first time for an end-of-contract deal." He corrected himself. "The rest went fine, the paperwork was incinerated along with all her clothing, possessions, jewellery, everything."

Cristal appeared to relax and sat back in her chair, taking a long drag on her cigarette. Raposa took the opportunity to change the subject in a hurry.

"I assume Symanski signed up? I saw he's in number five."

Cristal looked at him knowingly but allowed the change in conversation.

"He did, so that's fifty, and as it's only a month to the anniversary of the opening I talked him into signing up for next year, plus the last month of this term. About seventy percent have already renewed for another year. Jacobs and Russo did when I spoke to them."

Raposa smiled. "That's good news – so are we going ahead with the second resort?"

Cristal nodded. "If I secure that property on Seven Mile Beach we will. But that will bring a whole new set of challenges we'll have to face."

"Securing a facility in the middle of the busiest part of the island will be difficult for sure. A lot of temptations for the girls close by. At least here it's easier to isolate them," he pondered.

"The main thing is the model has worked, and come together faster than I ever imagined," Cristal said after letting out a long stream of cigarette smoke. "We capped it at fifty members here; if we get the Seven Mile Beach property, we should be able to create six villas again, so we'll double the membership to one hundred. The dues will be higher as the location is so much better, and more expensive, but I'm thinking of introducing gold, silver and bronze level memberships. Gold would be the beach resort exclusively, silver a fifty–fifty mix and bronze would be here at the current rate. We charge $250,000 currently for annual dues, plus twenty grand a night. I think we can charge three fifty for Seven Mile Beach and twenty-eight a night. By my calculations that will cover the additional cost of the location and still increase our margin."

Raposa's mind tried to keep up with the math; he'd not been the scholarly type, but working the streets had quickly taught him to figure out numbers and percentages. It all added up to a ton of money, that much he could piece together.

"It's also a lot of girls we need to find and train – we're going to outgrow the Cova do Leão. I tell you, we should think about training the girls somewhere else, then just using the boat to deliver them here. We could use it to run more trips for the guests that way. It would be cheap to set up a facility in Jamaica, Haiti, anywhere like that."

Cristal nodded her agreement as she took a last drag and stubbed out her cigarette. "I agree, I think it's time now the system is up and running. Be much easier to sort and assess the girls there, weed out the ones we don't want."

Raposa felt pretty pleased with himself for turning Cristal's demeanour around in his favour but still decided not to bring up the girl from town. No point pushing his luck. She was hard and fast on her no locals rule but that's because she hadn't seen this girl. He also hadn't recruited her yet so no point having an argument over something that might not happen. These kids were so young and unpredictable, they didn't think with reason, most were street kids that simply reacted to each situation they found themselves in. Cristal needed to see this girl in person, see those eyes, before he told her she was local. He was taking Hallie out to the Cova do Leão tomorrow to hopefully seal the deal, then he'd introduce her to Cristal. He realised Cristal had returned to her computer and was ignoring him, so he took the opportunity to leave. He opened the door but she stopped him.

"Raposa."

He turned and smiled, but she wasn't smiling; her expression was back to how they'd started.

"You're still on my shit list until this thing with Carlina goes away."

He nodded and before he closed the door, he heard her add,

"And you better hope it goes away."

16

WEDNESDAY

Reg stood on the deck of one of his dive boats, and stared down at the puppy running around excitedly. The little Cayman brown hound mutt sniffed every nook and cranny and enthusiastically wagged its tail. Reg's wife, Pearl, chuckled and slid an arm around the big man. She was a pretty lady with wavy blonde hair and a full figure which she made sure she was snuggling against her husband. Pearl beamed up at him, knowing he couldn't resist her smile, or her ample bosom nestled up against him through the colourful sun dress she wore. She'd turn fifty-eight later in the year, but with her bright smile and energetic demeanour she appeared a lot younger. AJ and Thomas had just finished cleaning their boat at the end of the day and were walking down the Yacht Club jetty.

"Oh great," Reg grumbled, "you've even arranged for reinforcements."

AJ looked at him as they stood on the pier, having not seen the puppy who was feverishly exploring under the bench.

"Reinforcements for what?"

The puppy, hearing a new voice, popped his head up and stretched his front paws as far as they'd reach up the gunwale to peer over.

"Oh, how lovely is that little fella," AJ gushed, melting at the sight of the puppy's face.

Reg just shook his head. "Bloody hell, same as last time; no point me even pretending this ain't gonna happen, is there?" He looked down at his wife, a foot shorter than him, and grinned through his thick grey beard.

Several years ago, she'd brought a puppy home and persuaded him to keep it. They'd unfortunately lost him after a couple of years to an illness they were never able to fathom. They'd both taken it badly, but it had now been about a year, and Pearl had decided their house was ready for a dog again. She smiled back up at him.

"What do you want to call him?"

AJ and Thomas stepped down to the deck, and AJ immediately got down on the floor to fuss with the puppy.

"Yeah, what's his name, Reg?"

He laughed. "Well, seeing as he's new to me, I haven't had a chance to give it much thought."

"He from Canine Friends Cayman?" Thomas asked Pearl.

"Yeah, they had a stray they picked up a while back, turned out she was pregnant, had the litter in the foster home. You know my friend Casey? Used to run Neptune's Divers, now she works for the Department of Environment. She's helped CFC for years. Anyway, she called and told me about the pups, and I picked this little chap out a month ago."

"See." Reg waggled his finger. "Conspiracy. Wait till I see Casey next."

"Give it up, you old grouch," AJ teased. "Smallest one of the bunch I bet?" she added, looking up at Pearl.

"Course he was, had to get the misfit no one else would want. How'd yer think I ended up with this one." She laughed, bumping Reg with her hips.

"Come on, you gotta think of a cool name, something worthy of a strong, fighting fella like this, Reg," AJ said, with the puppy on its back, wrestling her arm with his over-sized paws.

"A tough fellow, a good British fighter," Reg mused.

"Gotta be Henry bloody Cooper then, doesn't it?" Pearl burst out laughing.

"Perfect," Reg agreed.

"I like it," AJ said, tickling the puppy's tummy, "Henry Cooper. Which will undoubtedly be shortened to Cooper. No! Coop! That's brilliant, Coop is a great name."

"Yeah, that'll work," Reg smiled. "Coop it is."

"Who's Henry Cooper?" Thomas asked to the amusement of the English contingent.

"He was a famous boxer in England, love, well before your time," Pearl clued him in. "Speaking of names, isn't it about time you named your boats, AJ? They ought to have a moniker of some sort don't you think?"

AJ thought for a moment as she continued playing with Coop. She had considered it from time to time but could never settle on any names she liked enough. It was common practice to name the boats, especially if you had more than one in the business. It had been easy for her not to as one was the RIB, and the other the Newton, very different boats, so she and Thomas referred to them as the big and small boats. Reg had named his from the beginning: first was Golden Pearl, then Blue Pearl and the newest the White Pearl. He'd steered clear of the Black Pearl because of the *Pirates of the Caribbean* movies, but he was running out of pearl colours to use, so he'd probably use it if he bought another boat.

"I guess we should," she finally said, looking at Thomas. "Any ideas?"

Thomas looked around the group, seeming a little unsure. "I always figured the RIB should be named after your grandfather."

It had been AJ's grandfather's story, from his time in the British Navy during World War Two, that had set AJ and Reg on the hunt for a lost German U-boat scuttled seventy-five years ago, somewhere off Grand Cayman. AJ had found the sunken vessel a few years back in a dramatic race to preserve it against the greedy Argentinian son of a Nazi officer. Arthur Bailey had passed away when AJ was a young girl, the same year she first scuba dived in

Grand Cayman. A trip that happened to be with Reg's dive operation and began their friendship.

"That's a great idea," Reg said, to Thomas's relief.

"I love that too, but I'm not sure 'Arthur' is a good fit with Mermaid Divers?" AJ said looking at Thomas. "I'd considered it before but couldn't come up with a way to make it fit."

"How about 'Arthur's Journey' or something like that?" Pearl offered. "Sounds nautical enough and doesn't clash with Mermaids, even if it doesn't match exactly."

AJ nodded. "That's better, maybe something along those lines would work."

"Hey," Reg interrupted, "before I forget, could you do some DSDs Friday afternoon? I got a call from a resort we've taken some people out for in the past; they have three guys that want to try diving. I have all my boats running morning and afternoon Friday."

AJ started to answer, "We have Jack Benson's group all week..." But then she stopped herself. "You know what though, they're flying out Saturday midday so they can't dive that afternoon. Yeah, we should be able to do that. None of them are certified? They all want to do the intro course?"

"That's what the bloke who called said," Pearl replied.

"Where do they want to go?" AJ asked.

"North is fine I believe; I think the resort is this small place tucked away in Salt Creek. I'll let you know if it's picking up there, or in the past I know we've collected them from a yacht they have. Bloody nice Hatteras, you may have seen it around the island."

"Okay, well either way it's easy if it's north," AJ confirmed.

"Quest!" Pearl said enthusiastically. "How about Arthur's Quest? Sort of describes the story behind the name don't you think?"

"I like that," AJ said, mulling it over in her mind.

"Odyssey would be good too," Reg suggested. "It definitely was a long journey to find that submarine. Good tie-in to Homer's poem and all that."

AJ laughed. Reg often surprised her with references you wouldn't expect from a working-class sailor who'd worked with his hands his whole life. But Reg was a keen reader, and a smart man.

"Arthur's Odyssey. Yeah, I think that's good." AJ looked up at Thomas. "What do you think, Thomas? Could you get used to calling the RIB 'Arthur's Odyssey' instead of the small boat, or the RIB?"

Thomas beamed his toothy smile. "I think I'd be happy to get used to that, boss." His face turned a little more serious. "What about the Newton then?"

AJ looked back down at Coop, still playing with her on the deck. "Gotta be 'Hazel's Odyssey' doesn't it?" she said quietly.

Hazel had been a woman AJ had grown close to when she arrived on the island the year before to dive with Mermaids. Turned out Hazel was looking for more than just diving and had a story of her own she was pursuing the answers to. After some perilous diving on a wreck called the Raptor, off the north-west corner of the island, Hazel was murdered by a drug lord who'd been hunting her for years. It happened on the RIB and AJ still had a hard time being on the boat without seeing images of her dying friend.

Pearl stepped over and put a hand on AJ's shoulder. "That's a good name right there, my love, a good name."

17

WEDNESDAY

Nora strolled up to the door of villa number five and knocked firmly. The routine was old hat to her these days after ten months at the resort. Early on she had hoped it wouldn't be her picked, but then she stressed out when other girls were chosen as hosts, worried they'd terminate her contract before the year was up if she wasn't popular. After a while it became clear that all the girls appealed to some of the guests, some of the time, and she relaxed enough to enjoy the quiet times, and brave it through the busy weeks. Most clients were pleasant enough, or at least they weren't offensive. She'd only had a few that were keen to play with her immediately after they'd spent a hot, humid day fishing or golfing. She'd managed to persuade them into an intimate shower and washed away the stench before they spent the night. Most of the clients were older men, and with a bottle of wine in their system and a good dinner, their libido didn't last long. She could shuffle to the other side of the king-sized bed and get some rest.

Symanski opened the door and smiled but wasn't sure where to look.

"Hey Joe, nice to see you again," the seventeen-year-old girl said, taking control of the situation as she'd been trained to do with shy clients.

"Good evening Nora," he said, pushing his glasses up the bridge of his nose and stepping aside to let her in. "You look lovely, as you did yesterday."

"Thank you, Joe," she said softly as she glided by him, being sure to brush lightly against him. She'd chosen her short, silver dress, with the plunging neckline which had been a successful go-to outfit in encouraging the meek ones to find their courage. The night before they'd enjoyed a lovely dinner, she'd coaxed him into sporadic conversation, and they'd relaxed on the settee and watched a movie. But that was it, and despite her carefully making advances, he'd politely thanked her for the evening and shown her to the door. While she revelled in a night alone in her own bed, she was well aware she needed to make sure the client was happy to spend; what she'd learnt over the ten months was they paid a small fortune. She'd been confident he'd ask for her again, he seemed obsessed when she was around him, but she also knew she needed to get him past his shyness and give him an experience worth the price.

Nora entered the villa and nodded pleasantly to the Hispanic lady preparing dinner. There were seven women, one per villa, plus one for the main building, who prepared all the evening meals for not only the guests, but the girls as well. They were culinary wizards, but they also cleaned the rooms, including the girls' dormitories, and never seemed to take a day off. Nora often wondered what arrangement they were on. All seven appeared to be in their thirties, and uninterested in any interaction outside the absolute necessities. Uninterested, or afraid. They didn't even appear to converse much with each other. The ladies were always pleasant but their ability to speak English varied greatly depending on the circumstance. Somehow, they always understood the client's needs, but rarely conversed with the girls. All the girls had theories about where the seven women were from, but nobody knew for sure. It wasn't Brazil like Miss Sombrio and Raposa, as they spoke

Spanish not Portuguese, but the women wouldn't say, so the mystery went on.

Nora moved past the open-plan kitchen and dining area to the lounge where the ceiling opened up, making the room feel expansive. The bedroom and master bathroom were upstairs, above the kitchen and dining area, with a railing along the front edge overlooking the lounge. With full-width glass from the floor to the second storey ceiling, surrounding French doors overlooking Salt Creek, the Caribbean view from the whole villa was impressive. Standing by the French doors, she smiled at Symanski, who shuffled about nervously, clearly unsure what to do with himself. Several times he glanced back at the chef and appeared embarrassed. Or perhaps worried about being with such a young girl in front of a witness. Nora nodded towards the deck and opened the doors, beckoning him to follow. He seemed relieved to step outside and took a seat next to her on the outdoor sofa.

"What is she making for us? I can ask her to hurry and leave if you'd prefer?" Nora asked, trying to read the man.

He smoothed the fabric of his slacks and shifted in his seat, "I'm not very hungry actually, so whatever you'd like is fine. I think she was preparing some local fish."

Nora smiled and put her hand on his arm, "Let me go see and I'll get us a drink. What would you like?"

Symanski began to rise from the seat but she put a hand on his shoulder and stopped him. "Please, Joe, just relax, remember you're on holiday. I'll be right back."

The villas were stocked with a selection of fine wines along with a full liquor cabinet, so Nora opened a bottle of Châteauneuf-du-Pape red wine and grabbed a couple of glasses. He'd drunk red wine the night before so she guessed it would be a safe bet, as he couldn't manage to tell her. She stood at the entry to the kitchen and looked at the chef, who was busily chopping vegetables and ignoring her presence. Nora noticed rice steaming on the stove top and two beautiful fillets of fish waiting to go in the pan. Her stomach groaned at the opulent meal about to be wasted, especially as she was quite hungry.

"He says he's not hungry, so perhaps a cheese and fruit plate? I'm really sorry."

The woman made no obvious indication she'd heard or understood Nora's words and finished chopping the vegetables. When she was done slicing, she walked to the stove and turned the rice down to low before taking some cling-film and covering the fish. Nora shrugged her shoulders. "Thank you. I think he'd like some privacy once you're done."

Not expecting a response, she returned to the deck, where Symanski politely stood until she took her seat. She poured two glasses of wine and handed him one.

"Cheers, Joe," she said, holding up her glass, "Why don't you tell me about your day? Did you have fun on the island?"

He tapped his glass to hers and stared into her eyes as he took a long, slow sip of the wine.

"We played golf, but I'm not very good. They enjoy it more than I do. Al and Bill that is. Al wants to get out on the water tomorrow, I think I'll like that better. What did you do today? What do you do all day?" he asked, surprising her with a touch more boldness than the night before.

"I waited for you, Joe," she said with a sly smile, her bright blue eyes locking on his.

This time he didn't look away, but took another long sip of his wine, and for the first time she noticed how dark his eyes were. He had a nervous intensity like a wound-up spring and also for the first time she felt a pang of concern about the man. He wasn't very tall, couldn't weigh more than an average woman and appeared to be soft like he'd never done anything physical in his life, but for a brief second Nora sensed there may be a sleeping tiger behind the kitten facade.

"That's sweet," he said warmly, and her foreboding passed as quickly as it had arrived. "Why don't we step inside and get more comfortable?"

• • •

It was 2am. Nora had glanced at the bedside clock before she'd quietly gathered her dress and shoes and tip-toed downstairs. She was supposed to stay the night and have breakfast with the guest, unless they asked them to leave. But she'd lain awake and tortured herself back and forth, finally settling on an excuse of not feeling well if he complained. She carefully closed the door and gingerly stepped away in her bare feet. Her whole body ached. The tiger had certainly been awoken, and what a cold, harsh animal he was. Nora had been with clients that liked to be physical, but none who had really hurt her, or sometimes some soreness, but this had been different. As unimposing as the man was physically, he made up for it with a strange aggression that had terrified her. He'd held her down and several times she'd struggled to breathe with her face forced into the bed. She shivered, despite the hot and humid tropical night air. With her elfish Scandinavian looks and tall but skinny frame, she looked even younger than her seventeen years, but Nora had experienced a lot in her short life, and felt like an adult. She didn't think like a child or act like a teenager, but as she stumbled along the path back to the main building to what, for ten months, had felt like the safety of home, she wished she could curl up in her tiny bed in Oslo, cuddle her overstuffed teddy bear, and sleep like a child. She began to quietly sob as she trudged up the stairs to her dormitory.

18

THURSDAY

AJ piloted the Newton out of their berth at the Yacht Club, and idled around the end of the marina by Bacaro restaurant. Thomas was down on deck helping Jack's group stow their bags and setting up their BCDs on tanks. It was a pretty morning, with the sun low in the eastern sky off the port side, and a gentle cooling breeze coming from the north. AJ was first boat out of the marina this morning – it helped having the same group all week, so everyone knew the drill. They'd have their choice of dive sites when they reached the north wall. She passed by Morgan's Seafood restaurant off the starboard side, one of her favourites, and cleared the Yacht Club headland to enter Governors Creek. Looking back towards the Yacht Club boat ramp she noticed an impressive motor yacht moored at the fuel dock. Looked like a Hatteras, she pondered, an American boat builder that has been around for 60 years making high-end fishing boats and luxury motor yachts. Surfing their website was like a trip to the ocean lover's sweet shop. She figured this boat had to be at least 75 feet long so was probably a few million dollars, even if it was ten years old. She wondered if it was the boat Reg had mentioned yesterday. It often amazed her the wealth and opulence on the island. Most of the lavish homes lining the water were holiday homes for rich Americans and Europeans. These folks had millions to spend on a house they spent less than three weeks in each year. She could only imagine what their primary residences were like.

AJ owned a condo on the west side, but she didn't live in it. She'd bought the property with money she'd made from the world-wide fuss over her U-boat discovery. Her mother, a barrister in England, negotiated the rights to a documentary about the amazing story, and the windfall went towards the condo and the Newton dive boat AJ now steered into the channel leading to the North Sound. She still lived in a tiny apartment in the grounds of a large house overlooking Seven Mile Beach. The owners were from Atlanta, Georgia and rent was greatly reduced in exchange for AJ keeping an eye on the place, and taking them diving when they came to the island. With her condo rented out, and no need for a big place, she was happy to keep her amazing view. Most of the time it was just her anyway. The man she was dating, Jackson, worked for Sea Sentry, an environmental non-profit that had boats in various waters of the world, campaigning against illegal fishing, poaching and cruelty. He visited whenever he could, which was usually only a few days every couple of months, and was used to living on a boat, so the small apartment didn't bother him. Jackson tried to live a minimalist existence and AJ, never one for accumu-lating possessions, found herself trying more and more to reduce her impact on the island's overburdened landfill.

Thomas joined her on the fly-bridge as she opened up the throttle on the Newton, having reached the open sound and cleared the no-wake zone of the channel. The big boat eased up on plane and glided across the mirror-flat water of North Sound towards the cut, two and half miles away.

"Another perfect Cayman morning, boss," Thomas said, with his broad smile, and AJ was relieved to see him back to his usual self. They'd both learnt, having worked together so long that their moods deeply affected the other's state of mind. AJ wasn't really a morning person, although her lifestyle dictated she be up before dawn. Thomas on the other hand seemed to wake up with enthusiasm, ready to go, and his infectious spirit worked better than coffee on AJ.

"We'll have our pick of the sites," she replied. "Where do you feel like going?"

"Let's head east, maybe all the way over by Rum Point; we could do Penny's Arch for the second dive, they haven't been there yet this trip," Thomas answered, clearly having thought about it already.

AJ liked the idea of staying away from the west side, where they'd found the girl, and was sure that was Thomas's motivation as well.

"I like that idea," she said and turned the boat on a more easterly heading towards Rum Point Channel, the cut in the reef closer to Rum Point. "How about Andes Wall for the deep dive?"

"For sure, I've had good luck there, especially early like this. Maybe we'll spot them a shark if we're lucky," Thomas said, doing a little dance. "And today, I'm feeling lucky. That beautiful little island sweetheart's gonna call me back, lucky. Mama's made fish run-down for supper kinda lucky. Oh yeah, I'm feeling sharks at Andes Wall lucky today."

AJ laughed as Thomas spun around the fly-bridge in his happy dance but as she was about to turn on some music for him, her mobile buzzed with a text message. She checked the sender and saw it was Reg.

'Tomorrow's DSD, 3 guys, pick them up from their boat, Cova do Leão, 80' Hatteras, meet outside Governors Creek channel 2pm.'

AJ stared at the message a moment, and Thomas, seeing she was distracted, finished his jig.

"Problem, boss?"

AJ shook her head. "No, just an odd coincidence."

Thomas looked puzzled, "How's that?"

"Did you notice the big Hatteras at the fuel dock when we were leaving this morning?"

Thomas leaned against the framework. "That sleek-looking

motor yacht? That thing is really cool, gotta be able to cruise anywhere in that boat."

"That was Reg who texted; looks like that's our DSDs for tomorrow. We're meeting that boat outside the channel at two o'clock," AJ replied. "Just weird, I've never noticed that boat before today and now we're meeting them to go diving."

"Maybe it just got to the island?" Thomas thought a moment. "But I think I've seen it around before: stays way offshore most of the time."

"Hmmm, come to think of it," AJ looked up at him. "It could be the one we've wondered about before; always seems strange it hangs out in the deep water. I just figured they were fishing."

They reached the cut and Thomas started towards the ladder, heading down to prepare for the first dive. As he turned to step down, he paused and added, "Didn't have any outriggers and I didn't notice a fighting chair. If they were that keen on deep-water fishing you'd think they'd be set up better. In fact, that boat really doesn't have a cockpit big enough to fish from, not for the big game you'd find offshore like that."

AJ looked over her shoulder to reply, "You're right, that's a cruising motor yacht, not a fishing boat. Who knows? Guess we'll find out tomorrow when we meet them."

19

THURSDAY

Cristal held Nora in her arms and let her quietly sob against her neck. She'd found the girl in the dormitory lounge when she did her usual morning rounds to see what drama had ensued. Nora was curled up with her arms tightly wrapped around her knees in one of the overstuffed chairs. Once she had seen the bruising on the girl's arms and back, she led her to her own private apartment, and let Nora spill her guts about the night before. She felt the girl's body lose all its tension and melt into her embrace after Cristal told her she'd take care of the brute.

Walking Nora back to her dorm room that she shared with one other girl, Cristal told her she wouldn't be working for a few days until she felt better, and the bruising had gone away. Nora asked her if she'd have to see Symanski again, and Cristal assured her she wouldn't. The young girl looked so innocent and frail as Cristal tucked her back into her single bed and left her to get some rest. Cristal couldn't help a wry smile as she headed to her office. She knew she had that wimp Symanski by the balls now – the pervert would pay dearly for this.

. . .

She sent Raposa a text to come and see her, and lit a cigarette while she waited. Sitting at her desk, she clicked through the latest paperwork on the Seven Mile Beach property. The deal was close, finally. She had started out playing hardball with the seller and offered low, but the market was strong, and the man knew the land would continue appreciating the longer he sat on it. As the seller's estate agent loved to point out, 'there's only seven miles of Caribbean paradise on the famous Seven Mile Beach; once it's gone, it's all gone.' Cristal wanted to punch the man in the face, but unfortunately, he was correct. She'd sneaked up her offer bit by bit until he'd finally countered with a number she could work with. With the big corporations strong-arming the government to allow them to build taller, her four-storey structure would slide right through planning permission. Buildings used to be restricted to five stories for hotels, preserving the island aesthetic, instead of looking like a downtown city suddenly met a beach. In the mid 2000s, post hurricane Ivan, it was raised to seven levels, but then, under developer pressure, quickly became nine storeys which in turn accidentally evolved to ten when a particularly powerful developer argued over where the ground was actually located. They wouldn't blink at four levels and she would stack the villas two to a building, making sure each maintained a perfect ocean view.

Raposa knocked and entered, appearing a touch tentative after yesterday's scolding.

"Did you see Nora this morning?" Cristal asked before taking a long drag of her cigarette.

Raposa shook his head and Cristal could tell by his blank expression he was waiting to see if he was in some kind of trouble. She hid a smile, as she let out a long exhale of smoke. She loved having power over people, especially men. For her, power over other women was too easy; she preferred the challenge of the male species, the bigger and stronger the better.

"The new guy, Symanski, worked her over pretty good. Guess his Napoleon complex got the best of him, the little shit."

"Is she hurt badly?" Raposa asked, sounding concerned, which she knew he was. Concerned he'd have to deal with another body.

"No, she's fine. Bruised, and walking like she'd worked a night on a Rio street corner, poor little thing. She was too embarrassed to tell me what he'd used on her; must have been something though, 'cos I guarantee that twerp's little dick couldn't make a nun flinch."

Raposa laughed loudly, and she could tell she shocked him sometimes with her course language. She sometimes wondered what he'd be like in bed. She'd watched him perform, and he seemed to have a flair, but she had never experienced the man for herself. Either way, it wasn't worth throwing away a good employee over a fling. She preferred to never see her lovers again after she'd had her fill. Relationships were for the weak.

"Make sure Symanski knows he's screwed up; I was perfectly clear that damaging the girls was strictly forbidden. This will play out nicely for us."

Raposa nodded knowingly. "I'll go and find him."

Joe Symanski looked like a schoolboy caught stealing crayons. Raposa remained standing to tower over the little man, who stared at the tiled floor of his villa and mumbled apologies.

"What the hell were you thinking, Mr. Symanski?" Raposa laid it on.

"I'm sorry. I have an enthusiastic sexual appetite; I may have got carried away," he whimpered but wouldn't look up. "Is she okay? I certainly didn't mean to harm her, she's a lovely girl."

"No, she's not alright, she looks like she's gone three rounds with Ronda Rousey. She can't work for at least a week." Raposa leaned in closer, "The rules were made clear, sir: hurt the girls and you're out, no refund."

The accountant finally looked up, the mention of financial loss hitting home, and Raposa was surprised at the rage in the man's beady eyes.

"I just transferred a quarter of a million dollars to the damn resort, and you're telling me because one little tart moaned about a bruise or two you're keeping that? Think again. Do you know who my two friends are?" He started to stand but Raposa pushed him effortlessly back into his seat.

"Calm down Mr. Symanski. We do thorough background checks on everyone; believe me, we know just who your friends are, and we know everything about you. Your nasty divorce, your daughter you never see, the three allegations of rape that you've managed to get away with," Raposa said calmly, learning from his boss.

Symanski looked up, his anger now replaced with fear, and a touch of confusion. "They're not people to meddle with," he said with less conviction.

"What makes you think we are, Mr. Symanski?" Raposa said, staring coldly into the man's eyes. Symanski quickly returned his gaze to the floor.

"We're businesspeople, Mr. Symanski, we would prefer to resolve this issue in a mutually beneficial way," Raposa added, his voice softening.

Symanski looked back up. "Really?" A glimmer of hope in his eye, before suspicion crept in. "What exactly are you suggesting?"

"I'm just saying, you have certain tastes, and we're in the business of providing solutions to a client's unique needs." Raposa smiled pleasantly at the accountant.

Symanski slid his glasses up his nose. "Go on."

Raposa wondered why a man with his kind of money wouldn't find a pair of glasses that stayed in place. A stray thought about nailing them to the little creep's forehead crept in, but he stayed focused; this was going well.

"We can provide young ladies for you, that's what I'm saying. But it wouldn't be the girls we usually offer. This would be a special set of circumstances, so we have to bring someone in specifically for you. We'd need at least four weeks' notice."

Symanski shuffled in his seat but Raposa could see he was salivating at the idea put before him.

"What would the restrictions be?" he asked tentatively.

"There wouldn't be any," Raposa verified.

"No restrictions... at all?"

The hook was set. "None," Raposa replied firmly.

Symanski sat back, almost looking relaxed, "And what does this 'special' service cost? I assume there's an additional cost?"

Raposa smiled again. "Firstly, we'll overlook last night's indiscretion, and the loss of Nora's time while she recovers."

"Of course, of course," Symanski said, waving his hand impatiently.

"We have to recruit and house this young lady separately, you understand, and she'll not receive the in-depth training the others go through. But we'll select an appropriate candidate – she'll meet all the usual criteria for looks..." He paused to choose his English word carefully. "...and maturity."

Symanski just kept looking at him with a frown, waiting for the bottom line.

"Seventy-five if she walks out, a hundred if I have to carry her out," Raposa said, as though he were quoting the current rate for mowing a lawn.

Symanski didn't flinch. A strange smirk took over his mouth and his dark little eyes flitted from Raposa to the floor and back. "What about Nora? How much to provide Nora for me again, no questions."

Raposa was taken aback for a moment; he hadn't been prepared to consider that option. He could provide either a girl they recruited who didn't pass the training, or one straight from his contact on Dominican who wouldn't meet their standards in some way. Drug issues, or unwilling. It would cost him the price of fuel to collect a girl and the five grand he paid his contact, but Nora was a different story. They had a lot more invested in the girl, plus the price of replacing her. But she was nearly at the end of her contract, he remembered; she only had six weeks or so left. That might be perfect. She'd be leaving them anyway – may as well get paid for that too.

He shook his head, "That's probably not possible, I don't think Cristal would allow that, sir."

Symanski tilted his head to one side and smiled. "Bullshit. There's a price for everything; skip the play and tell me the number."

Raposa nodded. "Okay then. Two hundred. It would have to be on a day I'll give you, about five or six weeks from now. She'd be one night only; once she discovers it's you, she'll go crazy, she'll create mayhem. And not here, it'll be on the boat, offshore. Is that what you want?"

The corner of Symanski's mouth twitched, and he blinked rapidly. "Give me the date."

20

THURSDAY

AJ stood on the swim step with her gear on, ready to go. She looked out across the wide-open ocean in front of her, and then back over her shoulder at the north side of the island. Thomas stood behind her with a hand on the top of her tank in case they were rocked by a wave, but there was little chance, the seas were almost dead calm.

"Last chance, Bodden, you know I'm gonna see a shark down there. You already did your lucky dance, sure you don't want to lead this one?" she asked.

He laughed. "Nah, this is my gift to you today. I've arranged with the sea gods for plenty of eagle rays and at least one shark."

AJ shrugged her shoulders and replied with a smile, "Well, thank you Thomas." She took a giant stride into the water to follow the group of divers already gathering on the sea floor.

The first thing AJ noticed was the incredible visibility; she could easily see Jack, Sherry and their group at the mooring pin sixty feet below and a hundred feet ahead of her. She descended swiftly, and observed the soft corals and fans, looking to see if there was any significant current, often a problem at Andes Wall. The branches and intricate fans were almost stationary, barely a gentle sway as best she could tell. This promised to be a memorable dive, and she felt a pang of guilt that Thomas had insisted she take it.

A couple of raps on her tank got the divers' attention, and she finned gently across the top of the reef at sixty feet towards the drop-off. The whole landscape felt alive with movement. Schools of grunts, blue Chromis and schoolmasters weaved between coral heads and soft corals that reached five feet into the nutrient-rich waters. A large Nassau grouper hung with his mouth wide open and gills flared, while tiny gobies and wrasses gave his system a good cleaning. Their first eagle ray swooped by as AJ reached the top of the wall before dropping down the face to around ninety-five feet. She paused to let the others follow, before choosing to go east, and rolling over to look up at the almost sheer coral face above her. The light flickered and glistened on the surface, silhouetting Hazel's Odyssey, as the boat gently bobbed ten stories above. AJ rolled back over and did a visual sweep of the vast, dark, open water below her, and to the north. Two more eagle rays appeared from the deeper water, barely moving their massive wings to glide effortlessly over the divers towards the reef above.

Finning further along AJ spotted a chain eel poking his head from a crevice in the coral. Dark brown with a latticework of yellow, chain-like lines, the small eel watched her fin by with his bright yellow eyes. She pointed it out to the group and soon the photographers gathered, and flashes lit up the wall. She loved seeing the divers' reaction to an interesting find and, now entering her tenth year on Grand Cayman, she was delighted to feel the same enthusiasm underwater as the day she arrived. AJ checked her dive computer on her wrist, and seeing they were nearing twenty minutes' dive time, she angled up to go shallower, and start their return on top of the reef.

At first, she wasn't sure she'd actually seen anything; the deeper water can play tricks on the eyes and the lens effect underwater makes everything appear bigger. A twelve-inch ocean trigger at a hundred feet away could appear to be three feet long, until it came closer. But with a second movement she knew there was really something out there. The slow sway of the body gave away the shark before AJ could really see it properly. Below them, and well ahead, it slowly emerged from the darker water, and swam steadily towards the group. She dared not bang her tank in fear of spooking the beautiful creature, and hoped everyone had seen her pointing with an outstretched hand. As the image became clearer, she squealed into her regulator; the fish had the unmistakable, wide, extended brow of a hammerhead. Oh Thomas, she thought, what a gift indeed. Hammerheads patrolled the edges of the reef around the Cayman Islands, but were generally shy and stayed away from human activity, making them a rare sighting. Behind her, the group, including the photographers, stayed patient and let the big fish make its way towards them, apparently curious. Once he reached twenty feet away from AJ, the shark veered up and over the wall, heading for the sand flats in search of a stingray to pin down with his strong, mallet-like head.

AJ turned to look at her divers' reaction. Several were finning up towards the reef to catch a last glimpse, but the rest were wide eyed and frantically signalling their joy to each other. She eased over the top corner of the wall and started west back towards the boat. The few who had chased after the shark, who were the eager photographers of course, re-joined her and pointed south, indicating the direction the hammerhead had disappeared.

She took the return leg at a leisurely pace, allowing the group to explore the many cuts, ravines and coral heads. Once she neared the mooring pin, she pointed to the Newton above them and the group began ascending to fifteen feet for their safety stop. They'd spent quite some time deep and with the top of the reef still at sixty feet everyone was low on air, and even lower on no-deco time, with their bodies nearing the limit of nitrogen build-up. Hanging from the stern of the boat was a long, weighted regulator hose, attached to a tank on the boat. AJ and Thomas routinely provided the emergency supply in case anyone ended up too low on air to complete their safety stop. It also made a perfect fifteen-foot depth marker. After three minutes, allowing some of the gas to dissipate throughout their systems, the divers climbed the ladder one by one, until only AJ was left below the surface. Looking to the south she couldn't believe her eyes. The hammerhead cruised from the shallows right beneath her and, with a swoosh of its tail, returned to the deeper water beyond the drop-off. She decided that might have to be her little secret; she didn't have the heart to tell Jack and his friends they'd missed the second sighting.

AJ broke the surface and slung her fins up on the swim platform at the stern. Stepping up the ladder she looked up at Thomas beaming down at her.

"You're welcome," he said with a huge smile.

21

———————

THURSDAY

Raposa drove slowly down Rock Hole Road, trying to recall where the dirt path to the girl's shack was. He didn't need to. Looking ahead, he saw Hallie standing on the pavement watching him approach. She was wearing the same sun dress he saw her in the other day, and had a small blue rucksack thrown over her shoulder. He also noticed the same trainers, and chuckled. He pulled over to the kerb and parked, expecting her to open the door but she stood there peering into the Range Rover Evoque. He opened his door and stepped out, removing his sunglasses.

"Morning Hallie. You want to get in?" he said, smiling. He had forgotten how cautious and wary she was.

She nodded in way of a greeting and slowly opened the heavy car door, checking again inside the vehicle.

"You alone?" she asked, looking from the car up to Raposa.

"Of course. Look, Hallie, if you feel scared at any point just tell me and I'll pull over and let you out," he said reassuringly.

"I'm not scared," she said abruptly. "I'm careful."

He laughed. "That you are, and I understand why. Take your time, and like I said, anytime you want me to stop, I will. We're driving from town over to the Yacht Club on the North Sound, take us ten minutes, tops. The boat I told you about is there for you to take a look. Okay?"

Hallie slid into the passenger seat and looked around the luxurious interior of the car in awe. Raposa smiled to himself; he would have had the same look when he was her age. The look, the touch, the smell of an expensive car was completely foreign to a kid raised on the streets. He pulled away and watched from the corner of his eye as she marvelled at the ice-cold air streaming from the vents and chilling her light brown skin, causing her goose pimples.

As he drove along Esterly Tibbetts Highway she looked over at Camana Bay, the high-end outdoor mall, before they went under the expansive new bridge built to expedite access to the beach from the shops and condos in the complex. Raposa glanced at Hallie who was staring out the window.

"Have you been to Camana Bay? The shopping centre there?"

She looked over at him. "Of course. But not lately, the security is much tighter there. I only just got away last time, so I didn't go back. That was last year sometime."

He nodded and smiled, wondering how far she indeed travelled by foot, or maybe using the expansive bus system on the island. He decided to wait until he knew her better to pry any more – he didn't want to spook her. After five minutes of successive roundabouts along the highway, he turned right onto Yacht Drive, half expecting her to get concerned as the road was narrow and lined with mangroves. Apparently, she'd finally relaxed, or she knew where the Yacht Club was. He figured it was the latter. The boat was moored against the concrete sea wall, farther back from the fuel dock, where visiting boats were allowed to tie up. Raposa parked the Evoque and got out, waiting for her to do the same, before locking the vehicle. Hallie stared at the eighty-foot yacht across the car park in front of them. He could only imagine the thoughts running through the girl's head.

"Come on," he said softly, "I'll show you around."

She followed him across the car park and watched as he took the steps down to the spacious aft deck. He offered her a hand, but she jumped athletically down, and seemed to quickly assess the new surroundings, or more specifically her exit routes. He liked this girl. She was a gorgeous-looking kid, and those mesmerising eyes were incredible, but she reminded him of his own youth, and the friends he had on the streets of Rio. She was smart, but she was also agile and quick, like a wild cat. He was pretty sure if she decided to bolt he wouldn't be able to catch her. He walked across the aft deck, past the teak table and moulded-in couch, and beckoned her to follow. He opened the door to the salon and walked in, holding the door for her. Hallie tentatively followed, giving one more look over her shoulder at the steps back to the dock. Once inside her eyes grew wider and she was captivated, as she had been in the Range Rover.

Van Heerden and Marguerite stood in the back of the salon and gave the girl a moment to take in her new surroundings. Her eyes finally fell upon them and she immediately tensed. Raposa quickly stepped forward and started introductions.

"Hallie, please meet Captain Peter Van Heerden, and our training manager aboard the Cova do Leão, Miss Marguerite."

Hallie surprised everyone present by striding forward and firstly offering a hand to Van Heerden, and then to Marguerite.

"Pleased to meet you both, and thank you for allowing me on your boat," she said boldly.

Van Heerden laughed and looked at Raposa, who shrugged his shoulders.

"It's our pleasure, young lady," Van Heerden said when no one else spoke. "Would you like a tour?"

Hallie looked beyond the two at the stairs and doorways behind them.

"Yes please," she answered politely.

"Marguerite, would you show Hallie around the boat please," Raposa said, taking over. "Peter and I have some business to discuss, we'll be on the bridge when you're done."

"Of course," Marguerite answered with a slight bow of the

head, "I'd love to." She smiled broadly at the girl and stepped towards the galley with Hallie following.

"Where are the girls?" Raposa asked Van Heerden quietly.

"I sent them upstairs to the bridge. I wasn't sure when or how you wanted to introduce them," Van Heerden replied, walking towards the door to the aft deck.

"That's fine, she can meet them when Marguerite brings her upstairs. We'll kick them outside to the upper deck while we talk," Raposa replied as the two stepped out the door.

"I thought Cristal said no locals?" Van Heerden asked as they ascended the narrow steps to the fly-bridge.

"She did," Raposa replied slowly, "but, you saw the girl, what do you think?"

Van Heerden laughed. "Oh, she'll be the busiest girl you have." He paused on the upper deck and turned to Raposa. "If you can keep her under control. That kid's got fire in those beautiful eyes." He shook his head, "And then there's Cristal. She might not be so keen on breaking her own rule."

"She will," Raposa said confidently, "once she sees her. But until I get everything lined up, Cristal can't know, understand?"

"Sure." Van Heerden stroked his beard. "It's your balls she'll have removed – I'm just following orders."

Raposa slapped him on the shoulder. "I've got plans for my balls, she ain't getting them anytime soon. Don't you worry about Cristal, I'll have this wrapped and sorted by sunset today."

Van Heerden scoffed and opened the door to the fly-bridge. Inside, Abigay and Zoe looked up from the couch where they were sharing a magazine. "Hello gentlemen," they said in unison.

"Morning ladies," Raposa replied and looked the two over with a smile. "Don't you both look lovely."

They were both wearing two-piece bikinis with sunglasses propped on their heads.

"Thank you, sir," they managed in harmony again.

"Could I ask you ladies to step outside for a few minutes and enjoy the sun? The Captain and I have some business to discuss, and I'm sure it would bore you to tears."

They both rose and carefully smiled at both men as they slipped past and stepped outside.

Raposa held the door. "We have a guest aboard, a candidate for the program. Marguerite will bring her up in a few minutes. Can I rely on you two to give her a friendly welcome, and tell her how wonderful life is with the International Fellowship of Lions?"

Zoe ran a fingernail down his arm. "Of course we will, sir."

"I'm telling you, man, that one is a bloody walking sex machine. She'll give the clients a heart attack," Van Heerden said, laughing, after Raposa closed the door.

Raposa watched the two girls arrange themselves on the outdoor seats, knowing they couldn't see inside through the heavily tinted windows. "She doesn't lack any confidence, that's for sure."

22

THURSDAY

On the second dive, the group was rewarded with a nurse shark sighting, two more eagle rays and a plethora of other smaller, yet interesting critters. The thirty-minute ride back in from Penny's Arch went by quickly with the photographers showing off their new pictures and excited chatter about the dives. AJ eased back the throttle as she approached the channel leading from the sound into Governors Creek, slowing the Newton to idle through the 'no wake' zone. The 150' wide channel was lined with mangroves off the port side and large, expensive homes off the starboard side. AJ gave plenty of room to a catamaran full of tourists heading out to Stingray City, the shallow sandbar in the sound, where dozens of stingrays gather to be molested and fed. The story goes that fishermen returning through the cut, from the north into the sound, would throw their scraps overboard as they cleaned the fish. Over time the stingrays learnt where to grab a free meal. Somehow that had evolved into a lucrative business, ferrying hundreds of people to a conveniently shallow spot, where they could splash around in the waist deep water and feed them squid imported in bulk. The Department of Environment had recently been given the green light to come down on the non-licensed operations, and capped the licences allowed to their current number, at least freezing any more growth. At over two hundred licences already in use it was probably a little too late, but at least something was being done. AJ smiled and nodded as the passing people waved enthusiastically.

She reached the entrance to Governors Creek, which opened up into a large bay, a mile long, and almost half a mile wide at its broadest point. To their south was Crystal Harbour, a development of homes along a series of canals and fronting the bay. To the north was the Yacht Club, which protruded into the bay as a spit of land with the two restaurants on the end and the marina on the backside. Jack's group planned to take a break for a few hours and have lunch at their condo before returning to the boat around mid-afternoon, when they'd go out for one more dive. AJ was happy to work around any schedule they chose; they had the charter all week, so it was up to them how many dives they'd like to do. Generally, if divers were spending forty-five minutes to an hour underwater each dive, and going deep for many of them, three or four dives a day is plenty when they're diving every day for a week. The body never has time to dissipate all the built-up nitrogen and although Caribbean recreational diving should be a relaxing, low-cardio pastime, the body's internals are working overtime, and it gets tiring. Most divers sleep like babies on their holidays.

AJ turned to starboard, making a wide arc into the bay, giving plenty of room for anyone approaching from the north. As they idled along in the warm, midday sun, she heard the rising pitch of an engine approaching rapidly. She turned and spotted two jet-skis flying out of the channel at high speed. The first swung wide of the Newton and turned hard right across the bow, throwing a huge wave of water in the air. AJ cussed the fool under her breath and tried to get a clear look at the rider. It appeared to be a heavyset, older man, by the bulging life-vest stretched across his portly frame. The second jet-ski had slowed considerably, and let AJ pass by, before cutting to starboard and chasing after his friend. The second rider was a skinny little man whose life-vest rattled around as though a child was wearing an adult vest.

Thomas climbed the ladder to the fly-bridge and rustled his still wet hair, looking back at the jet-skis heading south. "What the hell was that about?"

"Bloody fools," AJ responded, shaking her head. "I bet they're guests of someone with a house here. The residents know better."

"You'd hope so – marine police see that, and they could lose those fancy skis." Thomas chuckled.

"I see them do that again and the marine police will definitely know about it." AJ grinned. "Then we'll buy those skis at auction and sell them to the guys who rent them on the beach."

Thomas gave her a high five. "That's why you're the boss, boss, always thinking," he said, tapping a finger to his head.

They pulled around to their mooring in the Yacht Club and helped the group unload their personal bags to the jetty. After verifying their leave time for the afternoon, Jack led his people up the path to the car park, and the van they'd rented. AJ looked up and scampering down the jetty towards her was Coop. Ears flapping, tail wagging and tongue hanging out, he skidded to a halt behind the boat and immediately sat and looked at AJ.

Not sure what to make of it, she laughed and said, "Come aboard!"

The puppy jumped up and leapt over the water to the swim platform, bounding past the open transom of the dive boat to AJ's feet, where he wriggled around excitedly as she made a big fuss of him. Reg had followed the dog down and stood on the jetty smiling.

"That's the first trick he's learnt. He's not allowed aboard a boat until he's granted permission. As it should be."

"You taught him that already?" AJ asked, amazed. "He's young to be picking up any training."

Reg stepped to the swim platform as Thomas uncoiled the air-fill line from their locker.

"Never too young I reckon. Besides, he's smart as a whip. Not quite up to speed on the potty training as yet. He gets a bit excited, as you may have noticed."

Thomas joined them on the boat and knelt down. Coop immediately shot over to the new admirer and took another fuss.

"Pearl playing tomorrow night, Reg?" Thomas asked between belly scratches.

"She is, make sure you make it, she's got some new songs she's been working on, great stuff," Reg replied. His eyes gleamed whenever he talked about his wife and her singing.

"We just have your DSDs in the afternoon, so we'll be there to help set-up if you like?" AJ offered.

"Sure, she'd appreciate it," Reg replied, stepping back to the jetty.

"Hey," AJ called out, thinking of the DSD clients. "These guys we're taking out – was that their Hatteras at the fuel dock this morning, Reg?"

"It is still there now," Thomas said. "I noticed it just after the jet-ski idiots came around."

"That's the boat," Reg said. "But I don't believe these guys own it. Belongs to a private resort, that's who contacts me. They're just guests or members, or whatever they call them at that place. It's the small resort they built a year or so ago, tucked away in Salt Creek. You can just see the tops of the buildings over the mangroves."

AJ shrugged. "I've seen the driveway to it, I remember when they were doing the construction. Odd site for a resort, hidden back there."

"I suppose it is really," Reg said as he turned to leave.

Coop scampered back across the deck as his daddy walked away up the jetty. He made the leap to the dock and sprinted until he was alongside Reg, looking up at the big man.

"Good boy, Coop, good boy," Reg muttered.

23

THURSDAY

Hallie felt like she'd disappeared down a rabbit hole; it reminded her of the stories her mother read to her when she was a small child. Downstairs, the boat housed a warren of rooms off a main hallway, and each one seemed to be a bedroom with its own bathroom. Every detail from floor to ceiling was pure luxury. Subtle LED lighting shone off gleaming, varnished wood and mirrors made every stateroom feel larger. The beds were neatly made and the only hint that anyone stayed in them was a book or magazine on the nightstand, and toiletries in the bathrooms. Marguerite had pointed out features of the rooms in detail as they toured through each one, but Hallie was only catching bits and pieces as her senses were bombarded with sights and smells that she'd never imagined. She stood in the master bathroom off the full-beam-width stateroom with a king-sized bed, staring at the tiled shower. It had been years since Hallie had taken a real shower. The shack had a small sink and she used a flannel to wash herself. Outside, a hose from a spigot was how she washed her hair. There was only cold water for both, but the water in the pipes would get hot during the day from the bright sun, so if she ran the water slowly, she'd get lukewarm water for a minute or so. She heard Marguerite talking again.

"One of these rooms would be yours during your training, which usually lasts three to eight weeks, depending on the work needed before graduating to the resort itself."

The woman spoke with a hint of an accent Hallie couldn't place, beyond knowing she wasn't Caymanian. Her uniform was a neatly pressed white shirt with lapels, and a black skirt. She had a hard time guessing how old the woman was, but she supposed it was around her mother's age, at least her age before the darkness set in, similar to her aunts and uncles. The woman seemed really nice, and while she looked like someone in authority by the uniform and efficiently tied-back hair, she was treating Hallie like an adult and an equal.

"The man, Raposa, he talked about training too. What do you mean exactly? Like schoolwork?" Hallie asked as Marguerite led her back up the wooden steps to the salon.

"Sometimes there's some studying, like schoolwork, but not often and I sense in your case you're well educated, and you speak English, which can be a main focus if it's not a girl's first language. The training is more about how to conduct yourself in a sophisticated environment."

Marguerite paused in the salon and pointed to the ornate dining table. "For example, if I asked you to set the table for a dinner with a soup appetiser, a steak main course, and a creme brulee dessert, I'm guessing you wouldn't be certain which knives, forks and spoons to set out, correct?"

Hallie shook her head, unsure what a creme brulee was.

"Right, so you won't be serving clients dinner, but you'll need to know which utensil to use, so we cover that." She turned and pointed to the bar in the corner. "For example, your client may like a Long Island iced tea; we have comprehensive liquor and wine selections in each villa at the resort, and you'll often have to make or serve them a drink. We'll teach you how to mix drinks and how to serve everything from cocktails to fine wines."

Hallie had been given a beer once, which she thought tasted awful, otherwise she'd never knowingly drunk any alcohol. Water was free – why waste precious money on a drink in a can or a bottle? The array of fancy bottles lining the back of the bar seemed more than a little intimidating.

"I don't know anything about any of that," Hallie said sheepishly.

The woman gently placed a hand on Hallie's arm which felt surprisingly comforting. "That's why we spend plenty of time with you, so you'll be completely comfortable before you graduate."

Hallie looked at the floor, unsure how to ask the main question that had been burning in her mind since her lunch with Raposa. It wasn't just knowing how to ask; she had no idea what to ask. How could she ask about something she knew nothing about?

"What is it Hallie?" Marguerite asked reassuringly.

Hallie looked up at the woman she'd only met thirty minutes before. She had learnt to trust no one, yet here she was in a strange place, having ridden in a car with a strange man, and now involved in a serious conversation with a foreign lady. Normally her inner alarms would be sounding loudly, but both Raposa and Marguerite seemed so nice, so friendly, and they treated her like an adult instead of a child. Or a petty thief. She realised she liked them both. It felt good to feel at ease with another human being.

"I don't know anything about sex," she blurted out. "I'm pretty sure there's sex involved, and I don't know if I'd like that."

Marguerite laughed, but it was sympathetically, and Hallie cracked a smile.

"Oh, my dear girl. Everybody likes sex. We'll teach you every-thing you need to know, and I think you'll find it most enjoyable." The woman carefully reached out and took Hallie in an embrace. Hallie couldn't remember the last time she'd been hugged. It must have been years. She wrapped her lean arms around the lady and accepted the comfort. She didn't let go for a long time.

They walked up the curving steps from the aft deck to the upper level behind the enclosed fly-bridge. Hallie was startled to see two women lounging in comfortable chairs, sunning themselves. They were both stunningly beautiful, wearing the skimpy bikinis she'd seen the tourists wear on the beaches outside the fancy hotels. The darker-skinned girl had curvy hips and large breasts that were barely contained by her bright yellow top. Hallie found herself staring at the woman's chest as she rose and offered a handshake.

"Hi, I'm Abigay," she said with a heavy accent.

Hallie looked up as they shook hands and noticed the woman had lifted her sunglasses and looked Hallie confidently in the eye.

The other girl was slim and lean like Hallie, with a skin tone lighter than her own. Her features were the opposite of the soft edges of Abigay's face, but her appearance was striking, and she boldly stepped forward. For the second time in as many minutes, Hallie accepted an embrace. The woman hugged her briefly and stepped back.

"I'm Zoe," she said with a different accent again.

Hallie managed a smile. "Hello, I'm Hallie, nice to meet you both."

Marguerite put a hand on her shoulder. "Why don't you girls get acquainted, I'll see what the men are up to."

She opened the door to the fly-bridge and left Hallie alone with the two women she'd just met. They both made a big fuss and invited her to sit with them, asking her a bunch of questions about where she was from and how she knew Raposa. She was surprised they didn't know much about the island, and hadn't been anywhere but the boat since they arrived here. She learnt Abigay was from Haiti and grew up speaking Haitian creole, some French and a little English but had improved her English a lot on the boat in the past six weeks. Zoe was from an island Hallie didn't know, called Martinique, and her English was fluent although she said she grew up speaking French and some creole, but a different creole to Abigay.

They both complimented Hallie on her good looks and told her she'd be very popular, which made her blush. The women seemed so mature and worldly, completely at home on the luxury yacht and talked about hair products and make-up that Hallie had never heard of.

"How old are you?" Zoe asked, running her fingers through Hallie's long, dark hair.

"I'm sixteen," Hallie said, innocently.

The two women chuckled, and Abigay looked at the fly-bridge before replying, "Oh, you're good to go then."

Hallie was confused. "How do you mean? Good to go where?"

They laughed again. "To bed, silly, gotta be legal age."

Hallie felt a little stupid; she really didn't understand what they were talking about. Abigay nodded at Zoe.

"Zoe here is fifteen; she can't go to the resort until she's legal, so they've given her a passport that says she's older."

"Why is that a big deal?" Hallie asked, still unsure.

"'Cos most places it's not legal until a girl is seventeen or eighteen – that's why lots of Americans come to the resort." Abigay explained. "In Cayman legal age for sex is sixteen, even with older gentlemen."

24

THURSDAY

Whittaker sat at his desk in the central police station off Elgin Avenue in George Town. He shared the room with another detective and their desks faced each other, so they could both enjoy the view from the window. His compatriot had left for the day, but Whittaker sat, alternating between staring out the window at the sun lowering towards the horizon, and perusing his notes on the still unidentified girl. There had been plenty of fuss and pressure from his boss, and his boss's boss, and so on up the chain of command. Dead bodies in the pristine waters of the island was bad for tourism and anything bad for tourism became priority number one.

With a crime rate as low as the island enjoyed, any suspicious death was priority number one in Detective Whittaker's mind; he didn't need government blowhards informing him of the fact, but investigations took time. Especially when the evidence was just about zero. He'd had no luck matching missing persons throughout the Caribbean, and facial recognition, after the artist had touched up the poor girl's face, had returned nothing. He was confident DNA would prove she was of mixed heritage, which they'd guessed by her skin tone and features, but that narrowed it down to a whole host of Caribbean islands, and possibly other countries farther afield. It was most likely Hispaniola, which was the island divided between Haiti and the Dominican Republic, but could easily be Cuba or Puerto Rico. Her age came back as seventeen or eighteen from the blood test; again, no surprise based on her appearance. The girl had been stripped naked, she had no tattoos, no jewellery, no significant scars, nothing he could try to trace. What he needed was something more to work with. Hearing footsteps in the hallway, he stood and hoped to hell the break he needed was walking towards his office.

Rasha entered Whittaker's office followed by a short man with a balding scalp and a portly midriff, wearing a sports coat and tie. Beads of sweat dripped from the man's face as he towed a heavy-looking rolling briefcase with an extended handle.

"Detective Whittaker?" the man asked in an American accent, offering his hand across the desk.

"Welcome to the Cayman Islands, Doctor Harding," Whittaker responded, shaking the man's clammy hand.

"Thank you," Harding responded. "It's very hot here." He dropped into one of the chairs and wiped his brow with a sodden-looking cloth he produced from his pocket.

"That's why it's called a tropical island, sir," Whittaker said pleasantly, looking at Rasha with a slight grin. She shrugged her shoulders and raised her eyebrows.

"I'll leave you two to it then," she said.

"Thank you, Rasha, I'll see you tomorrow," Whittaker replied and sat down. "Thank you for coming all this way Doctor Harding, I wish it was for more pleasant reasons," he continued.

Harding finished mopping his face. "I'm rarely anywhere for pleasant reasons, Detective, that's the life of a forensic pathologist. Someone is always dead."

Whittaker suppressed a laugh at the man's ironic truth. "I suppose," he managed. "Well, we indeed have a body. I'm sure Rasha explained, we found the girl on Monday in the water off the north side of the island. We determined she'd been in the water for approximately nine to ten hours, but so far, we've had no luck identifying her. I'm hoping your examination will give us some direction to pursue."

"Yes, well, I'll perform the autopsy and examination tomorrow," Harding replied sternly, "So you'll have a very preliminary report by the end of the day. But the full report will be three or four weeks; there's a lot of lab work to be done, and then I have to write up the report itself. I'm afraid I have quite a backlog at the moment, Detective." He waved a tired hand in the air. "Identifying her, and finding the perpetrator, if there was one, is your business of course. I can only inform you of the forensic evidence."

"Of course," Whittaker agreed. "Well, I'm sure you're weary from your travels so I'll let you get to your hotel, sir." He rose from his chair. "You'll be at the Marriott on Seven Mile Beach. I think you'll enjoy the resort. The view is quite nice."

Harding wriggled up from his seat, huffing and frowning, "It'll be fine as long as it has air conditioning, and a good Internet connection, Detective."

Whittaker guessed the man was exceptional at his job; his credentials were certainly impressive. It was undoubtedly the rest of life the man may struggle with, he thought with some amusement.

"It does, sir. I believe our own pathologist will be ready for you at 8am, Doctor Harding. Our autopsies are performed at the morgue, here in town at the HSA hospital. He usually sits in, when we have the rare necessity for a forensic examination. I hope that's satisfactory?"

"That's fine," Harding replied, dragging his briefcase towards the door. "I'll get everything done tomorrow. Believe me, I'm as eager as you are to get this finished." He paused and turned back to Whittaker from the doorway. "It's not this hot in Iowa, Detective – I didn't think it was this hot anywhere, besides the surface of the sun."

Whittaker watched him leave and stared at the empty doorway

a moment. Surely, he's got to be really good at his work, he pondered, but he seems to think paradise is hell.

25

THURSDAY

Cristal walked to the dockside at the back of the Yacht Club and stood admiring her motor yacht. Over her right shoulder, the sun was getting low in the western sky, throwing a rich tangerine glow over the glistening white fibreglass. She saw Raposa step from the salon and come down the steps to the aft deck to meet her. He offered her a steadying hand as she used the moulded steps from the gunwale down to the aft deck.

"So, what's all this mystery that's had you missing for the afternoon, and brought me down here? It had better be quick, no one's watching the resort with both of us here."

She knew how to knock people off balance in most situations – bold, decisive and slightly threatening usually did the trick. Raposa smiled and she knew he'd seen her tricks too many times.

"This won't take long at all, thanks for coming over." He walked towards the door to the salon. "I have something you'll like, come and see."

Cristal nodded, wanting to smile, but she wouldn't give him the satisfaction of deflecting her tough greeting. She followed him inside the salon. Seated on the settee to the left was a stunningly beautiful young girl. Cristal stared at her with a stern expression, testing her mettle. The girl stood and stepped towards her with her hand outstretched.

"Good evening, Miss Sombrio, I'm Hallie."

Cristal shook her hand with a firm grip but couldn't take her stare from the girl's captivating eyes. They were like gazing into jars of swirling honey. She was wearing a thin sun dress Cristal recognised from the boat's wardrobe, her long dark hair was carefully styled, and her features were delicately accentuated with a touch of make-up. Cristal knew Marguerite had spent several hours making the girl look like she'd thrown herself casually together. Cristal looked at Raposa expectantly.

"Hallie is a friend I met recently. I felt she would be an exceptional fit for our resort, so I invited her aboard to discuss what we have to offer. She's ready to sign a contract with us, subject to your approval of course."

Cristal allowed her mouth to ease in the direction of a smile when she looked back at Hallie. The girl was petite and lean, with a nice figure developing, from what she could see. Her face was delicately soft, and her perfect tawny skin shimmered in the rich sunlight streaming through the windows. It was too difficult to find the delicate balance between the body of a young woman and the features of a younger girl, but Hallie had both. She knew if the girl was willing to do the work, she'd be the most popular host at the resort. She was perfect for most of their clientele.

"Where are you from, Hallie?" Cristal asked, knowing full well what the answer would be, if given honestly. She saw the girl swallow before replying.

"I am Caymanian, miss. But I have no family ties and I've been living alone for nearly a year now. My mother is dead, and my father was never around."

Cristal glared at Raposa. "Outside."

She wheeled around and marched out the door to the aft deck and lit a cigarette while Raposa took his time following, no doubt instructing the girl what to do next. She had to admit he'd prepared her well, and she certainly was a money maker, but she had rules for a reason. Raposa closed the door and waited. Smart, Cristal thought; he's seeing how badly I'll react.

"Do you think I'm a fool?" she said calmly.

"Of course not," he replied quickly.

"Do you think the rules we have are foolish?"

"I do not, I think they're well thought out. But I also think, occasionally, there's cause for an exception," he said as calmly as she'd spoken.

Cristal considered her position. She knew she should stick to her rule, she'd made it for good reasons. It was too easy for a local girl to run away, back to her family or friends. Too easy to run to the authorities, and bring unwanted attention to the resort. Most of what they did was perfectly legal, but technically, if someone could actually prove it, they were running a brothel. Using illegal foreign nationals, without work papers. The resort was set up as a training facility, so on the books the girls were students taking a one-year hotel course. The story would hold water until the first client buckled under police scrutiny. Only a couple of the girls were under sixteen and they had false papers for them. One was actually fourteen, and the new girl, Zoe, was fifteen.

"Is she clean?"

Raposa nodded. "Her mother was a druggie, she won't touch the stuff; Marguerite checked her arms. She's never had a drink, doesn't smoke, already speaks English and she's smart. I can have her ready to replace Nora in six weeks."

"Where did you find her?" Cristal asked, her voice softening more than she intended.

"In town. She lives alone in a shack, no one else. Any family has lost all contact with her, she's been totally self-sufficient since her mother died a year ago. Just watch your handbag, she's a demon pickpocket." He laughed. "She took Marguerite's watch off her wrist without her even knowing. She handed it straight back to her but she's really fast. Kid's lived on the street, fending for herself for a long time."

"Was she hooking?" Cristal asked suspiciously.

"You won't believe this, Marguerite said she's a virgin." Raposa grinned.

"Hmmm… You haven't taken her to the resort, have you?"

"Of course not. No way I'd show her the whole operation until you approved," Raposa assured her. "Honestly, there's really no need to show her anything more until she passes training."

Cristal chewed it over in her mind, taking a long last drag of her cigarette, before callously flicking the butt into the bay. It made her anxious to go against her own rule, but Raposa was right, the girl was perfect, and they'd been struggling to get girls that were good enough lately, they were lucky to have these next two lined up. Cristal tried to maintain twelve girls at all times, so a client could stay once a month and never have the same girl twice. They hadn't had much luck keeping it at that number, and now, as they approached their one-year anniversary, the remaining girls from the opening were coming to the end of their contracts. She could persuade a couple to extend, but again, the clients expected fresh hosts, which is why they'd initiated the one-year limit in the first place.

"Fine. She can begin training," Cristal said firmly. "But if this goes wrong, it's on you." She tapped her finger on his chest. "And I'll carry your balls around in my purse if this turns into a mistake."

Cristal brushed past Raposa and stepped up to the dock without looking back. She really felt uncertain about the Caymanian girl, but she'd made a decision and there was no way she'd appear indecisive. That showed weakness. She clicked the remote start to her British racing green Jaguar F-Type, so the air conditioning would start running as she crossed the car park. She slid inside the leather sports seat and looked back at the Hatteras as the last light of daytime was slowly surpassed by the dock lights lining the sea wall. This girl could be a sensation with the members and Cristal was well aware that keeping the members entertained and happy was paramount. Especially with the new resort about to happen. These businessmen were paying big money to get what they'd be jailed for, or at least destroyed in the press, at home. The majority of their members were American, or at least based in America, where the age of consent varied by state. Some states were sixteen, some were seventeen and many eighteen, but there were also restrictions of age difference in many states. Regardless, most of them had wives and families, including daughters this age. Ditching the wife and taking up with a sixteen-year-old would have the shareholders running for the hills, stock prices plummeting, and the federal government taking a keen interest. Cristal provided the whole package, a beautiful resort on a tropical island with championship calibre golf just up the road, seven miles of the best beach in the world, fishing, diving and exotic young girls with zero attachment or baggage. Want a different girl, no problem. Two girls, certainly, we'll charge your account. Even younger, that can be arranged. The whole thing was a tax write-off as an executive's membership, akin to Young Presidents.

But the girls were the key. These men could buy condos on beaches, and memberships to clubs, but they paid for the discretion. They all had a taste for girls considered much too young, and the supply of such girls was worth the price of admission. Cristal's challenge was maintaining that supply. With those thoughts in her head, she finally justified keeping the Caymanian girl, and put the Jaguar in drive.

26

FRIDAY

AJ rolled over in bed and peeked at the clock on her bedside table. 6:20am. She almost always woke up before her alarm went off, which this morning would be 6:30, but she reached over and turned it off. Sunrise would be in fifteen minutes, but it would be another thirty minutes until the blazing orb rose over the low-lying island and fully illuminated the landscape. Her tiny apartment was dark apart from the glow from the clock, and the red light signifying the automatic timer on the coffee maker was operating. The grounds of the big house had landscape lighting in the evening, but in the pre-dawn mornings the gardens were unlit unless the motion sensors were tripped. AJ stretched and reached across the other side of the queen-sized bed, and wished she was touching Jackson. Being apart for such long stretches of time was taxing on them both, but they were committed to each other, and she was prepared to wait as long as it took. She supported and respected the work he did with Sea Sentry, but hoped he'd find a way to join her full time on the island. They hadn't talked about marriage, and AJ wasn't someone who needed a ring and a piece of paper to feel committed, or to be faithful, but she felt it may happen once they were together.

Kicking the covers off, she slid out of bed and rubbed the sleep from her eyes. She walked to the living room window, which was only a few steps from her bed, and pulled the curtain back so she'd see the light on the water once the sun rose. The kitchen was open to the living area and the smell of coffee drew her to the gurgling machine, turning the kitchen light on as she went. An eager cockerel crowed from somewhere in the neighbourhood, keen to be the first to meet the sunrise. AJ poured herself a cup, and after taking a sip, she placed her mug on the small dining table and went to find a tee-shirt to put on. She used to drink her coffee with milk and sugar, but over time, and under Reg's influence, she'd simplified the process and learnt to take it black without sweetening. Finding a Mermaid Divers shirt that she guessed was clean, AJ went back to the table and sat down at one of the two chairs. Her mobile lay on the table, plugged into a wall charger, so she picked up the phone and quickly scanned her emails. Several requests from customers for future bookings, a thank you note from a family she'd taken out last week, and five or six newsletters or daily blasts from email lists she subscribed to.

Thoughts of the girl in the water crept back in, as they seemed to have done all week. She couldn't shake the image in her mind of the zippered mesh closing over the young girl's face. She thumbed her way to her mobile phone contacts and scrolled until she found the number for Detective Whittaker. She pressed the button to create a text, and with her thumb hovering over the keyboard, she paused and thought about what to say. Or ask? What could she say? Nothing she would say could un-drown that poor girl. Whittaker must have far better things to do than fuss with her anxiety and concern, she decided, and clicked back to the contact page. She hit edit, and added 'Roy' between 'Detective' and 'Whittaker'.

Fifteen minutes later, AJ was leaving the West Bay Fosters supermarket with a couple of bags of ice, and a box of fancy fairy cakes with icing as a treat for Jack's group's last day. She pulled her fifteen-passenger van onto West Bay road and started the arduous two-mile commute to the Yacht Club marina. Dawn's light bathed the island in a pale glow and AJ's mood began to perk up as she worked on her second cup of coffee in her travel mug, and thought about the morning's dives.

The marina was alive with activity as once again most of the dive operations were running from the north side, as the superb conditions continued. Boat captains and divemasters swarmed about, loading boats with daily supplies and a few filling the tanks they didn't get to the night before. Thomas was already at Hazel's Odyssey and had most of their divers' gear brought up from the bow cabin already. Thomas always beat her to the boat. She'd tried leaving home earlier and he'd still be there before her. She decided he either had a sixth sense, or a tracking device, but she could never be there first, so she stopped trying.

"Morning sunshine," she greeted him brightly, and threw a paper bag in his direction.

He caught the bag and beamed with delight, pulling out a sugary frosted doughnut. "You're spoiling me, boss." He took a big bite and carried on setting up gear. AJ couldn't believe the young man's ability to consume food. They led an active lifestyle for sure, but he could put away prodigious amounts of food of any kind, and remained as skinny as a rail.

Hearing the patter of tiny feet, she turned and saw Coop approaching down the jetty, dodging between the feet of the boat crews. Arriving at the back of the Newton, the puppy sat down, still wagging his tail enthusiastically, and looking at AJ. Thomas stood behind her.

"Now that's uncanny. I can't believe he'd be that obedient, this quickly."

AJ laughed. "I know, he's a boat dog for sure." She held up her hand. "Come aboard."

Coop leapt down to the swim step and scurried over the deck, his whole body wiggling like a rubber band, before throwing himself upside down at AJ's feet, ready for a fuss.

"Looks like he wants to be on your crew more than mine," came Reg's booming voice, having followed the dog down the dock.

AJ looked up from scratching the puppy's belly. "First Thomas, and now Coop, no one's safe around me, Reg."

The big man grinned and waved her off, heading back up the dock.

27

———————

FRIDAY

Hallie woke up with a start, blinked a few times, then lay perfectly still, unsure where she was. The room was dark, except for the unfamiliar glow of LED numbers on a clock, and the bed covers that enveloped her felt soft and sumptuous. For a moment she thought she was dreaming and not awake at all, but as her mind cleared from the best sleep she could ever remember, the events of the day before began to return. The gentle rocking confirmed she was aboard the Cova do Leão, in her own stateroom, as they'd called it, and according to the clock, it was 7:35am. She reached to where she recalled the light switch was located above the queen-sized bed, and illuminated the room. They'd given her the smallest of the three guest staterooms, as the other two girls already had the slightly larger bow and port rooms. Hers was on the starboard side and about the size of her shack she'd lived in for the past two years. But this room had a carpeted floor and a luxurious bed. And air conditioning. Wonderfully dry, cool air conditioning.

She pushed the covers back and rose from the bed, looking at herself in the mirror above the small chest of drawers by the door. They'd given her a fancy nightie to wear but she'd felt almost naked in the thin, partially see-though garment, and worn her usual tee-shirt and soccer shorts she'd always slept in. Raposa had asked when she wanted to return and collect her possessions from her home, and she'd pointed to the tatty rucksack she'd brought with her. "I brought everything," she'd told him, and he seemed surprised. Why, she had no idea. You could only wear one set of clothes at a time; why would you need more than two? Had to have two otherwise you had nothing to wear while you washed the other, but she'd been baffled by the pictures in the magazines of these rooms, twice the size of her home, that people had nothing but clothes in. It made no sense to Hallie.

Marguerite had told her she would come for her at eight o'clock, they'd pick out some new clothes that would fit her, and then her training would begin right away. She couldn't hear any activity from the other staterooms, so she guessed the girls were still asleep. They'd both seemed really nice and treated her like an equal, which still felt strange, but refreshing. She cracked her door open and slipped across the narrow hallway to the bathroom, or head, as they'd called it. She was used to using a toilet in the corner of the open room, so having a separate bathroom was much nicer, something she remembered from when she and her mother had lived in a small house. She used the facility, splashed some water on her face and marvelled at the softness of the cotton towels. Returning to the hallway that ran down the centre of the lower deck, she moved towards the stern. At the end of the hall the stairs curved up on the starboard side and ahead was the master stateroom they'd told her was reserved for clients, or when Miss Cristal stayed aboard. Hallie went quietly up the steps and peeked into the salon. Seeing no one, she walked into the kitchen, which she'd been told was a galley, and looked around, opening some of the cupboards. She found a beaker and filled it with water from the tap, and took a long drink while she decided where to go next. There was a door on either side of the galley leading outside, so she chose the starboard one, and found a narrow walkway along the side of the boat between the edge of the cabin structure and the safety rail. She went forward until she found a flat area, where the bow came to a point, and sat down cross-legged so she could look out across Governors Creek in the low morning light.

Her shack was hot and humid inside, even at night, with very little air blowing through it, sheltered by a pair of logwood trees lining the dirt path. Hallie usually rose with the sun and made her way to the harbour front to enjoy the cooler morning air and breeze off the water. The peace and quiet before the workers arrived at the finance houses, banks and shops was her favourite time of day. As she sat on the bow of the multi-million-dollar yacht, that same wave of tranquillity washed over her and she sipped her water and watched the sun rise ahead of her in the eastern sky. A dive boat motored across the water before her from Yacht Club marina, heading to the channel leading out to the North Sound, its engine gently burbling as it idled by. A bunch of people appeared to be organising things on the deck that was lined with tanks against its railings. She wondered what it was like to breathe underwater and see all the fish and coral reef that she'd seen so many glossy pictures of. A woman with purple streaks in her blonde, shoulder-length hair was steering the boat, and Hallie thought how cool that must be to drive a big boat like that.

"Hallie," came Marguerite's voice from behind her, and she turned to see the woman leaning out the galley door. Marguerite smiled and beckoned her to come inside. Reluctantly, Hallie left her secluded spot, and walked back towards the doorway. She was nervous about what lay ahead with their training. Some things they'd told her she understood, but much of it was beyond anything she'd ever experienced. To her a bottle of wine was a bottle of wine, she had no idea there was all these different types, and then all these different people who made the different types. She didn't see how she could remember all that.

"Good morning, my dear," Marguerite greeted her, as she stepped through the doorway. "Would you like some breakfast before we start?"

Hallie thought for a moment. She didn't really eat breakfast. Her shack had no power and therefore no refrigerator and the bugs were problematic enough without food luring them in. She did remember, years ago, when life was more normal, she'd have a bowl of cereal before school.

"Do you have cereal?" she asked nervously, as though she were asking for a lobster and caviar omelette.

Marguerite smiled and opened a cupboard. "Weetabix or Raisin Bran?"

Hallie peeked at the packages having never heard of either one. "Raisin Bran, please," she decided, based on the purple box. She liked the colour purple.

Van Heerden walked into the galley and grunted good morning to them both. He headed straight for the coffee pot that Hallie assumed Marguerite must have started, and poured himself a mug. Hallie watched curiously and took in the aroma of the Columbian roast.

"Want some coffee?" Marguerite asked.

"I don't know," Hallie answered, "I've never tried it."

Van Heerden held his mug out, offering it to her, but Marguerite quickly intervened, "No, no, don't try his, you won't like it."

"What do you mean?" Van Heerden asked with a grin, "This'll put hair on your chest."

Hallie glanced down at her chest and then at Marguerite questioningly.

Marguerite laughed and slapped Van Heerden on the arm. "Don't listen to him. Here, try a little with some milk and sugar."

She poured half a mug of coffee and added a spoonful of sugar and some milk. Hallie took a sip of the hot liquid and let the flavour fill her senses.

"Mmmm," she said, taking another sip, "I think I like that."

Van Heerden left the galley chuckling and Marguerite tipped some cereal into a bowl. As she added the milk, she quietly explained. "So Peter used an anecdotal phrase when he said, 'it'll put hair on your chest.' It won't literally make hair grow, it's a phrase meaning the coffee is strong."

Hallie looked at Marguerite. "I know what anecdotal means, I've just never heard that phrase before."

Marguerite handed her the bowl and a spoon. "Good, I'll learn as we go the things you know, and the things you need to know. Did you enjoy school when you used to go?"

Hallie ate a spoonful of cereal, and the sugary taste, which was stronger than fresh fruit, surprised her. It also had an odd aftertaste she didn't remember, sort of like drinking a soda. "I liked it and it wasn't very hard, but I had to stop to take care of my mother."

Marguerite took two more bowls down from a cabinet as footsteps and voices echoed up from downstairs. Zoe and Abigay burst around the corner, chatting and giggling and Hallie stopped eating her cereal and stared at the two girls. Both wore silk pyjama bottoms and not another stitch of clothing. The only fully developed bodies Hallie had ever seen naked were her own and her mother's. Marguerite didn't bat an eye. Hallie, mortified and frozen to the spot, had no idea what to do apart from hold her cereal bowl out of the way as Abigay threw her arms around her, and kissed her on the cheek.

"Bonjour, ma belle," she said joyfully as her full breasts pressed firmly against Hallie's.

Hallie noted neither girl had any hair on her chest.

28

———

FRIDAY

Coop had decided he'd gotten the best of the fussing available, and trotted back up the jetty to Reg, before AJ had eased the Newton away from the dock. The sun was low in the sky but rising fast, and AJ took a deep sigh as she delighted in the shimmering light on the calm water. As she piloted Hazel's Odyssey beyond the marina peninsula, into the main body of Governors Creek, she looked over the starboard side and noticed the big Hatteras motor yacht, still moored against the sea wall on the backside of the marina. The boat had beautiful, sleek lines and she could only imagine what the inside was like. Sitting on the bow, looking out over the bay, she could see what appeared to be a young girl with long dark hair. Impressed that a kid who must be from a wealthy family to be on that boat, was up and catching the sunrise, AJ continued on her way, idling towards the channel.

Once clear of the channel, AJ opened up the motor, and brought the Newton up on plane for the ride out to the reef. After a few minutes, Jack and Sherry joined her on the fly-bridge, standing either side of the pilot chair, leaning against the framework.

"Been another great trip for us, thank you AJ," Jack said and squeezed her shoulder.

"I love the week you're here, you always bring a good group," AJ replied. "It's fun for Thomas and me." She truly meant what she said as well. They often had divers who were with them for a week or so at a time, but usually the boat was filled up with a mixture of other divers on different timings. Having one group of similar skill level, and in this case very experienced divers, was relaxing and rewarding. A lot less hectic.

"Sorry about the one issue," AJ added, realising she was talking about a great week in which a young girl died. Somehow it didn't seem right, but there again, should a stranger's misfortune ruin an event these people looked forward to all year, and spent a lot of time and money on? She didn't know. It was hard to reconcile in her mind as life seemingly went on, in disregard of the tragedy. What she did realise was that as disturbed as she was to have seen the corpse, she felt a far greater sadness she couldn't explain. She didn't know this girl; she'd never met her and knew nothing about her. Yet, there was a pain in her soul whenever she thought of her, floating alone in the ocean. And those thoughts wouldn't go away.

Sherry rubbed AJ's shoulder. "Nothing any of us could do about that. Very sad, and so unlike this island. Best not to think about it too much, and hopefully the police will find out what happened."

"Detective Whittaker is a good man, he'll figure it out," AJ said quietly.

They rode in silence for a few minutes until Sherry took the reins to lighten the mood. "Speaking of our week here, can we get a week around this same time next year?" she asked. "This timing seems to work well for our folks. We had to turn some people away for this trip; probably could have sold it twice over."

"I already pencilled you in the calendar, so absolutely. Would you want to bring more people?" AJ asked.

"No," Jack replied quickly. "It gets too big and unmanageable for us with more people. Can't get restaurant reservations, don't all fit comfortably in one van. Too much stress on everyone. This size group works well."

"Jack and I were talking last night about maybe adding a second trip though," Sherry said. "Perhaps in autumn or early winter. Do you think you could find us a week around that time?"

AJ opened the calendar on her mobile and scrolled through to the later months in the year, checking her bookings.

"We always take the boat out of the water for two weeks in September for service, as that's the quietest time of the year. After that, we have an open week in late October and that's about the only time we have a completely free week."

"Put us down for that week and email us the dates, we'll make it work at our end," Jack said keenly. "Might be exactly the same crowd as we have here; this lot would sign up again in a heartbeat."

AJ typed into her mobile, adding Jack to the calendar and then sending him an email with the dates.

"Alright, you're set, and you should get an email confirming the dates. Thomas and I will look forward to it." She put her phone down and made a small steering correction as they continued across the smooth water of the sound.

"Where to guys? What do you fancy for last day dives?"

Jack and Sherry looked at each other and thought for a minute.

Sherry finally settled on a suggestion. "How about ZZ Top? We haven't been there this trip."

"Maybe we shouldn't go over there," Jack said before AJ could reply. "You know? It was over there we found the girl."

AJ took a deep breath, "You know what, maybe we should dive over there and pay a little homage to the kid. If you guys are okay with it, I am too." She didn't feel ready to face it, which made no sense as it wasn't like the girl was still there, or even entered the water there. It was like going to the restaurant where you broke up with a boyfriend: the place could never be the same again. But some of AJ's favourite dive sites were in that area, and Mermaid Divers had to go back at some point, so may as well make it today.

Jack nodded. "Yeah, let's say a prayer for the kid and enjoy the hell out of diving there, in her honour."

AJ managed a smile, glad Sherry hadn't suggested Ghost Mountain. She didn't feel ready for that yet.

29

FRIDAY

"Girls, girls, girls," Marguerite said, clapping her hands and quieting Zoe and Abigay. They'd all finished breakfast and the two had been sitting on the couch in the salon, braiding each other's hair, talking excitedly about moving to the resort. They looked over at Marguerite, who stood in the doorway to the galley. Hallie peeked around her, still standing in the galley, pretending to sip her coffee she'd finished a while ago. She had no idea how to handle being around the half-naked girls. She didn't know where to look, or what to say, it was simply too foreign.

"You need to prepare for your final review. Chop, chop, go get dressed, and then you can study up here. I'll have a lunch menu for you to set the table and prepare drinks for, and then again for dinner. Tomorrow morning, Cristal will be here, so you better be ready." The two girls dutifully left the couch and hurried downstairs. Marguerite turned to Hallie and smiled.

"That was uncomfortable for you, wasn't it?"

Hallie looked at the floor at a complete loss what to say. Marguerite stepped towards her and gently lifted her chin.

"It's okay my dear. You were startled when the girls came in without their tops on, weren't you?"

Hallie nodded. For a year she'd had almost no one to have a conversation with. There were a few homeless guys she'd chat to in town, but they didn't make much sense, and were usually drunk. She generally tried to avoid talking to people in fear of them figuring out she was living alone, and reporting her to the Department of Children & Family Services. Being asked pointed questions, and conversing about anything important, was something she hadn't experienced since school.

"Why do you think that is?" Marguerite persisted, in a pleasant tone.

Hallie shrugged her shoulders and felt her cheeks blushing. Marguerite placed a hand on her arm and looked at her with a warm and caring expression.

"You should be proud of your body," she said softly. "Zoe and Abigay were like you when they arrived, they were shy and unsure of themselves." She chuckled. "Well, less so with Zoe. But most of the girls we work with are from troubled pasts and difficult circumstances; their self-worth has been suppressed. The first thing we must teach you is how to be comfortable with your own body. I will show you how to understand the strength and power your body has, especially with men." She shrugged her shoulders. "And with women too. It's perfectly natural to be affectionate, and even sexual, with a woman as well as with a man."

Hallie had never heard anyone speak in such a way before. When she was last in school, she was fourteen, and sure they talked about boys, and some of the girls were going on dates, but she had too much to worry about at home to be fooling with any of that. The kids at school seemed so immature when she had so much responsibility to deal with.

"Do you trust me, Hallie?" Marguerite said, warmly.

She did. It felt strange to Hallie, but she realised she really did trust this woman. After years of trusting no one, not even her own mother, she finally had someone who really cared, and it felt wonderful.

"I do," she said quietly and managed a smile.

"Good," Marguerite replied. "Let's begin your first lesson then."

Marguerite led her down the curving stairs to the berths and turned left, into the master stateroom. Once Hallie had followed her into the room, she turned the lights on and closed the door. Hallie felt butterflies in her stomach. She didn't feel threatened, just unsure of what was about to happen. Zoe and Abigay seem so happy and confident; whatever this is, it can't be that bad, she thought. She really wanted to possess some of that confidence they had.

"We're going to take our time Hallie, and there'll be no physical contact, you understand?" Marguerite said, standing a few feet away. "I want you to remove your clothes now."

Hallie felt a surge of panic, but she felt another sensation as well, the same strange feeling she felt when she saw the two girls in the galley. She'd felt this before when, alone in her shack, she'd looked at some of the gorgeous men in the glossy magazines advertising colognes and clothing. Clothing they weren't wearing much of. The same feeling she had when she'd touched her private parts to see how it felt.

Marguerite smiled and took a few steps back, giving Hallie more space. "Take your time, start with your shirt."

Hallie noticed her hands were shaking but she slowly lifted her tee-shirt up and over her head, discarding the garment on the bed next to her. Her arms instinctively crossed in front of her and covered her breasts.

"You're doing wonderfully, my dear, now remove your shorts," Marguerite encouraged her and Hallie noticed her eyes remained on Hallie's face the whole time, her motherly expression never changing. Hallie reached down nervously and slipped the shorts over her slender hips and let them fall to the floor. She stood completely naked. She was in the lavish bedroom of a luxury yacht in front of a virtual stranger, yet just yesterday she lived in a dirt floor shack, and stole to live. The surreal circumstances were so far from anything Hallie could relate to; it all began to feel like a dream. When Marguerite asked her to put her hands on her hips, she did so.

"Perfect," Marguerite said, and her eyes finally left Hallie's face. Hallie took a deep breath and tried to suppress her feelings, feelings of embarrassment and exposure, but also the other strange feeling.

"You have an absolutely beautiful and mature body, Hallie. Here, come with me." She led Hallie to the large master bathroom where mirrors adorned the wall above the twin sinks.

Marguerite pointed at the image of the young woman in the mirror. "See, look at that gorgeous woman; this is what we mean when we say be proud of your body. You should see yourself for what you are, not what society or circumstance tells you to feel. I see a sexually mature, strong and healthy woman, who's ready to take on the world. I want you to see yourself that way too. Do you see how vibrant and attractive you are, Hallie?"

Hallie looked at her lean physique she'd always considered to be skinny. She did notice in the bright light and large mirror that her body had changed since the last time she'd stood in front of a large mirror. That was when she'd had a normal life, in a house. Her breasts had filled out, her hips had shape and her face had lost the rounded, plumpness of youth and her cheekbones were more accentuated. She finally took her eyes off her own reflection and looked at Marguerite in the mirror. She nodded and managed a smile.

"Good girl," Marguerite said quietly. "Now, I want you to take your morning shower and I'll be right here."

Hallie looked at the expansive tiled shower with clear glass doors, then back at Marguerite with uncertainty returning.

"It's perfectly alright, Hallie. This is all part of becoming aware of your strength, and getting comfortable with your body and sexuality. You will learn to be in control of these situations by realising the power your body has over others. When Abigay hugged you this morning she used her sexuality and confidence to exude strength, and you felt that right? You were the one uncomfortable and intimidated, yet she was standing there topless."

Hallie nodded and everything Marguerite said made sense to her. She wanted that confidence and wanted to be happy and confident like the other girls. She opened the shower door and stepped inside, turning to face Marguerite. She put her hands on her hips and pulled her shoulders back, accentuating her bust. She felt like the picture of Wonder Woman she'd seen in the magazine, when the movie had been advertised; she felt like she could do anything she put her mind to.

30

FRIDAY

It was two days since she'd hosted that man, and Nora felt more sore and achy now than the day after. It hurt to raise her arms, and her shoulders felt like they did after she'd made a really long swim one time. That had been another bad situation with a man. She'd begged a ride on his sailboat from the Turks and Caicos to the Bahamas, and he'd been a perfect gentleman. Until they approached Nassau Harbour. He became agitated when she thanked him and said she'd be getting off when they moored up, and then angry when she declined his offer for her to pay for her trip in the bedroom. She dove in the water and swam from the middle of the channel to shore, leaving her meagre possessions behind. She wasn't opposed to trading such favours to cover her passage, but not with that smelly, old guy. She remembered then that the soreness was worse on the second day. Her bruising had also taken on some interesting shades of green and purple, so she kept a long sleeve shirt on to hide the embarrassing marks on her forearms.

Sitting at the small table for two by the east-facing window of her dorm room, she stared outside at nothing in particular. Their dorms were on the second floor of the main building, so the two-storey villas partially blocked the view, but she could see Salt Creek to her north, and mainly trees and mangroves, with a few roofs, to the south-east. It was days like these that the girls looked forward to, and then hated. They weren't allowed any form of outside communication for 'security reasons', or so they were told. Not even television or radio. There was a large selection of movies on Blu-Ray disks in the lounge, but she'd seen all the ones that appealed to her. Each girl was issued a Kindle tablet with a broad selection of books and games, but no Internet connection. There was a small gym in the building, but she definitely didn't feel like working out. She'd been reading most of the morning, a book about some kids in England on sail boats called *Swallows and Amazons*. She knew it was intended for younger kids, but she couldn't stop reading it anyway.

Movement from the car park below caught her eye and she watched a guest walk over to one of the fancy cars the resort provided them. The man was short and chubby and walked with a waddling gait. She recognised him from the airport trip as Jacobs. She'd been relieved he didn't select her to host him when they arrived: he was ugly and talked loudly. But her roommate had told her he was a pussycat. So now, feeling her aches and pains, she regretted it. Jacobs retrieved something she couldn't see from the car, as Russo appeared from his villa. He was in number four, next to the main building. He was easily the best looking of the three, and seemed to be their ringleader. She'd heard a rumour he'd asked for two hosts each evening, but she hadn't spoken to any of the girls that hosted him. Her stomach clenched, and a lump formed in her throat, as she watched Symanski saunter across the car park and join his two friends. He sure doesn't look like a man that's been 'taken care of' Nora thought, at least not in the way Cristal had led her to believe. He looked more like he'd been given an upgrade and a door prize; the creep swaggered with more confidence than when he'd arrived. The three men gathered and walked towards the dock area, laughing and slapping each other on the back. They were wearing swim shorts and tee-shirts, so she guessed they were going out on the jet-skis or maybe the boat.

As they disappeared from view, Nora sank back in her chair, and thought about the series of events and tribulations that led to her current predicament. She'd grown up in a regular working-class home in Oslo. Her parents were normal, hard-working people who raised her and her brother with love and care. Her mother was a teacher and her father a mechanic at a small boatyard. Nora loved spending time on the water, whether it was summer sailing with her dad in a small Hobie Cat he'd borrow from the yard, or skating on the frozen surface in winter. She was an average student in school, mainly because she'd rather be outside than studying, but everything changed shortly after she turned sixteen. All the girls liked the young geography teacher, Mr. Paulsrud. But Jørgen Paulsrud paid particular attention to Nora. How he could sit in the teachers' lounge and chat with her mother over tea then take Nora's virginity in a cheap motel room was puzzling to her, looking back. But at the time she was besotted, and she would have done anything for the man. Anything, except let him leave her for Kaarina Salberg. Kaarina was the same age as Nora, and although they weren't friends, she knew the girl. Nora was beside herself when he said he couldn't see her anymore, and enraged when she saw him talking to Kaarina. It was the look he gave her. His 'it's our little secret' wink and a smile.

Nora asked Paulsrud to meet her at the boatyard on a quiet Sunday morning. It was late summer, and a cloudy but warm day with a steady breeze. He obliged and she took them out on the Hobie Cat, saying they should be alone on the water and talk – she needed his help and advice to get her over their relationship. Her intention of course was to win him back, and she hoped her sailing skills and the beauty of the Inner Oslo Fjord might sway the balance. He wasn't much of an outdoorsman, and complained most of the time about the chilly wind and how far they were from shore. He told her he had no intention of rekindling their relationship, and she needed to find a boy her own age. Devastated all over again,

Nora turned the boat around and sailed back between the scores of small islands, with tears streaming down her face. Tacking against the wind, she skillfully manoeuvred the craft, often carrying one hull of the little catamaran high above the water. Paulsrud was completely out of his element, and struggled to comprehend where he was supposed to be to help balance the boat, as Nora worked the sails and swung the boom back and forth. Getting increasingly irate, he swore at her, yelling she should stop screwing about, zigzagging around, and get them back to the yard. Nora had recounted the next moment a million times in her mind, but the more she relived it, the more unclear and fuzzier her memory became. What she knew for sure was she swung the boom to tack to port, and Jørgen was still shouting. When she completed the turn, Jørgen was no longer on the small boat, and the scenic cut between the uninhabited rocky islands of Skogerholmen and Terneholmen went back to silence, outside the wind filling her sails.

Turning once more around the tip of Skogerholmen, she rejoined the main fjord and picked up the following wind. Not looking back, and unable to think clearly, she simply sailed. Fifty miles she sailed throughout the day to the estuary of the fjord into the North Sea. Hugging the coast to the west she found a quiet inlet and spent the night huddled against the cold under the boat's trampoline, the canvas deck strung between the two hulls. The next morning, still confused and traumatised from the previous day's events, she pulled the Hobie back in the water and sailed into the next fjord. In the small town of Brevik she bought a hot coffee and a newspaper. The front-page story was about a schoolteacher and one of his students, missing after being seen sailing away from a boatyard in Oslo. She stared, bewildered at the photographs of her and her former lover. She ran back to the Hobie she'd left tied to the sea wall under the small bridge that connected the island of Sylterøya to the mainland. Terrified that every person she could see would recognise her, she hurriedly sailed back down the fjord to the southern tip of Gjermundsholmen island where the east side of the rocky point was out of plain view. Dismantling the Hobie she shed the parts into the water for the outgoing tide to wash down the fjord.

It took an hour for Nora to walk the two miles back across three bridges, and through the little town of Brevik, to find the commercial port. Wandering around, acting like a curious kid, she asked every seaman she passed where his boat was heading. She finally got the answer she was hoping for, and waited until sunset to sneak aboard the freighter, bound the next morning for Portsmouth, England.

Nora stood on her sore legs and walked to the door; may as well get some lunch, she thought to herself. She took her time hobbling down the stairs, and walked across the dormitory dining area that opened to the lounge and the large windows overlooking Salt Creek. Motoring into the little bay was the Cova do Leão and standing on the dock awaiting their ride were the three men. She moved to the side, in case Symanski turned and saw her, although she knew the windows were heavily tinted. She may not be certain what had happened in the fjord, she pondered with a clear head, but she'd swing a boom at that arsehole any chance she had.

31

FRIDAY

Back at the marina, AJ helped the last of the divers from the boat to the dock, and turned to Jack and Sherry.

"Thank you both so much, I can't wait for October, I get to see you twice in one year now."

Sherry gave her a long hug and they both started to get a little teary.

"Alright you two," Jack laughed. He shook Thomas's hand as the latter stepped over from the boat. "People will think you're not looking forward to getting back in the quarry after all this nasty, clear, warm water, and colourful reef."

Sherry released AJ and wiped her eyes, "Well we can't have anyone imagining that," she said, slapping Jack's arm playfully.

Jack hugged AJ. "Thanks again, young lady, always a pleasure, we'll be back before you know it."

They picked up their bags and followed their group up the jetty, towards the car park. AJ sighed. So many of their customers were returning divers; some went as far back as her early days working for Reg, people he had encouraged to switch to Mermaid Divers, to help grow her business. Relationships and friendships were established, and continued to grow every trip – it went well beyond a normal customer–supplier interaction. It helped they were providing an enjoyable pastime, in a gorgeous part of the world, but spending hours at a time in the close quarters of a boat led to conversations of a more in-depth and personal nature than time spent with most service providers.

"Here," Thomas said, extending a wad of folded-up cash to AJ, "looks like they were generous as always."

AJ smiled. "Yeah, good people." She felt guilty counting the tip the group had left, so she pocketed it for later, when she and Thomas would split it evenly, as they always did.

"Okay, I'll get the air line to fill some tanks, if you want to find Reg," she continued. "He was grabbing us our lunch from Greenhouse. Jen texted me, said she's testing a new sandwich on us, so it should be something really tasty."

"Sure thing." Thomas beamed, and strode speedily up the jetty with his long legs. AJ always wondered how the guy could look so casual yet move so fast; she figured it had to be a special island gene. She certainly didn't have it with her short legs. She amusingly claimed to be 5' 4", but that was with her hair fluffed up and heels off the ground. She opened the small locker at their boat slip and pulled out their air fill hose. Each slip had a quick disconnect plumbed through the dock to a big dive compressor so all the dive operations could fill their tanks right there in their slips. After connecting to the outlet on the dock, she ran the line onto the boat, and began hooking up their manifold to a series of tanks. The manifold was essentially a six-into-one connection that allowed six tanks to be filled simultaneously from one feed. Opening the first stages on the tanks released a mass of hissing air, as the system equalised itself from the varying amounts of air pressure remaining in each tank. AJ turned the main valve at the manifold which opened the system to the compressor, and the tanks began to fill.

She looked up to see Thomas making his way back with a bag in his hand, and Coop merrily trotting along beside him. She couldn't help but smile at the little mutt, working hard to keep pace with Thomas's lanky gait. Apparently, the pup liked the smell of Chef

Jen's concoctions too – his little brown nose sniffed at the air and his tongue hung out of his mouth. Thomas and AJ ate their sandwiches while the tanks filled, pausing their lunch every once in a while to move the manifold to the next set of tanks. Coop sat as patiently as a puppy could, occasionally unable to contain himself and jumping up, giving them the starving puppy eyes treatment. The dock was a busy place, as all the dive operations refilled their tanks, and welcomed their afternoon customers aboard. At one thirty they'd finished their lunch, AJ had texted Jen with their rave review of the sandwiches, and the tanks were full. A loud whistle from down the jetty sent Coop scurrying back to Reg, who stood by his boats, hands on hips, looking intimidating as usual. Until Coop arrived. Then he bent down and made a big fuss of his new dog like the softie he really was.

Thomas freed the stern line before walking down the side of the slip and releasing the bow, stepping aboard with the line in hand. AJ eased into the throttle and piloted Hazel's Odyssey clear of the dock and down the channel between the berths. She felt a little melancholy after the goodbyes with the Bensons, and for some reason she wasn't too excited about their afternoon gig. She had no idea why, but she carried a strange sense of uneasiness that she couldn't put her finger on. Reg didn't tolerate lousy customers, so surely these people were fine? He'd dealt with them before and he'd sent them her way.

"How many divers we have, boss?" Thomas asked cheerily from the deck below.

"Three, I was told," she shouted back. "But no idea what size they are, so just get regs ready and we'll grab BCDs once we see who we have."

"Sounds good," he replied, and his upbeat mood radiated throughout the boat, as it always did. AJ's funk began to lift without her even realising.

32

FRIDAY

They cleared the channel to the sound and sure enough, AJ spotted
the big Hatteras anchored off to the side, clear of other boat traffic.
She idled over and Thomas dropped their bumpers over the starboard side as she pulled alongside, aligning sterns. An older man
in a captain's uniform helped tie them off at the bow and a good-
looking man, close to AJ's age, lashed the two boats together at the
stern.

"Hi, I'm AJ, this is Thomas, we're Mermaid Divers. Reg at Pearl
Divers arranged for us to do your DSDs this afternoon."

The younger man, wearing only board shorts, smiled, and AJ
couldn't help but notice he was not only handsome, but clearly in
good shape.

"Hello, thanks for meeting us out here. We have three clients
who'd like to dive with you," he said in an accented voice. "May I
come aboard?" he asked, obviously knowing the maritime rule of
never stepping aboard another person's boat without permission.

"Please do," AJ replied, starting to think the afternoon may be
more pleasant then she'd been thinking, cursing herself for being a
pessimist.

The man stepped over to the Newton's swim step and offered

his hand. "Raposa." After shaking hands he pointed back to the boat where the uniformed man had made his way to the stern. "And this is Captain Van Heerden."

"That's a beautiful Hatteras, is this the boat we sometimes see offshore around the island?" AJ enquired.

The man who introduced himself as Raposa briefly glanced back at the Captain. "Perhaps. We take members on fishing trips and cruises out on the water sometimes, or to other islands around the Caribbean."

Thomas leaned on a dive tank and peered over at the pretty lines of the luxury yacht, "She's beautiful, sir," he said, addressing the Captain. "How long is she?"

The man looked down at Thomas from the aft deck without changing his stern expression. "Eighty feet."

Thomas continued unperturbed by the man's gruff tone. "Could we take a quick tour when come back in, sir?"

The man remained expressionless. "This is a private yacht for our members, we don't do tours."

Raposa quickly took over the conversation. "We have three clients for you today, none of them have dived before so you'll do the orientation, or I think it's called the resort dive, with them, yes?"

AJ didn't like the Captain's demeanour, which brought back her sense of concern, but she continued the conversation.

"It's called 'Discover Scuba Diving' these days, DSD for short, and yes, it's basically an introductory dive where we give them some basic safety instruction and then guide them on a half-hour dive. Maximum depth is thirty feet. We'll take them to the shallow reef outside the sound, it's a beautiful dive."

Raposa leaned a little closer, and spoke quietly. "Can you give these guys a little extra time? Maybe a second dive? It would be great if you can take care of them for me, you know, a little extra."

AJ made a point of looking at the Captain and then back at Raposa. She wasn't sure he'd get the hint that 'maybe if your friend up there wasn't an arsehole, we'd be more inclined', but she went through the motions.

"We'll pay extra of course," Raposa quickly added, so she assumed her message was received.

"We'll see how they do, but yes, we should be able to do two dives."

Raposa gave her a broad smile, and she was pretty sure he was laying on the sultry, Latin, smouldering eyes too. She didn't have the heart to tell him he was lovely to look at, but not her type at all.

"Perfect, thank you so much," he said, in the tone of a man used to getting his way. "Our clients are in the salon, let me bring them aboard." He turned and nodded to the Captain who walked across the aft deck and opened the door to the salon. A minute later he returned with three men in tow. AJ surveyed the clients, quickly assessing sizes for BCDs and weighting.

"Good afternoon gentlemen," she greeted them brightly. "Thomas and I will be taking you diving today, please come aboard."

Thomas and AJ helped the three men step across from the Hatteras, and Raposa traded places, back to the Cova do Leão, as AJ had noticed the yacht was named. She didn't speak Portuguese but knew *leão* meant lion, so she guessed the rest. Lion's Den, she decided, didn't sound very inviting to a female.

"I'll leave you guys in good hands," Raposa said, waving to his clients. "See you back here in a few hours."

They cast the lines off, pushed Hazel's Odyssey away from the Hatteras and Thomas idled the Newton away, AJ remaining on deck to outfit the customers and start their instruction.

"What's all this weight stuff for?" the man who had introduced himself as Al asked loudly. He looked somewhat familiar to AJ, but she couldn't place him, and didn't recognise his voice.

"I'll explain it all once we've got you geared up, but suffice to say, without it you'll bob on the surface like a cork," she replied patiently, figuring she must be remembering someone similar, as she couldn't recall where they could have met.

"Why has Joe got less than I got?" the man barked, pointing at Symanski.

AJ wanted to say 'because he's skinny and you're fat, and fat floats', but she smiled instead, "You ballast based on body weight, and you two aren't the same weight, I'm guessing."

The man laughed. "Hear that Bill? Five minutes on the boat and this chick's busting my balls about being fat."

The tall, quieter man, Bill, grinned. "Al, maybe your wife paid her to weight you down so you don't come back up, ever consider that?"

The three men thought that was really funny. AJ thought she might like his wife. But there again, the woman married this buffoon, so maybe she wouldn't. She handed Bill his weight belt and asked them to sit on the benches while she went over some basic instruction. The rest of the ride out to the reef was spent attempting to teach the men a few key elements of scuba diving. Information and skills to keep them safe, and make the dive go smoothly. The rotund man, Al, was clearly the jester; Bill seemed to be the sensible one – he actually asked a few intelligent questions; and Joe, the scrawny little man, was just plain creepy. His beady eyes darted about and the only time they lingered it was on AJ's cleavage. She felt like leaning over and lifting his chin up to look at her face, but she really didn't want to touch him, the man made her uncomfortable. AJ wondered what these three did for a living, and how they knew each other, they seemed unlikely friends. But unlike with her customers who had just left, she wasn't interested enough to ask; her goal was to keep them safe for the next few hours, and hopefully never see them again.

33

___

FRIDAY

Hallie thought she'd died and gone to heaven. The shower had been even better than the one she'd taken last night in the bathroom across the hall from her room. The water felt like a warm rain shower firmly sprinkling down so it doused her and ran the lather away from her body. And the soap, she closed her eyes as she thought about it again, it smelled like a flower garden. Once she'd decided to ignore the fact that a strange lady was watching her, she'd lost herself in the opulence and sheer delight of bathing in hot water she didn't have to splash over herself. Marguerite had then had her try on what felt like a hundred different clothes, from swimsuits to evening dresses to fancy shoes.

Hallie had never walked in heels before and they agreed she needed some time to figure that out, hopefully mastering it before she broke an ankle. She'd worn a one-piece swimsuit when she went swimming as a kid, but she couldn't believe the image in the mirror when she tried on a two-piece bikini. The bikini top hitched her breasts up and made them look quite a bit bigger, not like Abigay's, but still, for a girl who had been hiding her figure, trying to remain unnoticed, it was a pleasant surprise. She still didn't understand what all these clothes could possibly be needed for, but she'd quickly been consumed by the immersion in the extravagance. Marguerite had left her to put her new clothes away in her stateroom and told her to come upstairs in thirty minutes. It wasn't until she sat down on the bed, that she realised she'd been stripping down naked between each piece of clothing she tried on, and had stopped feeling self-conscious about it. For the first few she'd still been shy, and it felt awkward, but soon the excitement had taken over, and she didn't think about it again. Maybe she could do this, she contemplated; of course that was in front of a woman, it would be a different story in front of a man. That odd feeling tickled her stomach again, and a little lower down.

Then there was lunch. When she went upstairs after thirty minutes she was greeted by a small feast, spread across the dining table. The salad, she was told, was goat's cheese, walnut and orange with a vinaigrette dressing. What she would have called snacks, the Spanish called tapas, she learnt, and were really tasty bite-sized portions of raw tuna with other things on a crispy biscuit. Marguerite told her she needed to remember all the names but there were too many things she'd never heard of.

All three girls helped clear the table and clean the dishes, while Van Heerden and Raposa disappeared upstairs to the fly-bridge. The girls had been kept downstairs when the other men were aboard; Marguerite said they were resort members and they weren't allowed to see new girls until they had graduated to hosts. Hallie's curiosity was burning, and she figured she'd try and sneak a peek when they came back. After they'd cleared everything away from lunch, Marguerite asked Zoe and Abigay each to mix her a drink and told Hallie to watch. She gave them the name of the drink, which Hallie hadn't heard of, and the girls went over to the bar in the salon. Hallie expected them to pour whatever they'd been asked for from a bottle, and hand it her. But the girls took a different-looking glass each, Zoe dipped hers in something, Abigay stuck olives on a stick, and they both poured, shook and concocted some weird potion before finally adding it to the glass and setting it on the bar. Hallie was dumbstruck. How did they possibly remember all that to make one drink? There's no way I can do that, she thought in a panic.

Marguerite came over and instructed the girls to try a sip of their own drinks. They both did. They then tried a sip of each other's, and finally Marguerite tried them both.

"Well, Zoe? How did you do?"

"I think I added a bit too much triple sec," she answered, "Otherwise it's good."

"And what about yours Abigay?" Marguerite asked.

"A bit of blue cheese fell out of its olive." She giggled. "Apart from that it's goooood," she added with a sexy wiggle of her hips and she and Zoe both laughed.

Marguerite smiled. "I thought they were both excellent, well done girls. Blue cheese escapees happen sometimes, it's not the end of the world, dear, and yours was a touch strong on triple sec Zoe, but I happen to like that. The important thing is you're able to tell."

Marguerite turned to Hallie who was listening intently, trying to follow along.

"Why don't you try them, Hallie."

Zoe picked up her glass and handed it to Hallie with a grin. "Here you go, try my Cadillac Margarita."

Hallie took the glass and said the name several times in her mind, determined to remember it, hearing it for the second time. She took a big gulp of the drink, which tasted sweet but burned her throat, and she came away with salt all around her mouth.

Zoe and Abigay laughed and Zoe leaned over and licked the salt from around Hallie's mouth, then gave her a quick kiss on the lips.

"Okay Zoe," Marguerite intervened, taking the glass from Hallie's hand. "Poor girl's only been here a day, let's not get ahead of ourselves."

Zoe just grinned and winked at Hallie who had no idea what just happened, or what she was supposed to do, let alone feel about it.

"Hallie, you might try sipping the drinks; this is not beer to be swigged like a sailor, my dear."

"Sorry," Hallie said, blushing from everything that had just happened. "I'm used to drinking water when I'm thirsty, I just drink it."

Abigay handed her the other glass. "Take it easy, just a sip, it's a Dirty Martini with blue cheese olives."

Hallie held the oddly tapered glass carefully. It seemed a silly way to make a glass as it didn't hold very much, and was easy to spill, but what did she know. She took a gentle sip and reeled at the sharp taste, wrinkling her nose.

"I like the sweet one much better," she said, picking up the margarita and taking another drink to wash away the taste of the martini. She felt the salt around her mouth again and quickly looked at Zoe in case she came in for another kiss, but Zoe just grinned suggestively and winked again.

34

FRIDAY

AJ looked down the mooring line to the reef where Joe and Bill were waiting, holding the rope as asked. Al, the mouthy guy, had a hard time descending, predictably, despite the extra weight AJ had added. He insisted on blabbering and was clearly nervous, despite claiming to be perfectly calm. The average male's lungs hold over a gallon and a half of air, and even when exhaled efficiently contain nearly half a gallon. Combine that with all the other air spaces in the body, plus anything buoyant being worn, such as a wetsuit, and a human is akin to a pool floaty. Athletes, and people who exercise regularly, subconsciously learn to exhale more fully, allowing more fresh oxygen to be brought in on their next breath. Al Jacobs hadn't set foot in a gym in his life and was taking quick, shallow breaths, keeping his lungs fully inflated. After five minutes of floating and coaching, AJ finally persuaded him to shut up and exhale in a long, easy release, and down he went. She took her time descending, reminding him via hand signals to clear his ears from the pressure increase, much like a plane changing altitude, and after another minute they joined his friends at twenty-five feet.

Releasing the line to the mooring pin, AJ glided away across a sand flat and beckoned the group to follow. Symanski kicked away and dropped straight to the bottom, where AJ met him and, pushing the button on his inflation line, dumped a little air from his tank into the bladder of his BCD. He rose from the sand and hung in the water, blinking at her through his mask as though she'd performed a levitation trick. Fortunately, Bill seemed to be doing fine, hanging in the water, neutrally buoyant, but of course Jacobs let go of the line, took a big gulp of breath and immediately began ascending as he tried to fin towards the others. AJ kicked up and grabbed his leg to stop him popping to the surface, and signalled for him to breathe easy. He soon settled down enough that she felt comfortable letting go and finned away, leading her ducklings in line behind her.

She stayed over the sand for the first few minutes, running parallel to a coral finger, until she was confident the guys were getting the hang of it. Once they appeared settled enough, she turned over the reef and began a long arcing circle, staying above thirty feet. The shallow reef was the ocean's nursery, where every coral head housed colonies of small, colourful fish and invertebrates. Light from the sun loses most of its visible spectrum within 33 feet of the water's surface, making the reef appear more beautiful at lesser depths. For the new diver, experiencing the underwater world for the first time, it seems like a rainbow had exploded and scattered its vivid palette across the seascape. Everywhere they looked something was moving, swaying or pulsing, and when a small hawksbill turtle paddled by, the group was transfixed.

AJ had taken great pains to drill into the three men that touching anything that didn't come from the boat with them was harmful to the living coral or creature, and strictly prohibited. She used her 'many things down there sting or bite' line, which normally made anyone think twice. But sure enough, one of them took off after the little turtle. What surprised her was which one of the guys it was. The little, beady-eyed guy seemed too nervous of life itself to be so bold, but there he was, kicking with all his puny might towards the unsuspecting sea turtle. AJ took a few long, full strokes with her lean, muscled legs, and swiftly caught up with the man as he reached for the turtle's hind flipper. She grabbed his arm and held it firmly, allowing the startled turtle to surge away to the safety of deeper water. Symanski turned and AJ was shocked by the venom in the man's eyes, glaring at her through his mask. By the long stream of bubbles flowing from his regulator he was breathing hard as well, not all from the swimming effort, she gathered. He wrenched his arm back and she noticed his fists were clenched. She held out a hand and slapped the top of it with her other hand, then wagged her finger at him, reminding him not to touch anything. He quickly turned away and the other two joined them, playfully shoving their buddy as though he'd just been caught by the teacher in a junior school classroom.

The rest of the dive was uneventful and after they'd made their way back on the boat AJ and Thomas began switching their gear over to a new tank. Bill and Al laughed, and enthusiastically talked about what they'd seen, asking AJ and Thomas to name some of the fish they described. Joe stayed off to the side, busying himself with his mobile, or something else in his bag, staying quiet. Finally, he stepped closer to AJ, surprising her.

"I'm sorry about the turtle," he said quietly. "I forgot about the touching thing for a moment down there."

AJ wasn't sure quite how to respond. She was amazed he was apologising, and it was good he was acknowledging the error of his ways, but she wanted to ask him what the rage was all about. He hadn't known her long enough to develop that much contempt for her, surely, so maybe he was just an angry guy inside. Perhaps he hated authority or being corrected, she wondered. She guessed he'd not been mister popular in school, so perhaps he carried a chip on his shoulder, or was it because she was a woman? Whatever it was, the man had anger issues, and she'd be happy to see the back of him.

"I appreciate you saying something. It's easy to get excited down there, there's a lot of new stuff to see."

He nodded and returned to his friends. She knew she'd let him off easy, but decided his dive guide for a few hours was probably not going to fix a lifetime of issues, so best make one more dive and move on.

She explained again about breathing compressed air at depth, and allowing nitrogen from the air to dissipate in their systems, which is why they were taking a break before going in again. Three uninterested faces stared back so, knowing they had been shallow for only thirty minutes, and hadn't accumulated enough nitrogen to be a problem, she told them to gear up and they'd get back in. Thomas helped them into their BCDs and made sure the tanks were on. When he walked across to help the last diver, AJ stopped him and whispered, "I'll go again, I know what to expect with them."

Thomas looked at her uneasily, and she could tell he wanted to debate the issue; he always wanted to pull his weight, but she subtly shook her head, and he let it go. Jacobs managed to descend with the others for the second dive and no one tried to harass any wildlife. By the end of the thirty minutes, AJ had actually relaxed enough to enjoy the view, but she was looking forward to a cold drink and some fish tacos at the Fox and Hare later. It had been a long week, with an odd mixture of good times, a tragedy and the usual hard work. Back on the boat, the group seemed happy, and AJ released them from the mooring to head back in. Thomas piloted Hazel's Odyssey through the cut and began the run across the sound, getting the Newton up on plane to speed across the flat, calm water. AJ busied herself rinsing the dive gear with their freshwater hose, and stowing it below. The three men laughed and joked, ribbing Jacobs about how much weight he had to carry, and he fired back, insulting the other two. Maybe they're just normal blokes having a guys' trip, she thought, and started to believe she'd been too harsh and judgemental. Perhaps it was a reaction to the Bensons leaving? She hung the last BCD on its hanger and dropped the fins into a basket they stored them in. The cabin was always hot and steamy, especially with damp dive gear, but something she heard made her freeze a moment, and strain to hear the men's voices.

"You finally got up the nerve to nail that little Scandinavian broad, and you damn near ruined it for all of us," she heard Al's voice, growling at one of the others.

"I told you Al, I smoothed it all over, there's nothing to worry about. It's costing me a pretty sum, but I sorted it out." She made out Joe, the creepy little one.

"Are they screwing you over? If they're screwing you over, you know I'll take care of it," Bill reacted, and AJ stayed below in the sweaty cabin, transfixed.

"No, no." She could tell it was Joe again. "I think it's fine, it's a lot of money, but it's worth it, I'll get what I want."

She heard a loud laugh, which had to be Al. "I'm sure, you freakin' weirdo, I don't want to know what that is! Bet she'll have more than bruises though, right?" He cracked himself up alone, or at least so loudly AJ couldn't hear if the others laughed.

"This whole deal is expensive, but it's clean and easy, right?" came Bill's voice of reason. "We don't have to worry about a thing, they have all the aggravation, we have all the fun, and we get to write it off."

"No way we could make something like this work back home; someone would blow the whistle and we'd be up shit creek," Al said more quietly than usual. "I look forward to this trip every month or two."

"I tell you what I'm looking forward to," Bill said, just loud enough that AJ could still hear. "Getting back to the resort, and having two of them little girls give me a full body massage."

"Now this man's a lion," Al crowed loudly.

This time she heard all three laughing, so she made a lot of noise coming out of the cabin, making sure they'd know she was back. Their conversation reverted to talking about the dive as the engine note changed and Thomas brought the boat down off plane.

It took a few minutes to offload the three men back to the Hatteras, and Raposa was present again to help.

"Thank you for taking them out, everything go okay?" he asked as AJ prepared to cast off again.

"Sure, went fine, I think they had a good time," she replied, still confused and conflicted by what she'd overheard. "Reg will sort out the bill with you."

Raposa nodded and gave her a big smile, the three guests having already disappeared into the salon of the yacht. With a short thanks, and no tip. "Until next time then." He waved, and followed his guests.

AJ went up the ladder to the fly-bridge and joined Thomas at the helm.

"Thank goodness that's over," she said quietly as they idled away. "I hate to listen to people's conversations," she started, "but I couldn't help hearing them, and it really creeped me out." She looked at Thomas, but he was staring back at the Hatteras, apparently not hearing a word she was saying. She turned, and there, on the upper aft deck behind the enclosed pilot house, stood a girl. The same girl AJ had seen on the bow that morning. Thomas looked mortified.

"Do you know her?" AJ asked.

Thomas came out of his trance, and met AJ's curious gaze. He appeared confused. "I'm pretty sure that's Hallie Bodden. My cousin."

35

FRIDAY

Harding sat across from Whittaker in the detective's office at the central police station. Whittaker could not understand how anyone could sweat so profusely, going from an air-conditioned hospital, to an air-conditioned car, to an air-conditioned police station. Maybe he did jumping jacks as he walked from one cool environment to the other, he thought. The man wiped his face with the soaked cloth he had used the day before. Maybe not, Whittaker decided, looking at the man's rotund figure.

"Thank you for dropping by, Doctor Harding, I'm sure you've had a busy day."

Harding shoved the rag in his pocket. "Yes, yes, well I know everyone's always in a hurry for these things."

"Were you able to determine anything of consequence that might help my investigation?" Whittaker asked, hopefully.

"As I said before, it'll be weeks before the full report, but there's a few details I'm confident in sharing," he said, as he reached into his expansive rolling briefcase and pulled out a Manila folder containing a multitude of papers. He shifted uncomfortably in the chair as he selected the sheet he was looking for and tugged at his tie as though it were choking his chubby neck. Whittaker looked sympathetically at the chair, straining under the man's weight, and made a mental note to ask the cleaning lady to bring up some Lysol spray after he left.

"She indeed drowned," he started, without ceremony. "The blow to her head was not the cause of death, although it was significant, and may have rendered her unconscious. Hard to know what caused it, except that the object was round. Difficult to determine exact diameter as the indentation was shallow."

"A blow delivered, or did the girl hit her head on something, like a fall?" Whittaker asked.

Harding frowned at the interruption and examined his paper before replying, "As I was about to get to, it's indeterminable. Without the location of the incident available to study, it's impossible to say for sure. She had bruising to her right shoulder which would be consistent with a fall, possibly after being struck on the head and rendered unconscious, where she'd be unable to put her hands out to break the fall. But it's also possible the head wound came from a railing of some sort, and her shoulder contacted something else at the same time. An accidental trip that caused both. If we had the location, we could attempt to reconstruct the incident; without that, it's all assumption."

Whittaker nodded, jotting down notes of his own. Harding shuffled in the chair some more and wiggled his tie, which curiously continued to strangle him.

"It's after five, Doctor," Whittaker offered. "Perhaps you'd like to remove your tie and relax a little?" Before he could stop himself, he continued in his attempt to have the man enjoy his stay. "Later this evening, if you'd like to join my wife and me, we'll be having dinner at a local pub. Wonderful food, and a lovely singer will be performing?"

Harding stared at him blankly, and for a moment Whittaker wondered if he'd insulted the man in some way. Finally, once again shifting awkwardly in his seat, the doctor managed a bumbling reply.

"Very kind of you, err, Detective, but my wife will be expecting my call at 8pm, and I really must rest for the journey home tomorrow."

Whittaker shrugged his shoulders, slightly relieved the man didn't take him up on his offer – he'd have some explaining to do with his own wife, dragging this fellow along on their date night.

"Understandable Doctor. Please continue."

Harding played with his tie again, but didn't remove it, and Whittaker decided he was done trying to make the man comfortable; some mountains were just too tall to climb.

"Where was I?" he muttered to himself. "Oh, right, so we covered the head wound."

"You mentioned the size of the round object that contacted the head was difficult to determine, correct?" Whittaker asked, tapping his pen on his notepad.

"I did, yes. The wound had been disturbed post mortem – the fish I would assume – so any paint chips or evidence from the object was not present. Of course, if it was a metal pole, or even a hardwood, such as a baseball bat, I wouldn't expect any particulate to transfer," Harding answered.

Whittaker thought a moment, and Harding waited for his question.

"Possible to narrow down at least a range of size the object may have been?" he finally asked.

Harding looked irritated – he clearly didn't like to be put on the spot – but he shuffled through his papers and pulled out a page with multiple photographs printed on it. He held the paper for Whittaker to see. "Very difficult. You see, the human head is far from round and when struck by, or on, a round object, only a portion of the object makes contact. If the skull is fractured then we have a little more shape to work with, but in this case the scalp indentation and the wound is all we have." He pointed to one of the pictures showing a close-up of a cleaned wound, with the girl's hair shaved away.

"See here, the wound is concentrated in the centre and tapers away either side, indicating it was not a flat object but a rounded one. If it had been sharp, or had an edge, then the wound would have a narrow, deeper profile and wouldn't taper away such."

He returned the sheet to his folder and Whittaker continued to look at him questioningly.

"Right, yes, an approximate size. Well, it was certainly no smaller than 25 millimetres around, and no bigger than, let's say, 75 millimetres. I'm comfortable with those dimensions."

Whittaker made more notes. "Thank you, so between one and three inches."

Harding nodded and continued before he could be asked something else he didn't want to answer. "Moving on to the ankle wound, where I was able to retrieve some fibres."

Whittaker looked up from his notes. "Really?"

"They're consistent with a nylon braided rope. The wound, again, had been disturbed, but several fibres remained, deeply lodged in the heel wound. The depth of the wound varied radially, consistent with the woven strands of a braided rope. Oh, and the rope was black."

Whittaker finished adding those details to his own notes and looked up. "Unfortunately, just about every boat on this island is moored with a nylon rope of some sort; won't be easy to trace anything based on that."

"No, I'm sure." Harding almost smiled. "But once I run my full tests in my lab, I may be able to narrow down the manufacturer, and at a minimum I'll be able to compare it to a rope you can provide me. Find a suspect and give me his rope."

"May be enough to hang him?" Whittaker chuckled at the joke, but Harding just looked at him strangely.

"Whatever the other end of the rope was tied to exerted a considerable strain on the ankle," the doctor continued. "I can tell by the wound from the ankle, all the way to the tip of the heel. Evidence suggests the rope was in fact pulled over the heel."

"Could she have been strung up by her ankle, you know, hung upside down?" Whittaker asked, now regretting his hanging humour.

"I don't believe so. The ankle wound happened underwater, I can tell by the nature of the wound and particulate found in ocean water, embedded deeply in the flesh. And, she wasn't hung upside down in the water – at least, she didn't die that way, as her own mass underwater wouldn't be enough to make the gouge in her ankle. In fact, as you know, she'd float."

Harding tucked his Manila folder back in his briefcase, indicating he was finished.

"Age, ethnicity, height, weight and all that you already knew but will be in the preliminary report I'll email you before I get on the plane tomorrow. If there's nothing else, Detective, I'll make my way to the hotel."

Whittaker stood and extended a hand. "Thank you, Doctor, I appreciate your hard work and I look forward to both reports. I do hope you've had an enjoyable stay on our little island."

Harding struggled to his feet and shook hands. "Yes, well, thank you, it's a bit too hot here for my taste I'm afraid, and I'm not one for beaches. All that sand. Damn stuff gets everywhere; be better off concreting the coastline, make the pavement meet the water. Anyway, good luck. I'll be in touch."

With that, he dragged his briefcase to the door and left. Whittaker looked out his window while he cleaned his hand on a wipe he pulled from a packet in a drawer of his desk. The sun was making its way down the western sky to disappear beyond the horizon, and orange tones began to separate the blue water from the blue sky. He sat and read over his notes. He was no closer to a suspect. If he interviewed every person on the island in possession of, or with access to, a black, braided nylon rope, he'd have to interview the whole population. Nothing the doctor had provided helped him find his culprit. It confirmed what he already knew: he was indeed looking for a culprit, and it may have given him the evidence to convict a suspect. A suspect he currently had no idea where to find, or even where to start looking.

36

———————

FRIDAY

Thomas had given AJ the background on his cousin, as best he knew it, on the ride back to the Yacht Club. She was actually a second cousin. His father's cousin's daughter. He'd explained how Hallie's mother had passed away a year ago, after struggling with a drug addiction. Thomas had to call his mother and ask her when she'd last seen or heard from the daughter. Hallie hadn't come to her mother's funeral, and Thomas couldn't recall the last time he'd seen the girl. Had to be three years at least, he decided. His mother told him, word was she was taken in by the family of a school friend, living in Spotts, an area to the east of George Town on the south coast. The Bodden family, which was expansive and scattered throughout the island, had tried to take the girl in, but she'd told everyone she was fine. The more Thomas tried to recall the girl's face, the more he started to doubt himself. After all, it had been years since he'd seen her, she was probably thirteen at the time, and would surely look quite different now. They were cleaning down the boat and he'd about convinced himself he was mistaken, when his mother called him back.

"Hey mama, what's up?" he answered, holding the mobile in one hand while he hosed fresh water over the deck with the other.

"I was telling your daddy what you said, about the girl," his mother said in a thick Caymanian accent. "He said, his uncle told him a month back he thought he'd seen her in town. Said he tried to talk to her, but she went running off. Said she looked all grown up and dressed fine and all, so he didn't think much of it."

"Which uncle? Was it her granddaddy?" Thomas asked. "He ought to know her you'd think."

"Naw," his mother answered. "It were ole Philman, he's your granddaddy's sister's husband, he ain't a Bodden, don't recall what his last name is right now, but he ain't her granddaddy." She chuckled and spoke a little quieter. "He been known to tip a bottle or two an' all, so he ain't the most reliable source. Whether it were her, or not, I don't blame her for running."

Thomas thanked his mother and hung up the phone. He and AJ finished washing down Hazel's Odyssey, and filled the tanks for the next day. AJ was excited. They had a writer and photographer from America chartering the boat alone for the day. AJ usually took Saturdays off, borrowing Carlos, Thomas's future brother-in-law, from Reg. Then AJ and Carlos would go out Sunday, giving Thomas his day off. But tomorrow she was keen to go herself. Nick Sullivan was a bestselling writer of suspense books based around scuba diving, and she loved his stories. He was also an enthusiastic and amusing character to be around, so a day with Nick promised to be fun. Thomas wasn't big on reading novels, but he'd been hooked on them too. They both secretly hoped they'd find their way into one of his tales someday.

Thomas kept thinking about the girl, and since his mother's call he'd swung back the other way. He certainly wasn't sure it was her, but he was sure it could have been, and that was enough that he ought to pursue it. She was family. He couldn't go out to the Hatteras and ask them, the captain wouldn't even let them step aboard, so next best thing was to find out if she was where she was supposed to be. Telling AJ he'd see her later at the Fox and Hare, he headed towards George Town on his bicycle.

It was about five miles and Thomas cut over to West Bay Road, where he weaved around the busy beach traffic. Twenty minutes later, with sweat glistening on his dark skin, he stopped by the fish market on the last piece of sandy beach left on the edge of downtown. Three small canopies, each with a wooden bench underneath, made up the tiny market where some of the local fishermen made their catch available to anyone with cash, public and restaurant alike. It was late, and the fishermen had all packed up for the day, except for one old man picking his rusty bicycle up, about to go home.

"Philman, how'd ya been these days?" Thomas said, slipping into his heavy native accent.

The old man looked up and squinted, taking a moment to recognise him. "Jeremiah and Wilma's boy ain't it?"

"Sure is, sir. You're just the man I was looking for," Thomas replied, setting his bike against the low wall and stepping over to the beach.

"Oh, you were?" Philman eyed him suspiciously. "Why's that then?"

"You mentioned to my pap, a while back, you thought you'd seen Hallie Bodden, here in town?" Thomas asked politely.

"I did?" The old man said, looking confused. "Hallie Bodden you say? That's the girl with the crazy mother ain't it? Amelia? Didn't she up and die last year?"

"Yes sir," Thomas answered patiently. "That's the one, her daughter would be about sixteen nowadays."

"And Jeremiah said I'd seen her? Amelia, or the girl?" he asked, looking even more confused.

"The daughter, sir, Hallie," Thomas answered. He remained polite but guessed he'd ridden all this way for nothing; his mother had been right.

"I do recall seeing a girl," Philman mumbled. "Looked real familiar, but older than I remembered. Hard to keep up with all the family, you know? Everyone's got kids and grandkids, too many to remember."

"True enough, sir. But you think you saw Hallie?" Thomas allowed himself a hint of optimism.

"Them eyes," Philman muttered. "Ain't never seen no one with them eyes before."

"That's her," Thomas said excitedly. "Where, sir? Where did you see those eyes?"

Philman looked over his shoulder and pointed. "Right there. She were walking into town. Wouldn't have thought nothing of it 'cept she turned and I saw them eyes of hers. I called to her, but she just run off into the crowd."

Thomas left Philman to head home, or more likely the off licence, and rode into the harbour front. The last of the passengers were lined up at the cruise port, to be tendered back to the giant ships moored outside George Town's tiny harbour. The crowd was steadily switching over from the day visitors to stay-over tourists and residents, making their way to the restaurants for the sunset and an evening meal. Thomas was surprised to see Fabian, 'the dancing policeman', still manning the crosswalk, and enthusiastically helping folks across the road with a shrill whistle and a twirl. Thomas rested his bike against the harbour front wall, and jogged over to the zebra crossing at Harbour and Cardinal. Fabian held station in the middle of the road, whether cars were passing or people crossing, so Thomas couldn't really walk over and talk to him. As Thomas was about to give up the idea, Fabian blew his whistle for a final, long, piercing note, waved frantically at the cars and walked off the crossing to the pavement on the other side. Thomas sprinted over, dodging a few cars to reach the man before he disappeared. A couple of tourists halted Fabian for a photograph on their mobile, which delayed him enough for Thomas to catch up.

"Mister Fabian, sir, may I ask you a question?" Thomas asked, slightly out of breath.

Fabian turned, sweat spilling down his brow. "Sure, what can I help you with, young man?"

"I'm actually trying to find my cousin, and I was wondering if you may have seen her. I believe she may have been hanging out in town here recently," Thomas babbled out.

Fabian laughed, interrupting him before he could finish. "I see more than a few people around here, you'll have to help a little more. How long this girl been missing anyway?"

"I haven't seen her for a while, but she may be fine. I'm just concerned, so I'm trying to check in on her."

"I see," Fabian said, wiping his brow, "Well, what does this young lady look like? Maybe I've seen her."

"She's sixteen, really pretty girl with skin tone a little lighter than mine, slim and medium height, long dark hair and she has brown eyes." Thomas tried to find the right words.

"You just described half the schoolgirls on Cayman, man," Fabian laughed.

"I know, I'm sorry, but it's her eyes, that's how you'd remember her. They're brown, but they're this really light, vibrant brown, I guarantee you haven't seen anything like it before."

"Yah man, there's a kid that's always hanging around, she's a nice-looking kid but dresses real plain. Usually always wearing the same dress, come to think of it. She's always looking down, but I do recall she had really bright eyes. She was walking by one day and I nodded hello her way. She looked straight down and kept walking, fast as she could. But when I looked at her, I remember she went from seeming real plain and normal to looking like a model in a photograph. It was the eyes I think." He shrugged his shoulders. "But I don't know if that's your cousin, or a kid off a cruise ship."

"But you said you've seen that girl hanging around for a while?" Thomas queried.

"True, I guess I have, so you're right, she must be local. No idea where she lives, I'm afraid. Good luck finding her though," He went to leave then stopped. "But if you don't you might consider filing a missing person with the station."

"Thank you, sir, I will," Thomas replied and watched Fabian leave with a few fancy steps.

37

FRIDAY

Hallie had never worn a dab of make-up in her life. She'd never had a want, or need, when they'd led a normal life, and once they lived in the shack, if it wasn't a necessity, she certainly wasn't wasting money on it. The past year or more she'd spent trying to be invisible, so enhancing her features was the last thing she wanted. It had never occurred to her to use make-up to downplay her looks, but she didn't have the first idea how to apply it, or what to buy anyway. Abigay stood behind her in the master stateroom bathroom, pulled her hair back into a ponytail, and slipped a colourful hair tie over to secure it out of the way.

"Let's start with eyes," Abigay said in her songful creole accent. Hallie liked Abigay. Zoe was friendly, and full of energy, but she found her unpredictable. Like the kiss this morning. She didn't know what to make of that. Abigay was easy going, more relaxed, at least around Hallie, and she reminded her of friends she had had in school.

"You have the most beautiful eyes, so we need to accent them softly, you know, not too much." They looked at each other in the mirror. "My eyes are dark brown, they need more help, so I try to use a little more colour."

Abigay picked up a pencil from the counter. "Here, just some eyeliner, like this," she explained as she carefully applied the eyeliner to herself, before handing it to Hallie. "See how it frames the eyes and draws attention to them?"

Hallie took the pencil and held it close to her eye. Seemed to her this might be a great way of losing a perfectly good eye, and she'd prefer to keep her sight.

"Want me to apply it on you first, so you see how it feels?" Abigay offered sweetly.

"That's okay, I'll try," Hallie replied, still uncertain, but if she was going to poke an eye out, she'd hate to blame Abigay for the rest of her life, she liked the girl. Tentatively, she touched the pencil to the edge of her eye, which made her blink and put a stripe down the top of her cheek. She looked at Abigay in the mirror and they both burst out laughing.

Most of the next hour was spent perfecting eye make-up. Abigay also showed her some simple blush, saying their skin tones didn't need much, and then played around with lipstick colours, until they found a shade she liked best. As Abigay packed up her make-up case, Hallie looked out the starboard portholes at the sunset. She thought about the dive boat she'd seen earlier. The woman was the same one she'd seen that morning, pretty, with cool hair. She'd had a sweatshirt on earlier, but just a bathing suit this afternoon, so she'd seen the tattoos down her arms. Marguerite had told her they didn't allow girls with tattoos as hosts, at least nothing elaborate. The woman was too old to be a host anyway – you had to be young for the men to like you. There had been a Caymanian man too. She hadn't paid much attention to him as she'd been intrigued by the woman, but now it struck her as odd. What was he doing on a dive boat? Caymanians were traditionally fishermen; she'd never known a local working with the dive boats. For some reason it made her feel lonely. She thought of the large family gatherings she used to go to when life was normal. There would be a dozen kids her age to play with and adults fussing around telling her how much she'd grown since the last time they'd seen her. Imagine what they'd say now, she pondered. Hallie had spent so much time on her own, she'd lost the line between feeling lonely and, well, how she felt every day. This new pang of longing and emptiness surprised her. Why now, as she was finally surrounded by people, would she feel lonely? It didn't make sense.

"Okay, let's pick out your evening gown, and a little jewellery," Abigay said, taking Hallie by the hand and leading her out of the master stateroom.

Marguerite had her keep three nice dresses, which she laid out on the bed for Abigay to see.

"Hmmm, the silvery one is the sexiest, but the red one will be great with your skin tone," Abigay said enthusiastically.

Hallie picked up the red dress and held it up to herself, looking in the mirror. "This was my favourite one, the other two are... Well, there's not much to them, I sort of feel naked in them."

Abigay lay down on the bed, pushing the dresses aside and laughed. "Girl, you gonna feel a lot more naked when they get you actually naked."

Hallie laughed with her, but the idea scared her still. It was one thing taking clothes off in front of Marguerite – she already felt like her aunt, or someone close – but a strange man? She had chills at the thought.

"Put it on, let's see," Abigay urged her.

Hallie slipped her tee-shirt carefully over her head, so she didn't ruin her make-up, and turned to Abigay with her arms covering her bare chest. "Do you really get used to all this naked stuff? You and Zoe dance around without your clothes on, and Marguerite tells me I should be happy with my body, and it's okay to show it off. But it feels really strange to me, I'm too embarrassed."

Abigay sat up and looked serious, speaking quietly, "Look, Marguerite's gonna tell you a lotta stuff. Some of it makes sense, some of it, I don't know, I figure it's their way of getting you to do what they want. What you gotta decide is whether that money they're paying is worth a year of your life. For me, I'll take a year of living like this any day over the shit I had back home. Since Hurricane Matthew four years ago, my brothers and me, we been living in a shipping container they made into a house. My parents were taken in the storm, so this guy runs the house and rents out the beds to us. He decided I pay my rent in his bed. So, for me, if I gotta sleep in a king-sized luxury bed, in a gorgeous resort with some rich old guy, and get paid for it, that be a big improvement in my circumstances." She smiled. "Besides, you hot shit little mama, you should show off that body of yours any chance you get, them men come running."

They both laughed and Hallie dropped her hands away to take her shorts off. "I don't know about that, I still don't think I can be comfortable naked around a stranger – you think you can be?"

"Yeah, I always been shy, but I reckon I can do it." She grabbed her own breasts and shook them a little. "People just stare at these things anyway; I could have trees for legs and my head missing, they wouldn't notice."

They laughed all over again, and Hallie slipped into the red dress. "Do you miss home?" she asked as she pulled and tucked the thin, silky material into place. "I don't mean the container, but Haiti?"

Abigay sighed and thought a moment. "It seemed great when I was little, and my parents were alive, but it was all I knew. We were poor but so was everyone. I worry about my brothers, they good kids but it's easy to get into bad shit there. I worried they start getting in trouble."

Hallie turned to face Abigay and made a pose in the dress.

"Ummmm, you look good sister, that Latino hunk Raposa gonna love to get his hands on you. You best watch Marguerite, too; I think she'll like a piece of that tight little body as well."

Hallie wasn't sure what she meant but she laughed along as Abigay had tears running down her face. "Oh damn, I'm ruining my make-up now," she cackled, but couldn't stop laughing.

When they had settled down, Abigay fetched a small jewellery box from her room and opened it on the bed. She picked out an ornate Indian-style gold-coloured necklace and wrapped it around

Hallie's neck. Looking in the mirror Hallie couldn't imagine what a necklace like that must cost. She had seen similar things in the windows of the harbour front jewellery stores, alongside the fancy watches.

"This is gorgeous," she whispered.

Abigay rummaged around to find the earrings she was looking for, and held them up to the side of Hallie's face.

"Perfect," she said softly.

Hallie grinned at her friend in the mirror. "They are. But my ears aren't pierced."

They laughed some more and sat down on the bed, picking through the jewellery box and commenting on pieces they liked.

"Are you worried about the riots?" Hallie asked, casually.

Abigay looked at her. "What do you mean?"

"The riots at home. In Haiti. You didn't see the protesters are causing riots? It's been bad according to the paper."

Abigay shook her head, "They don't let us have a newspaper here. Or see news of any sort. They say we need to be focused on the resort for the time we're here and not distracted."

"They said there was no Internet, TV or phones, but I didn't care really, I haven't had any of those things. But I read the *Cayman Compass* every day, it's our local paper. I have one in my bag. I think it's the one with the article about Haiti." She jumped up and opened the wardrobe, retrieving her beaten-up rucksack and opening the main zipper. She searched around inside but couldn't find the newspaper. She looked at Abigay, confused.

"It's gone."

Abigay shook her head sullenly. "They ain't gonna let you see that stuff no more, girl."

38

FRIDAY

Thomas retrieved his bicycle and stood on the pavement, trying to decide what to do next. He was starting to believe his cousin was in George Town, but it didn't mean for sure she was living there. Cayman's bus system was extensive, and frequent, so she could be coming in from anywhere on the island. The sun was crashing through the horizon and some low, offshore cloud was making for a colourful event, which reminded him it was getting late. He glanced at the time on his mobile; it was 6:25pm and he was supposed to be at the pub by seven. He turned and pedalled away down North Church Street, starting towards Seven Mile Beach and West Bay. He'd have to come back on Sunday, his day off, and have a better look around. He rode past Fort Street and kept up with the slow-moving evening traffic, until it started backing up before Mary Street, just after the fish market. He quickly switched to the other side of the road and, keeping tight to the kerb, went against the oncoming traffic. At the junction for Mary Street he braked and waited for a car to turn, and when he slowed, he noticed Philman sitting on a low wall outside the Harbour Centre building. Making a spur-of-the-moment decision, he cut right and skidded to a stop in front of the old man. Philman looked up at him and shuffled the paper bag containing his beverage under his legs.

"Hey kid, thought you'd gone. I told ya everything I know," the old man slurred.

Didn't take him long, Thomas thought, maybe he stays topped up all day so a little extra in the evening tips him over.

"Sorry to bother you again, but I thought of one more thing. Hallie's mother, do you know where she was living when she was still alive?"

Philman looked up with a weird expression. "Why should I know that?"

Thomas was asking on a wild chance that the man might have known, he really didn't expect him to. But his odd reaction made him keep pushing.

"No reason. Just my pap always says, you're the man to ask about anything going on in this town. Guess this one slipped by you."

Philman squinted up at Thomas through an alcoholic haze, but Thomas could tell he'd struck a nerve.

"Damn right I know this town, your daddy's right about that. I'll outfish him any day, but he's right about that," Philman blabbered. "Course I knew where she lived." He reached down and picked up his bag. Giving Thomas a gruff stare he took a long pull, then coughed a few times. Thomas waited him out. The old man wiped his face and put the bottle back down.

"Off Rock Hole Road, right up there," he growled quietly, pointing at the junction thirty yards away, where Rock Hole Road veered off from Mary Street. "Little dirt path on the right, bit before Jersey Lane. Shack down the path there, that's where she lived, God bless her."

The old man waved Thomas away and slumped his chin on his chest. Thomas grabbed his bicycle and turned into Rock Hole Road, as the last embers of the sun gave way to the dark sky.

Thomas didn't know Jersey Lane, so he rode quickly, figuring he'd turn around once he found it. It was a tiny cul-de-sac on the left, which he almost missed, the crooked street sign partially hidden in the overgrown shrubs. Thomas swung his bike around and slowly cruised back on the other side of the street, in search of the pathway Philman had described. After fifty yards he found it. The path was barely wide enough for a vehicle but, rutted and unmaintained, he was pretty sure no cars used it. He got off his bike and pushed it tentatively down the path, which got darker and darker the farther from the dim streetlights he went. He was upon the shack before he even saw it, nestled in the trees and shrubs to his left. He foraged in his pocket for his mobile, and quickly turned on the torch function. The structure was wood panelled with a tin roof, one door, and a single window on each wall, as best he could see. A water spigot stuck up at an angle from the ground under the front window, with a short piece of filthy garden hose attached. The door had a latch for a padlock on the outside, but there wasn't a lock on it.

Thomas stared at the hovel in disbelief. Is this really where they had been living? He couldn't imagine it. Many of his extended family were poor, and several had run-down homes, but none lived in anything like this. The idea that Hallie may have been here, alone for the last year, was incomprehensible to Thomas. He took a deep breath and reached for the door handle.

"What the hell do ya think ya doing?" came a low voice from the shadows farther down the path. Thomas jumped back and instinctively shone the light in the direction of the voice. An old Caymanian man shielded his eyes from the torch.

"Point that thing down, damn it."

"Sorry," Thomas quickly responded. "Sir, I don't mean to bother you, I was looking for my cousin, I was told she was living here." Thomas kept his torch pointed at the ground near the man's feet, so the edge of the beam still illuminated him. He could see the man was sizing him up and was pretty sure he had some kind of billy club tucked behind his leg. Rock Hole Road was not the upmarket part of George Town, so the man had reason to be wary of strangers.

"Who's your cousin?" he finally growled.

"Hallie Bodden, sir. I'm Thomas Bodden, I'm actually her second cousin."

The old man mumbled for a moment, but Thomas couldn't make out what he was saying. Finally he spoke up again.

"If I knew this girl, and if I was to ask her, reckon she'd want to see you?"

Thomas thought it a moment. "Probably not, sir. But I don't think she's here."

The old man looked confused. "Then why you looking here for her?"

Thomas took a step back towards the shack, and gently pushed his foot against the door. "To see if I'm right," he said and watched the door swing inward.

The old man shuffled along to the doorway, dragging his feet, and Thomas wondered how the hell he didn't hear him coming before. Thomas shone his torch inside and they both peered in. The shack was surprisingly clean and tidy inside. A single bed sat against the back wall, neatly made. A towel hung from a nail next to the sink on the right wall, by the toilet. Both fixtures were scrubbed clean. To the left was a small table and two chairs, and against the wall a wooden cabinet. Missing were any clothes, toiletries or personal effects.

"When was the last time you saw her here?" Thomas asked.

The man looked Thomas over again and let out a long sigh. "Few days back. Kid keeps herself to herself, never any trouble. Quiet as a mouse." He scratched his balding head. "She paid me through the month. Always paid me on time, right at first of the month. Girl was the one used to pay me when her momma was still here." He shook his head. "Weren't so quiet back then, that woman had some problems. Tried to pay rent on that there bed one time." He chuckled. "I told her, unless she hiding cash money between her legs, I sure as hell weren't going there."

Thomas shone the light around one last time before stepping out of the dirt-floored shack.

"Sorry to disturb you, sir, you have a good evening."

The old man pulled the door closed. "You find her, tell that kid I said thank you. Girl came out good despite her mother's bad ways."

Thomas nodded and wheeled his bike back down the narrow dirt path, turning his torch off and slipping his mobile back in his pocket. He now knew, Hallie wasn't where she was supposed to be. He felt a pit in his stomach as he understood what that meant. It was probably her on the Hatteras after all.

39

———

FRIDAY

Tucked away in West Bay, the Fox and Hare was the best replication of a true English pub the ex-pat owners could put together on a tropical island, 4,750 miles from home. The building itself was a nondescript two-storey stucco, on the inland side of North West Point Road, at the corner of Bonaventure. But once inside, the place transformed into a slice of the old country. The bar itself was a hefty oak wood structure, lined with bar stools and a floated resin top over maps of England and the Cayman Islands. Pictures and memorabilia from the homeland decorated the walls. A picture of the queen took pride of place behind the bar, between rows of glass shelves holding every alcoholic option you could imagine. Twelve beer taps flowed various brews from Britain, two from the Caribbean, and one from America. The Miller Lite and island beer were served cold, all others at room temperature. The only time the owners advertised was for two Friday nights a month, when Pearl took the tiny stage in the corner. The place was packed by seven o'clock when she strummed her guitar and opened her first set with Stevie Nicks' 'Edge of Seventeen'.

Reg, who'd been there since six setting up Pearl's gear, took a table a few rows back, so some of the other patrons could get a good view. And from where he could keep an eye on them. The pub wasn't known for trouble, but Reg had no problem causing some if a drunkard disrupted his wife's performance. AJ sat with him, holding a chair open for Thomas, who was uncharacteristically late. Reg had seen Roy Whittaker and his wife come in, as they often did to see Pearl play, and invited them to join their group. The four of them tapped their feet and sipped their drinks, making small talk between songs. A Friday night at the Fox and Hare was more like a mini concert than ambience music in the background. Pearl had a big raspy voice, and the ex-pat locals, more than a few Caymanians, and the occasional tourist, generally came to hear her sing. Socialising was secondary, between sets.

AJ looked up and saw Thomas finally arrive, breathing heavily and sweating as he came through the front door. She waved and he spotted them, making his way between tables to join them.

"Where the hell you been?" Reg growled in his best intimidating voice.

"I'm sorry, sir, I was delayed in town, I got here as fast as I could," he panted, downing the glass of water AJ shoved in front of him.

Reg grinned. "You remember Roy Whittaker," he shouted over the music and Thomas leapt back to his feet to shake hands with the detective. "And this is his wife, Sonia."

Sonia was a large, Caymanian lady with a round face and a permanent smile. She nodded to Thomas, who greeted her politely, "Nice to meet you ma'am," and sat back down.

AJ leaned over and asked as quietly as she could, "Where have you been? You didn't even have time to change."

Thomas downed the last of the water. "I'm really sorry, I was in town, I went looking for my cousin."

AJ was surprised; the last he'd said was he didn't think it was her after all. "Did you find her?"

Thomas shook his head, "No. Well, yes, but no. I found where she's been living, and it weren't with family or friends – seems she's been fending for herself since her mother died."

"So you can go back and see her when she's there?" AJ asked innocently.

"No, she was gone, moved out. Man who owns the house, well, the shack, didn't know she'd left. Guessing it was last few days." Thomas looked worried. "Makes me think it was Hallie I saw on that boat."

Pearl wrapped up Alannah Miles' 'Black Velvet', finishing her first set to rousing applause, before the place quietened down and the house music picked up in the background. Pearl made her way over to the table to a round of compliments, and a kiss from Reg.

"You look like you just ran a marathon, Thomas," Pearl said, with a smile.

"I'm sorry I missed the first few songs, ma'am, I had some bike riding to do. Sorry for being all sweaty," Thomas replied without his usual exuberance.

"Everything alright? You look worried," Pearl asked. For a woman with no children she had a strong mothering instinct.

Thomas looked at AJ, seeming unsure whether to discuss his cousin or not. AJ figured it wasn't her place to make that call, but between the terse nature of the captain, the odd conversation of the resort members they'd taken diving, and Thomas's cousin being spotted on the boat, something wasn't right. She nodded to Thomas, hoping he'd open up. Wouldn't hurt for Whittaker to hear about all this.

"It's a cousin o' mine," Thomas said tentatively, still looking at AJ. "She's just a kid, but I think I saw her today on that big yacht we took some divers out from. Don't make no sense her on that boat." He tapered off, appearing unsure what else to say.

"Those customers we took out, there's something not right about that group," AJ picked up the conversation. "I'm used to being around men, their wolf whistles and bravado, all that bullshit, but these guys were different. They were talking about paying for girls, and leaving a girl with bruises. Why would Thomas's sixteen-year-old cousin be on a luxury yacht with these people?"

Whittaker leaned in. "If you don't mind me asking, who's your cousin, Thomas?"

"Hallie Bodden, sir. You may recall her mother, Amelia Bodden, she unfortunately passed last year." Thomas had a hard time keeping his eyes up. "She lost her way some, sir, drugs and what have you."

"I do recall Amelia, sad indeed. She had the misfortune to cross paths with the RCIPS a few times. So, who's been looking after the girl since her mother passed?" Whittaker asked and AJ was pleased he hadn't switched into his full detective mode. She guessed Thomas would likely stop talking if he did.

"We all thought she was living with the family of a school friend, but I guess she must have lied about that. Amelia had lost their house a few years back and it seems they lived in a shanty shack off Rock Hole Road. Hallie kept on living there." Thomas shook his head. "I went by this evening, but she's moved out. Maybe everything's fine, but I'm worried what's going on with her."

"Poor girl," Pearl said quietly.

"And who are these men on the boat? What boat are we talking about?" Whittaker asked, his tone turning more serious.

"The boat is the big Hatteras you may have seen around, belongs to the resort that contacted me," Reg said, looking concerned himself. "Done some charters for them before, never had any issues. The resort is that place they built a year or so back, tucked away in Salt Creek. International Fellowship of Lions is who they have me bill. I think it's a membership resort of some sort. As for the men, I don't know, who were they AJ?"

"Americans," AJ commented, trying to think how to describe them. "Two of them were older, fifty I'd guess. I can look at my paperwork for DOBs to be exact. The third one was younger, probably late thirties or forty. But he was a weird little guy, creepy. He was the one they said bruised a girl. They talked about a Scandinavian girl as well, they were ribbing the creepy one about finally, you know..." AJ hesitated to be crass in front of a policeman and his wife, although she was sure he'd heard everything before. "You get the point."

"The captain on the boat was strange too," Thomas added. "I asked if he'd let us see the boat and he was all high and mighty and said no, it was for members of the resort only."

"Unfortunately, being rude isn't illegal yet," Whittaker said without a smile. "But it seems odd your cousin would be on that boat. She's under seventeen so she's considered a child by social services. I could take a visit to the resort tomorrow, ask a few questions."

"Thank you, sir," Thomas enthused. "Could be she's fine, but it would mean a lot to my family to know. Hallie was always a good girl, sir, a good student until her ma got herself messed up."

Whittaker nodded and sat back, taking a sip of his beer.

"I feel terrible I sent you that bunch," Reg said, looking at AJ.

"You couldn't know, Reg," AJ replied.

"Besides, if you'd taken them out you wouldn't have known that was my kin," Thomas said. "If it was her. I still can't be completely sure."

"Yeah, but I saw that girl too, and it was the same girl I saw that morning when we headed out – she's just a kid."

Pearl got up. "Sorry guys, I have to go back up, I'm worried about all this now." She looked at Thomas. "But Roy will get you sorted out lad, don't you worry." She squeezed Whittaker's shoulder as she left for the stage.

"Anything on the girl we found, Roy?" AJ asked, thinking she'd change the subject and give Thomas a break.

Whittaker paused before replying slowly, "We have a few more details to work with, but still no suspects."

He looked at AJ thoughtfully. She immediately figured they were having the same thought. She regretted bringing it up, and turned to Thomas. Thomas shook his head and looked down at the table.

"I'm sure they're not connected, Thomas," AJ said, putting a hand on her friend's arm. "No reason to think they have anything to do with each other."

"No reason at all," Whittaker added. "Don't worry, young Bodden, I'll go by tomorrow. If your cousin is involved with those people, we'll see what's going on."

Thomas managed a weak smile.

The crowd applauded as Pearl started her second set with Pat Benatar's 'Hell is for Children'.

40

SATURDAY

AJ and Thomas both looked around expectantly as they idled clear of the channel into the North Sound. The morning light glinted off the calm, empty waters; the Hatteras was nowhere to be seen. It hadn't been near the fuel dock where they'd seen it before either.

"I don't know what we would have done if it was still sitting here anyway," AJ said. "The captain made it clear we weren't welcome aboard."

Thomas was at the helm and she saw the determined expression on his face. He looked tired too; she guessed he hadn't slept much. Thomas had the uncanny ability of sleeping anywhere, at any time, a talent AJ did not possess, so seeing him tired was rare. He didn't answer her.

"I better go down and get Sully sorted out, find out where he wants to go first," she said, squeezing Thomas's shoulder as she headed for the steps.

"Sure thing, boss," he replied absentmindedly.

Nick Sullivan was medium height, medium build, and giant personality. AJ always figured if his writing hadn't panned out he should have been an actor. He had one those faces that changed expression with every increment of thought and emotion. He lived in New York, but had grown up scuba diving with his family on regular trips to Bonaire, and now, as a bestselling author, enjoyed dive travel throughout the world in search of stories. He had dived with AJ for a few years, whenever he came to Grand Cayman, but this was the first time he'd chartered the whole boat for the day.

"Where would you like to start, Sully?" AJ asked, as she joined him at the table in the middle of the deck where he was preparing his camera set-up.

"I need a pinnacle, AJ," he said with a big smile, demonstrating a large column with his hands. Or maybe a phallus. She wasn't sure. She couldn't help but giggle.

"Oh, yes." He put his hands down and blushed a little, laughing. "Sorry, anyway, got any pinnacles?"

"We do," AJ answered, still chuckling. "The most prominent one on the north is..." She stopped when she realised what she was about to say, and where they'd have to go. Just yesterday she'd struggled to take the boat in the general vicinity, and had been relieved not to go to the actual site. Today, she and Thomas would have to face it. As she had tried to convince herself yesterday, it's just a name and a patch of ocean, it really had nothing to do with the girl. Her body happened to be passing through there when they found her. An hour earlier and she'd have still been out farther, over the deep, an hour later, and she'd have been heading towards the open ocean off the north-west corner. If she looked at it from that perspective, it was actually fortunate timing. The idea the kid would have drifted across the vast Caribbean Sea, slowly sinking to the depths and all the other horrible things that happen to a corpse as it goes through the process of returning to the earth, was a far worse thought.

"I'm sorry?" Sully looked at her quizzically. "Where were you thinking?"

"Ghost Mountain." AJ said firmly, "We'll take you to Ghost Mountain."

"Oooh," Sully said with a smile, wiggling his fingers in the air in a spooky fashion, "sounds ominous."

AJ smiled; best to leave it at that, she decided.

They splashed in to great visibility, and with it, all of AJ's anxiety washed away as she and Sully descended to the reef. He sported bright, lime green fins and a matching weight belt, both unmistakeable in contrast to his black wetsuit. Current was minimal and as she finned towards the drop-off, the bright morning sun lit up the corals like a flower garden. The water was so clear, AJ had barely left the wall at sixty feet when Ghost Mountain appeared, emerging from the dark blue ocean ahead of them. The pinnacle was connected to the steeply sloping wall at over two hundred feet, so it rose from the depths as a solitary spire, looming towards them as they seemingly swam into the abyss. Sully enthusiastically waved 'okay' hand signals to her and she watched his animated grin cause his face to wrinkle and lose his mask seal. She guessed this happened a lot as he cleared the saltwater from his mask in one sweeping motion and carried on grinning.

She descended to a hundred feet and began to circle the pinnacle until Sully halted them. He'd found a spot he liked. With the sunlight on the far side of the spire, it haloed the small, underwater mountain in a heavenly glow, and his powerful strobes illuminated the shadowed face. AJ hung back and took in the scenery while her client clicked and flashed away. A little deeper down, loitering below a giant purple elephant ear sponge protruding from the spire, she spotted an array of brightly coloured fins and spines. She wished she'd brought her spear down with her – the invasive lionfish would make some tasty tacos. Moving her gaze back to scanning the deeper water, she picked up movement at the far reaches of visibility. Often the ocean triggers or large jacks trick the eye into thinking they're something larger from a distance, but whatever she was seeing wasn't a trigger or a jack. It wasn't even a shark. Rather than tap loudly on her tank to get Sully's attention, she kicked over and tugged on his fin, pointing to the deep blue open ocean. It moved like a ray, but the top of an eagle ray is darker and spotted, and she realised this would be the biggest eagle ray she'd ever seen. As the giant manta ray swooped towards them its cephalic lobes – the soft, curved fins across the front of its mouth – became clear, and AJ squealed into her regulator. Sully almost dropped his camera as he fumbled to adjust a series of settings to capture the beautiful beast as it cruised past. The manta's wingspan was easily twenty feet across and its mouth gaped open as it sifted the water for plankton. Just like a whale shark, the huge fish fed upon the smallest creatures in the ocean.

Twenty minutes later they climbed the ladder and dropped their BCDs and tanks in the custom holders lining the benches. AJ and Sully looked at each with huge smiles, both at a loss for words.

"What?" Thomas asked, "What did you see? You're both grinning like a, what's your phrase?" He looked at AJ for help.

"Cheshire cat," She managed to say.

"Yeah, grinning like Chelsea cats," Thomas said, almost getting it right.

AJ laughed some more and couldn't speak.

"I am flabbergasted," Sully finally said. "I am gasted with flabber."

AJ laughed even more, and poor Thomas fidgeted around looking for an answer. "Come on, man, tell me what it was."

AJ managed to regain control. "A freakin' manta ray, Thomas, we saw a huge manta ray."

Thomas's mouth dropped open.

"I didn't even know you had mantas in these waters," Sully said, throwing his hands in the air.

"We don't!" AJ replied. "I've heard of an odd sighting over the years, but I've never seen one, and I bet Reg, who's been diving here forever, hasn't either."

"Right where we found her," Thomas said quietly and AJ looked up, a lump instantly forming in her throat.

"Damn," she uttered under her breath. "You're right."

"Who's her?" Sully asked.

41

SATURDAY

Cristal strode aboard the Cova do Leão, moored against the dock at the back of the resort. She wore designer jeans, a bright red sleeveless silk shirt, and her long black hair was slicked back over her scalp, obediently staying in place. She slid the door open to the salon and marched inside. Raposa, Marguerite and the two girls all looked up at her, clearly having been waiting.

"Well, don't just stare at me, let's get on with this," she barked, and smiled to herself at the hive of activity that ensued.

Sometimes she enjoyed acting pissed off to keep everyone on their toes, but this particular morning she'd woken up annoyed. Or agitated, or something she couldn't put her finger on, but either way she was pissed off, so everyone would know it. It was probably one of them causing her discontent, she just hadn't uncovered the reason yet. Cristal had an uncanny knack of sensing issues and problems before they arose, which often helped her steer around disasters. Her radar was on high alert this morning.

Marguerite had the girls sit at the table where she'd set out an assortment of cold breakfast foods. Apparently, she'd learnt not to rely on Cristal arriving on time. Cristal waved her hand, and Zoe and Abigay started their breakfast. She wandered around, pausing to pour herself a coffee, while the girls used butter knives for butter and sugar spoons for sugar, all delicately and precisely performed.

"Where's the new girl?" Cristal asked Raposa, who remained on the couch.

"Up top, with Peter. If she was farther along I'd have her observe, but she's not ready this soon," he replied calmly.

Cristal nodded as the girls finished their food, wiped their mouths softly with their napkins, and made sure their utensils were together, facing them on their plates, indicating they were done.

"Well done, let us adjourn to the bar," Marguerite guided patiently.

Cristal turned and watched the girls head across the salon. They were both wearing colourful sarongs with loose-fitting white linen shirts over their swimsuits, and sandals on their feet. Zoe walked confidently but Abigay had an island swing to her gait, and moved more slowly. Cristal registered every nuance of their mannerisms and movements. Matching girls to clients was an essential part of the process. She'd found the men had a look in mind, but often chose a host that came with a personality they didn't expect or desire if not guided. No information was available on the Internet, too risky. The members chose from the available hosts when they arrived, or often requested certain hosts for their next visit. Some regulars had girls they preferred every time, others asked for someone different each visit. Photographs alone could be deceiving, so Cristal had an electronic portfolio on each girl, viewable from the secure tablet in each villa. They were linked to a central server so updates could be made real time from the office. The portfolio included videos of the girls, short interviews and a description, carefully crafted by Cristal herself. The girls weren't allowed to see their portfolios, access was password protected, and members were supplied a new code every visit. She didn't need a girl getting her nose out of joint because she'd been described as 'sexually aggressive' or 'timid, likes to be led'. They were kids after all.

"I'd like a full-bodied red wine, something European, Zoe," Cristal instructed and turned to Abigay. "Whiskey sour."

Abigay went to work behind the bar and Zoe left for the wine storage, which was on the lower deck. When the drinks were completed Cristal tried both and set the wine back on the bar, keeping the whisky sour. Raposa got up from the couch and Marguerite put a slow Latin tune on the salon's sound system. Raposa held his hand out towards Abigay and, taking her cue, she stepped over, took his hand, and the two began a slow, romantic dance in the middle of the room. After a minute, Marguerite switched the song to an upbeat dance tune, and the two stepped farther apart and danced energetically until Cristal clapped her hands. Raposa nodded to Abigay, and extended a hand towards Zoe. The girls switched, and the strange scene continued as the big yacht bobbed gently in the calm waters of salt creek in the mid-morning sun.

With beads of sweat trickling down his brow, Raposa poured himself a drink of water in the galley while Cristal asked the girls a series of questions as they sat on the couch. The questions were all based around queries they could expect from resort members while they were in their company. Where are you from? How old are you? How long have you been here? What do you do in your spare time? The girls were coached to stay as close to the truth as possible but give away the minimum. What kind of money do you make here? That was a question Cristal threw at them, after a series of benign, innocuous enquiries.

"I'm a student here," Zoe replied assertively. "We're not paid."

Cristal nodded. "Good." She turned to Marguerite, who hovered close by like a mother hen. "Okay, downstairs."

Marguerite led the girls away, down the narrow stairwell to the staterooms. Raposa returned from the galley and looked at Cristal.

"What do you think?"

Cristal thought a moment. "They're both good, you and Marguerite have done well. Zoe will be a feisty one, she will only appeal to a few of the members. Most don't seek out young girls for them to act like older girls."

Raposa grinned. "Wait until you see the next part of the review, she'll have plenty of return customers, believe me. I would recommend her to our female clients too. She really doesn't care who's in the bed."

Cristal almost imperceptibly raised an eyebrow. Her mood was improving for a reason she knew no clearer than the instigator of her poor humour earlier. Perhaps it was two new hosts at a time they desperately needed some fresh bodies. They both walked down the stairs and turned left into the master stateroom. Zoe was lighting a series of candles placed around the room and, once they were lit, she turned out the lights. Cristal closed the door and leaned against the jamb. She wanted to light a cigarette, but she maintained a strict non-smoking policy in the resort, on the boat, and with the girls. Young girls weren't expected to smoke. Marguerite stood in the shadows of the doorway to the walk-in closet, and Abigay was absent from the room. Raposa stood in front of the bed.

"Undress me," he said quietly to Zoe.

Zoe pressed herself against the man's toned body and slid her hands across his chest to the buttons of his shirt. She slowly undid each one while looking him in the eye.

Cristal's mobile vibrated in the back pocket of her skintight jeans; she retrieved the device and answered the call in Portuguese. Raposa frowned at Cristal. Zoe didn't even flinch at the sound of Cristal's conversation, and continued with his shirt buttons until she reached his shorts, where she didn't stop.

Cristal watched with indifference, speaking quietly but sternly into her mobile. When she finished her phone conversation, Raposa and Zoe were both on the bed in the throes of energetic lovemaking. Cristal clapped her hands.

"Good enough," she said in a disinterested tone, noting Raposa appeared disappointed.

"Save your strength, lover boy, you got another one yet." She winked at him and he slid out of bed and started putting his clothes back on. Zoe began to do the same, but Cristal held up a hand.

"Don't bother getting dressed." She waved a hand at Marguerite, who quietly stepped forward from the shadows.

"Your turn," Cristal said, and Marguerite's face became flushed and her chest heaved with deep breaths. Cristal realised the woman may enjoy this part of her work more than she'd noticed before. She knew Marguerite preferred the fairer sex, but it seemed Zoe had quite the effect on her. Zoe walked boldly over to the woman and pushed her firmly down on the bed before she could say a word.

Raposa looked at Cristal as he buttoned his shirt back up, and gave her the 'I told you so' look.

Cristal clearly raised an eyebrow this time. Zoe already had Marguerite's clothes off.

42

SATURDAY

It was later in the morning than he'd planned by the time Whittaker pulled up to the impressive steel gates of the International Fellowship of Lions. He'd arrived at his office by 8am but spent over two hours researching the resort and its ownership, mostly getting nowhere. They had no website, no Facebook page, and no press about them that he could find. It was Saturday, so no one was working in the Land and Surveys government office, but through their online portal he'd discovered the land was registered to a Brazilian holding company, Leoa Empresa, LTDA. He could find nothing on the Internet regarding that company beyond the translation of the name: Lioness Enterprises. He learnt Leoa without the squiggly accent over the 'a' was a lioness, rather than a male lion. This titbit doubled his prior knowledge of the Portuguese language, so he didn't consider the morning a complete loss. The only useful name he found anywhere was the representative of the company who'd signed the paperwork: Cristal Sombrio. Further searches gave him several 'World of Warcraft' hits in Portuguese, which seemed to be, not surprisingly, a crystal of some sort in the video game. He found one older article from a Brazil newspaper about a shooting outside a restaurant; from what Whittaker could gather from Google Translate's best attempt, the Sombrio family had been gunned down. The only family member to survive was the daughter, Cristal.

An imposingly tall wall met the gates from each side, and several surveillance cameras peered down at the driveway, tracking the movement of Whittaker's unmarked Ford Explorer. He opened his window and looked at the security entry box on a metal stand. It had a sensor pad to electronically detect a swipe card or a transmitter, but no visible keypad. There was one button to the right of the pad. Whittaker pressed the button and a speaker amplified a digitised ring tone.

After a long wait the ringing gave way to a click. "Hola?" came a female voice.

"Hello, this is Detective Roy Whittaker with the Royal Cayman Islands Police Service. I was wondering if I may have a word with Cristal Sombrio?" He figured he'd throw the name out there and see what he got. There was a prolonged silence; finally the Hispanic lady's voice returned.

"Un momento por favor," she said, sounding nervous.

After several minutes, Whittaker was about to press the button again when a new voice came over the speaker, in accented English. "Good morning, how may I help you?" The woman said sternly, sounding annoyed.

"Good morning, this is Detective Roy Whittaker, I'm with the Royal Cayman Islands Police Service. Is this Cristal Sombrio I'm speaking with?"

The woman avoided the question. "This is a private, members-only resort, Detective, how is it I can help you?"

Without probable cause she could turn him away, but she had to know that would raise his suspicions. Besides, most people are curious when a policeman knocks on their door. Except guilty people. They don't answer, and then they usually run.

"I haven't had the chance to come by your resort since you

opened. At the RCIPS we like to get to know everyone running prominent businesses on our little island. In case we can ever be of service, or what have you; it's nice to put a face to the name."

After a brief pause, her voice came back on, still sounding annoyed. "We're extremely busy this morning, I can only give you a few minutes. Please hold your badge up so we can verify your ID."

Whittaker held his wallet up out the car window in the direction of the camera over the gate, open to his badge.

"Please hold it in front of the scan pad, Detective," the woman's voice came back.

Surprised, he held the badge in front of the scanner and heard an electronic clicking sound. He then heard a louder noise and looked up to see the gates sliding open. It's easier to get through the airport than this place, he thought, as he drove forward and saw the large main building ahead and what appeared to be guest buildings on either side. He parked in front and got out. In the parking to either side, by the other buildings, he noticed matching Range Rover Evoques, six in total, and one large Chevy Suburban. Beyond the Suburban he could make out the sleek nose of some kind of dark green sports car. The door to the main building opened, and a woman stepped outside. She made a striking first impression. Expensive-looking jeans hugging her slender hips, a vibrant red top, hair slicked back, bold red lipstick and designer sunglasses, which did not hide her beautiful face. Whittaker guessed late thirties, maybe forty at the outside. He ran some math in his head based on the newspaper article.

"Miss Sombrio?" he asked, still trying to verify as he extended his hand.

She shook firmly. "Nice to meet you, Detective Whittaker," was what she said, but her tone didn't sound like she thought this was nice. "As I said we're busy here this morning, so I'm afraid I only have a minute or two."

Whittaker looked around at the tranquil setting tucked away in the mangroves and scrubland surrounding Salt Creek. A few birds chirped and air conditioners whirred, otherwise all was still. Maybe like a duck, he thought, all serenity on the surface and frantic paddling below.

"No problem, miss, I understand. Perhaps you could tell me a little about what you do here?" he said politely, still looking around.

The woman he now presumed to be Cristal Sombrio lit a cigarette and blew out a long plume of smoke. He noticed she had one digit missing from her left hand.

"As I said, we're a private resort," she started, her voice a touch more courteous. "We have a limited membership, and cater to a discerning, and affluent, client. We offer an opportunity for businessmen, executives, entrepreneurs, owners of large corporations and the like to gather and share ideas, strategies. Obviously, we provide them with an idyllic venue to relax and conduct their business."

"Do you mind if we go inside?" Whittaker asked, pointing to the front door. The door and the windows across the front were all heavily tinted and he couldn't make out what was beyond the glass. She took a final drag from her cigarette before throwing it to the ground where she ground it with the bottom of her red-soled sandals. She glanced at the Rolex on her wrist, an unsubtle reminder his time was limited, but opened the door to the building. Whittaker expected a reception area, but it was more like a lounge; there was no desk or obvious place to check in. Six fancy-looking chairs surrounded a glass-top coffee table and a cupboard supporting a coffee maker was the only other piece of furniture. There were two doors against the back wall, one mark 'WC', one marked 'Staff Only'.

"Thank you, it's heating up outside," he said with a smile. "So this is your restaurant and guest rooms in this building?"

She shook her head. "The villas are for the guests, each has its own kitchen and a cook provided for the duration of the stay. This building houses our offices and our students. We also run an elite hospitality school; our dormitories are on the second floor."

"Really? You're also an accredited university?" Whittaker carefully probed; none of his searching had revealed anything about an educational facility.

"We're not affiliated with any traditional facility, it's a private training program we offer," Sombrio answered carefully.

"Interesting. May I see through there?" Whittaker asked, pointing to the door marked 'Staff Only'.

The woman gave him the watch performance again, and looked most put out. "Quickly then, but I really must get back to work," she replied curtly, but led him through the doorway.

They passed a stairwell and a door to a gym on the right. To the left were restrooms and then the space opened up into a dining area leading to an open-plan lounge and huge windows with a view of the creek. As they walked through the dining area he noticed a large commercial kitchen to the right. A Hispanic lady was busy preparing food. She was the only person he could see on the whole floor, besides the two of them.

"What a delightful view," he said, walking across the lounge area and standing in front of the French doors leading to a patio, and a concrete dock running the width of the property. Moored to the right of the dock was an 80' Hatteras motor yacht. Farther to the left was a small centre console and beyond that a floating dock, with six jet-skis.

"My, that's a nice boat. Does it belong to the resort too?"

She joined him at the window. "It does. As I mentioned, our members expect a certain level of amenities and hospitality."

"Wow, that sure is nice. So, your members meet for their conferences or what not in here?" he asked, turning back to look around the lounge that had seating for about a dozen or more people.

"No, they meet in the villas, this is for the students," she answered quickly. "I really do have to get back to my desk, Detective."

"Where's the classrooms?" he asked, ignoring her invitation to leave.

"We use the dining area; as you can see there's plenty of seating and tables. Most of the studies are hands-on anyway – as you can see, we have a full kitchen," she answered as she walked back towards the door they'd entered through.

"How many Caymanians do you employ here, Miss Sombrio?" Whittaker asked, still standing in the dining area and looking at the lady in the kitchen.

Cristal stopped, turned back and put her hands on her hips. "None. But I assure you all of our workers and students have the appropriate paperwork. Now, if you don't mind." She held her four-fingered left hand towards the door.

"I'm sure they do," he replied, smiling politely, but not moving, "Any Caymanian students?"

"No. All our students are from overseas. Now please sir, I've given you all the time I can." She stared at him impatiently, still holding her hand towards the door.

"Of course, well it's been most educational for me, thank you for your time." He finally started towards her but stopped when he heard footsteps coming down the stairs. A slender teenage girl, with white blonde hair and bright blue eyes, descended the stairwell, half watching where she was going, and half looking at a tablet she carried. As she neared the bottom of the steps she looked up and saw Cristal, and then the detective. Her face looked mortified, and Cristal appeared to glare at her.

"Class isn't for another twenty minutes, back up," she assertively instructed the girl.

"Just a moment," Whittaker said firmly as the girl was turning abruptly to leave. "Are you a student here, young lady?"

The girl looked at Cristal and didn't reply. Cristal did instead. "Of course, and she's supposed to be studying in her dorm room currently." The girl took the chance to start back up the stairs until Whittaker spoke again.

"Excuse me, I'm Detective Whittaker with the Royal Cayman Islands Police Service. Miss Sombrio here was kindly showing me around. Where are you from, Miss...?" He tapered his question off, inferring he was also asking her name.

"I'm from Belize, sir," the girl answered in an accent he couldn't place, avoiding giving her name. She wore white shorts and a long-sleeved, pale blue blouse. As she stood with her leg bent, one foot on the next step, he thought he could see a dark bruise on her thigh, just below her shorts.

"How are your business studies going? I'm sorry, I missed your name, young lady?" he asked with a pleasant smile.

"Nora, my name's Nora. And I'm studying hospitality. It's going well, sir, I enjoy the classes." The girl's eyes danced between Cristal and the Detective.

"Thank you Nora, run along now, the Detective is just leaving," Cristal quickly interjected and Nora took off up the stairs. Whittaker walked towards the door but kept an eye on the girl. Taking two steps at a time, she extended her hand to grab the railing and her sleeve pulled back on her pale-skinned arm, revealing a large greenish-purple mark.

43

SATURDAY

Hallie wished she had a window. They called them portholes. She didn't much care what it was called, she'd just like one. Even her shack had windows. As wonderful as her stateroom was, she couldn't see outside, and that bothered her. Especially right now, because something was going on and she didn't know what it was. She'd spent most of the morning sitting in the enclosed fly-bridge with Van Heerden, and she didn't much care for Van Heerden either. He pretty much ignored her, which was fine, but when they did speak, he talked to her like she was a child. Marguerite didn't do that, neither did Raposa. If Raposa had she never would have gotten past lunch with him. Van Heerden seemed permanently grumpy. While she was with him he spent the whole time cleaning and fiddling with boat stuff. She'd offered to help but he'd told her no, in quite a condescending way. She had wondered if the clients at the resort were like Raposa, or like Van Heerden. More and more she'd been imagining herself in Raposa's strong arms, and each time she would get that tingly feeling again. That tingly feeling was something she was starting to enjoy. She'd looked at Van Heerden and instantly lost any tingles, at least the good ones. She couldn't imagine touching a grouchy old man like that. Finally, she had sat quietly, looked around outside, and eventually taken a nap to pass the time.

After what had felt like all day, Raposa called up on the intercom and said she could come down – the girl's review was complete. When she entered the salon, Raposa didn't look as perfectly put together as he usually did. Every time Hallie had been around the man, he'd been dressed perfectly, not a hair out of place. The review must have been stressful on him, she'd decided: he looked flushed. Marguerite and the girls were downstairs freshening up, Raposa had said, and Cristal sat on the couch, talking on her mobile phone. She spoke in what sounded like Spanish, but Hallie knew a little Spanish from school and she didn't recognise a word of it.

It was then that all hell broke loose. A middle-aged Hispanic lady had come running onto the boat, shouting in Spanish. Hallie recognised a few of the words this lady said, so she knew it was Spanish. Cristal abruptly finished her phone call and barked some instructions to Raposa in the language Hallie couldn't follow. Then she stomped off the boat with the lady, shouting at the poor woman. Raposa told Hallie to go to her stateroom and stay put until someone came and got her. And here she still sat, thirty minutes later.

She was hungry; all she'd had all morning was some cereal, and that seemed ages ago. Marguerite was too busy getting ready for the review and had shooed her away to sit upstairs. She'd gotten used to feeling hungry, and it didn't bother her like it used to when she was a little kid. Sometimes, especially when the weather was bad and the cruise ships couldn't come to the island, her money for food would evaporate like the crowds of visitors. After the first time it happened, she made a point to squirrel away a little money. Storing food in the shack wasn't an option unless it was canned. Hallie had been careful to only work when she needed to. Every time she lifted a wallet or a purse there was a serious risk involved. If she did it every day, the odds dictated she'd be caught. If there were other areas that were easy to get to, and busy like the harbour, then she would have rotated around and worked a different patch each day. But people didn't pack together in a concentrated area anywhere else, that she knew about anyway, so she just worked the harbour. Besides, those people left the island the same day, or the next morning, they didn't stick around like the hotel tourists. Less time for them to harp on to the police and keep them wound up. As long as each score was a decent haul, it would last her as long as a week. Sometimes the wallets had nothing, or she'd not manage to pull anything from a purse and had to let it go for the day; couldn't be seen hanging around too much.

Hallie lay on her bed and stared up at the ceiling. The bed felt so firm, yet soft and cosy, she smiled every time she touched it. Her room was an odd shape, because one side was rounded like a boat, the other like a normal room. She traced the curve of the hull with her eyes and imagined the water lapping against the outside, right where she lay. They hadn't given her a computer tablet yet, but when they did, maybe she'd start reading books; she needed something to occupy her busy mind. She was really going to miss reading the newspaper every day. She had never had a mobile phone, and only briefly in school did she have access to the Internet, so she didn't crave those luxuries. When life had been normal, and she was a kid, they had a TV, but she didn't watch much; Hallie preferred to be outside playing. But the newspaper was her entertainment, her education, her distraction from the life thrust upon her by an unforgiving world.

Her thoughts continued to bounce around, and eventually made their way back to her family. She wondered if any of them ever thought about, or even remembered her. Her mother had cut all family ties and insisted that they couldn't help the pair of them anymore. Several times relatives would try to talk her mother, when they ran into them around town, but her mother wouldn't have it. Once her mother was gone, it seemed natural for Hallie to keep away from those people and fend for herself. That's what she'd been doing for ages anyway, fending for herself and looking after her mother. In a way, life got easier when her mother was gone. She felt guilty whenever she had those thoughts, but it was true. Her mother was better off dead than living the life she'd succumbed to. That's how Hallie felt about it, but the guilt was still there. As she lay, alone, in her new world, she began to wonder what it would be like to see her family again.

Raised voices upstairs snapped her out of her daydreaming, and she quickly sat up.

44

———————

SATURDAY

Nora sat nervously on the edge of her single bed in the dorm room. Her roommate was still buried in the covers, asleep. She wasn't sure what had just taken place downstairs, but she knew from Cristal's expression that she was mad. Nora had answered how they'd been taught, but the man, who'd called himself Detective something or other, kept looking at her oddly. Not menacingly, Cristal had that covered, but as though he recognised her somehow. She wondered if her past had finally caught up with her. She used to check the Norwegian papers online whenever she could, but she hadn't been able to do that for the past eleven months. The authorities had found pieces of the Hobie Cat on the coastline, but the body of Jørgen Paulsrud had never surfaced. Maybe it had now. Not even Raposa or Cristal knew the real reason why she'd left Norway; she'd made up a story close to the truth about having an affair with a family friend, and her parents throwing her out. She'd invented a last name to give them as she had no papers anyway, and hoped they wouldn't trace the story and see a picture. Even then, it was an older picture of her in school uniform with her hair shorter, they might not recognise it was her. Apparently, it had worked. Perhaps until now. She swung her feet, which didn't quite touch the ground from the bed, and started thinking about how she might escape a small Caribbean island, two hundred miles from the next land mass, with no money and no means of transport.

Cristal's voice echoed loudly up the stairwell and made Nora jump. "Nora! Get down here." *Appears her mood hasn't improved,* she thought, as she slipped her sandals back on and walked towards the door. Her roommate stirred under the covers and Nora wondered if this maybe the last time she would see her. They weren't close, but they'd shared the dorm room for several months since the Puerto Rican girl joined the resort, and she realised she'd miss her company. She trudged to the top of the stairs, on her march to meet what she'd now convinced herself was a deportation back to Norway, then halted when she saw Cristal looking up at her.

"Bring all your stuff, you're moving to the boat for a week or two," she said sternly.

It seemed like Cristal was still aggravated but Nora was surprised and relieved there wasn't a swarm of police waiting for her downstairs. Two weeks on the boat sounded like a break from the resort, a break from clients, and two weeks closer to being out of here. With a new spring in her step, Nora gathered up her things, which meant clothes, make-up, toiletries and her computer tablet, and rushed down the stairs.

"Did no one tell you to stay in your damn room this morning?" Cristal snapped at her.

"No miss, I've been asleep. I came down when I woke up," Nora replied, unsure what she'd done wrong.

Without another word, Cristal walked her through the dorm lounge and out the French doors to the deck. The Cova do Leão was docked snugly against the sea wall and Cristal strode aboard without helping Nora, who was struggling to carry the mound of clothes and hang on to the other items in her hands. By the time Nora made it through the open door into the salon, Cristal was standing in the middle of the room with her hands on her hips, and a finger poking in Raposa's chest.

"When I told you to keep all the girls upstairs, I meant all the girls!" she yelled, loudly. "Not everyone except Nora!"

Nora froze, unsure what to do while Cristal continued her tirade, so she stood there, balancing her bundle and trying to be invisible.

"I told her roommate, Nora was asleep," Raposa defended himself somewhat meekly.

"I knew I had a bad feeling today," Cristal blasted at no one in particular, before turning her wrath back on the Brazilian man. "That damn detective was asking all kinds of questions, then Miss 'Screw My Teacher' comes skipping down the stairs and the guy starts grilling her."

Nora was mortified. So much for them not knowing. Her heart was in her mouth and her mind raced. She felt nauseous. Did they always know, or did they just find out? Was it the copper who had tipped them off? That couldn't be or she'd be in handcuffs right now.

"He kept asking about Caymanian employees and students," Cristal continued. "Whether we had any here. I don't know if he was bothered because we weren't employing locals, or if he was looking for someone in particular." She put the emphasis on the last two words, which Nora noticed, but didn't think much about; she was frantically deciding where her own fate might lie. Part of her wanted to drop her things and run, but her fight-or-flight instincts were giving her few options either way. There was no clear path of escape from where she stood, and she was no match for Raposa in a fight. No match for Cristal either, she now realised. The woman had been kind to her, almost motherly and she'd looked up to her. She'd heard Cristal raise her voice before, but it was nothing like this; she was terrifying.

"So, what do you want to do?" Raposa asked, surprisingly calmly, clearly trying to settle the enraged woman.

Cristal paced around the salon, appearing deep in thought. Nora liked it better when she was confronting Raposa, and not looking her way; she was waiting for the wrath to fall her direction.

After all, she'd lied to them and they obviously knew about her fabrication. The armful of clothes began to feel like an anvil in her hands, but she dared not move. She felt like a rabbit hiding in plain sight; if she moved the hunter would see her. Stay perfectly still and maybe she could blend in enough to be overlooked.

Cristal stopped pacing and looked directly at Nora. Boom! She thought, rabbit for dinner.

"Keep them both here on the boat," she said. "This one can help train Hallie for a while. Keep them both out of sight."

Nora was relieved to hear this little bunny was to live another day, and wondered who Hallie was. Cristal still looked at her and she nervously fidgeted, trying to keep clothes from dropping to the floor. Cristal finally addressed her rather than Raposa.

"You only have about six weeks, and you'll be leaving us," Cristal said, her voice softer and back to normal. "I need you to be a good girl and help with the new trainee we have aboard. Can you do that for me?"

"Of course," Nora said, her voice still a little shaky from the turmoil. "And I'm sorry about... you know, my stuff back at home."

Cristal scoffed, "You think the girls here come from rose gardens and perfect homes, perfect lives?" She waved a hand in the air. "Everyone has a story, and everyone is running from something."

Nora didn't know what to say. She was relieved, but the idea her deception, or more accurately the knowledge of her deception, had in turn been kept hidden felt more deceitful somehow. She was glad Cristal carried on.

"You'll be a wealthy young lady in a few weeks, you'll be able to go wherever you want." Cristal smiled and took a step towards Nora. "I hope you're seeing the bigger picture here? We'll give you some time to feel better, and then keep you on light duty. It's only a few weeks and you'll be on your way, with a passport in your new name, and plenty of money."

Cristal took the bundle of clothes from her arms and dropped them on the couch. "But I need you to play along, understand?"

Nora wasn't certain she completely understood what Cristal was suggesting, but she sure as hell wasn't about to prolong this little chat.

"Of course, Miss Cristal, whatever you need me to do," she responded dutifully.

"Good girl." Cristal smiled at her again. "Now, we need a sensible reason for these marks on you, don't we? No point making the new girl nervous."

"I was thinking we could say I was mugged in town? A robber stole my bag and I wouldn't give it up so easily?" she offered.

Cristal looked at Raposa then back at Nora. "That's my girl, perfect, that's what we'll say to anyone who asks from here on, okay?"

Nora nodded, glad she thought of it on the spot. She'd hoped the 'I was thinking' part would ease their minds and take some heat off. It appeared her prior lies were done being discussed and she preferred to keep it that way. Cristal seemed to be her normal self again and even helped Nora gather her clothes from the couch. Nora had a burning question she'd been dying to ask for days, but had been hesitant to; maybe now they'd cleared the air and had a plan, together, she could ask. She took a deep breath.

"How is Carlina doing? Have you heard from her?"

Cristal was walking in front of Nora, carrying half her things towards the stairs. Her pace slowed and she took a moment to answer.

"She's good. As promised, once your contract is up and you leave, you're free to contact Carlina. I'll give you her email. We set up emails for all our hosts when they leave. It's part of the departure package to help you get started in your new life."

"Thank you," Nora replied eagerly. "That sounds great, we were close as we both started about the same time."

Cristal turned and smiled before starting down the stairs.

"Two of our original hosts, you both mean a lot to me and what we've built here." Marguerite met them at the bottom of the stairs in the narrow hallway. "Ah, Marguerite, good. Please move Zoe and Abigay into the resort. Let's put Nora here in the bow stateroom, it's a little nicer, and it has its own bathroom."

Nora smiled appreciatively. This all sounded lovely; she must be a lucky rabbit. But she knew too well, rabbits are prey animals; their life is spent finding food, and avoiding being eaten. Rabbits rarely died of old age.

45

SATURDAY

Hazel's Odyssey swayed gently on the mild swells rolling in from the north. The sun was nearing its zenith and the heat was only slightly dampened by the breeze that wafted over the boat. They were moored to a shallow site, taking a prolonged surface interval after making three dives on the wall. Sully had chartered the boat to have the flexibility of making more dives in the day, spending less time at each site to capture the biggest variety of scenery and lighting. Their first dive had been the longest, the next two they'd kept to twenty minutes each. After their break, the plan was to make four or five thirty-minute dives, no deeper than fifty feet on each one. The three of them sat in the shade of the fly-bridge, and Sully scrolled through his pictures on the LCD screen of his camera, alternating between cussing himself for missing a shot, and oohing over the good ones. Every once in a while, he'd hop up excitedly and show Thomas and AJ a shot he particularly liked.

AJ lay on one of the benches, with her sweatshirt balled up under her head, and she drifted in and out of a nap. The lapping of the water against the hull, and the soft wind over her face, put her to sleep like nothing else. Thomas needed no help sleeping. He sat in the corner with his head flopped at a weird angle and slept like a baby until Sully woke him every few minutes to show him another manta ray picture, and rub it in a little more.

All three jumped when AJ's mobile sprang to life, playing the theme to the 70s British TV show *The Sweeney*.

AJ sat up and answered the call.

"Hello Roy."

"Hey there AJ, my apologies for bothering you."

"No bother at all, how can I help you?" she replied. Thomas sat up with the mention of the detective's name.

"Are you anywhere near town? I was hoping you might be able to come by the station for a few minutes, there's someone I'd like you to meet, and share your statement from yesterday with."

AJ looked around at the vast open water surrounding her boat. "I'm afraid we're outside the North Sound right now, we won't be back in until late this afternoon. What's going on exactly?"

"Of course you are, silly of me, I should have realised you'd be working." He paused. "Let me think how we might be able to do this."

AJ gave him a moment to think, wondering what could possibly be happening.

"Could you take another call in a few minutes? If I phone back with someone else on a conference call, would that be okay?"

"Err, sure, of course. Whatever you need me to do," she stammered, figuring it had to have something to do with the boat and possibly the girl, but he wasn't giving anything away.

"Great, thank you, sorry for the trouble," he said politely, "Oh, and please be out of earshot of anyone else when we speak again, best keep things quiet for now please."

"Okay. It's just Thomas and me on the boat, and our customer – we just have one diver with us today."

"Right, okay, well, if it's possible to keep this all between just you and me for now, I'd appreciate it. I'll call back in a few."

Whittaker hung up and AJ looked at her mobile for a moment, unsure what she could tell Thomas, whose curious eyes she sensed staring expectantly at her. She met his gaze.

"That was Whittaker," she started with the obvious. "He's calling me back in a bit, he didn't tell me anything yet."

"Did he go by the resort place?" Thomas asked keenly.

"I don't know, Thomas, he literally didn't tell me anything. He asked if I could go by the station, but I told him we're out here. He just said he'd call back in a few."

"Oh my," Sully said. AJ had forgotten for a second he was sitting with them. After the manta ray dive, and the reaction Thomas and she had both had, they'd felt obliged to explain the story of the girl in the water.

"You're needed at the police station? We can take the boat in if you need to, we're just scuba diving out here, a police murder inquiry takes precedence over my pictures," Sully kindly offered.

"Thanks Sully, let's see, he's supposed to call back and we'll see what they need," AJ replied, and right after she'd finished the sentence, *The Sweeney* returned.

AJ hurried up the ladder to the fly-bridge and answered her mobile.

"Hello, Detective." She decided she should use his official title if someone else from his side was joining them on the call.

"Hello Miss Bailey, thank you for taking the call, I'm sorry once again for disrupting your work day. With me on the line is Judge Elmslie."

A lady's voice came on the line with a rich Caymanian accent. "Good day, Miss Bailey, thank you for agreeing to speak with us."

"Of course," AJ managed. She'd expected another policeman, someone else looking into the case perhaps, not a judge.

"Miss Bailey," Whittaker continued. "Would you mind recalling the conversation you overheard on your boat yesterday, for the judge to hear."

AJ took a deep breath, and ran through what she remembered hearing them say. She tried hard to repeat their words exactly, but it struck her how hard it was recalling a conversation from just the day before. The mind and memory had already twisted her recollections based on her own interpretation and bias, but she felt sure she'd conveyed the essence of the men's banter.

"Thank you, Miss Bailey," the judge said sternly once she'd finished. "And it is your impression that a woman, or girl, may well have been harmed in some way by these gentlemen?"

AJ thought it over for a second. "I'm confident that if what they were saying was true, then a girl had been engaged in sexual relations with Joe Symanski, money was exchanged in some part of the process, and she came away with bruises."

"And this girl they spoke of was described as Scandinavian?" The judge asked.

"I remember those words precisely as it was the first thing I overheard, and it pissed me off. He said, 'little Scandinavian broad'," AJ replied assertively. If any other recollections were shaky, that one wasn't, she had stored that in her memory banks. It was more the part about 'nailing' the girl that aggravated her, but still, she remembered it clearly.

There was a pause on the line and AJ waited, not sure if they were done with her or not. After a moment Whittaker spoke again.

"Judge, the girl I saw said she was from Belize, but she looked as Scandinavian as you can get, blonde, blue-eyed, fair skin, and as I said, I'm confident I saw bruising on her forearm and her thigh. The kid barely looked sixteen."

AJ stayed silent; she couldn't believe what she was hearing. She assumed the detective must have gone to the resort and seen this girl there. She wondered if he'd seen Thomas's cousin, but was afraid to ask anything.

"Yes, well, we should say goodbye to Miss Bailey," the judge said firmly, "and continue our conversation privately, Roy. I hear what you're saying, but you're not giving me much here."

"Of course. Thank you, AJ, we appreciate your time," Whittaker said, sounding a touch flustered. "Again, please keep all this to yourself."

"Sure, no problem," AJ responded, hesitating. "What about the Bodden girl? Any word on her?"

"No, nothing on her as yet I'm afraid, but let me speak some more with the judge here. I'm hoping I can persuade her to let me keep pursuing this."

The line went dead. AJ slowly made her way back down the ladder to a pair of inquisitive faces.

"Well?" Thomas asked first.

"Nothing on your cousin as of yet. Sorry Thomas," AJ said gently. "But we should put the VHF on the police channel. There's a chance things may liven up this afternoon."

"Oh my," Sully said, raising his eyebrows. "Sounds intriguing."

"You may have a story for one of your books out of this trip, Sully," AJ said, with more concern than enthusiasm.

46

SATURDAY

Hallie hadn't been able to hear what the ruckus was about until they'd come downstairs. By then everyone sounded calm and she figured out a new girl was moving in, and Zoe and Abigay were going to the resort. She wanted to look around the resort herself, and see what the place was like, but for now she was keen to see who the new girl was. Curiosity was about to get the better of her when a knock came on her door, and Abigay poked her head in to say goodbye. They'd hugged and said they would see each other once Hallie finished her training and moved to the resort as well. Abigay was excited, so Hallie was excited for her. Marguerite was in the hallway and told Hallie she could go upstairs; she was taking Zoe and Abigay ashore, but would be back later.

Hallie now wandered around the salon and the galley, opening and closing every cabinet and drawer. Since she'd arrived, she was constantly amazed by the amount of stuff these people apparently needed. She couldn't fathom what half of it was for. The cheese didn't know whether it was being cut with the knife you ate your dinner with, or the fancy one with the curved end designated 'a cheese knife'. It all seemed a waste to her, but what did she know, she was a kid who lived in a dirt-floored shack. She heard footsteps coming up the stairway and quickly put the corkscrews and wine stoppers she'd been playing with back in their drawer. When she looked up, she saw the coolest-looking girl she'd ever set eyes on. She had the blondest hair and piercing blue eyes; Hallie thought she must be the human version of a husky. She loved huskies; she'd seen them in magazines. The girl was slender and beautiful, but with almost child-like features. She had no idea how old she was, she could be anywhere in her teens. The girl looked lost in thought until she saw Hallie, and then her face lit up with a pretty smile.

"Hi, I'm Nora," she said with an accent Hallie didn't recognise.

"Hello," Hallie replied, still mesmerised, "I'm Hallie."

"I think I'm supposed to help you with your training," the husky said, going to the galley and finding a glass.

"You are? You're not new here?" Hallie asked, following her.

Nora laughed. "No, I've been here almost a year."

Hallie realised the girl was going straight to where everything was kept in the galley, clearly she knew her way around the boat. As Nora reached for orange juice on the top shelf of the refrigerator, Hallie noticed the bruises on her arm. Nora must have seen her reaction. She put the juice carton down and slid her shorts up a little to reveal a nasty-looking green and purple bruise. She then pulled both her sleeves back to show the same on her arms.

"I was mugged, here in town," she said as though it was no big deal.

"Really?" Hallie said, surprised.

Nora shrugged. "I should have just let the guy have my handbag, but I struggled so he knocked me around."

Hallie frowned. "What did he look like?"

"I'm sorry?" Nora asked, looking equally surprised.

"What did he look like?" Hallie repeated, "I know all the players downtown, I can tell you who it was if you describe him. But honestly, I'm surprised, you're not their mark. You have to be careful going after tourists, the government gets really mad when the island appears 'unsafe', and the police come after you. They'd lift something from your handbag, but it's odd they'd mug you."

Nora looked at her but didn't say anything. The sound of high-pitched engines came from outside, and echoed around the small bay. Nora moved to the salon to look out the windows. Hallie followed her and saw two jet-skis from the resort's floating dock doing circles in Salt Creek. One was ridden by a chubby man and the other by a skinny one. Nora noticeably tensed up.

"Who are they?" Hallie asked.

"Guests," Nora replied venomously.

"You know them?" Hallie asked quietly, sensing Nora's anxiety.

Nora turned from the window as the two jet-skis blasted down the channel towards the North Sound. "Unfortunately." She walked to the couch and sat down with a big sigh.

She patted the seat next to her. "Come, sit down, don't worry about them, and don't worry about my bruises."

Hallie sat next to the girl. "I want to know about you. You're from here, on Cayman?" she asked with a smile.

"I am, been here my whole life. I've never actually been off the island," Hallie said matter-of-factly. "They had a trip once, my school did. It was to Florida, but I couldn't go, we couldn't afford it. Where are you from?"

"I'm from Belize," Nora said with a grin.

Hallie looked at her. "We had a boy in my school for a year, he was from Belize, he didn't look a bit like you," she said quizzically.

Nora laughed. "Belize is what my papers say. I'm from Norway, but I was in the Caribbean already when I was recruited for the resort. Where did you live on the island? I thought they had a rule about no local girls, there hasn't been anyone from Cayman at the resort yet."

Hallie wondered if everyone from Norway looked like a husky. "Raposa kinda talked Miss Cristal into taking me, I guess. I lived in George Town, well, I grew up in West Bay, but then I was living in George Town when he found me."

Nora looked off into the distance thoughtfully. "I've been here almost a year, and I've never actually set foot in George Town, or been to West Bay," she said quietly, almost to herself. "Airport and back, that's it."

"But you said you were mugged in town," Hallie asked, confused.

Nora's shoulders sagged and she looked at Hallie; her beautiful bright blue eyes appeared sad. "That's the story they want me to tell, how I got my bruises, and it's the story you need to remember, that's all that matters. I've got another six weeks to get through, and then I'm out of here. I'm gonna take my money and find an island just like this one, but not this one."

Hallie couldn't really keep up with what it all meant, and she had a million questions she wanted to ask. She liked Nora, she sensed she was really nice, like Abigay, but she wasn't full of hope and joy like Abigay. Nora seemed tired and sad.

"Why not this island?"

"They didn't tell you that?" Nora asked, sounding surprised, but continued without an answer, "You can't stay here, it's part of the deal. You can go anywhere else, but you can't stay on Cayman. Carlina, she's the first graduate to leave, she was planning on going back to the Dominican, said it was the only place she knew. Maybe I'll go there."

"But I don't even have a passport," Hallie replied. "I can't leave the island." The idea hadn't crossed her mind she'd have to leave. When Raposa told her she could go anywhere she wanted, she thought of West Bay and finding a small apartment. One with a tile floor, and electricity.

"They provide all your paperwork and set up your bank account for the money, emails, stuff like that. That's what they say, anyway. I guess I'll find out in a few weeks," Nora said, less assuredly. "I'll contact Carlina then, we talked about starting some kind of business together."

Hallie was still trying to process the idea she wouldn't be able to stay on Cayman. She knew the world by the maps and globes she enjoyed studying in school. When she wasn't going to school any longer and she'd read a newspaper article talking about a place she wasn't sure about, she'd go into the library downtown. They had big atlases and she'd search the pages until she found the place. She knew just where Norway was, and she knew where the Dominican Republic was, but she had no clue where she could go if it wasn't on Cayman.

"When did Carlina leave?" she asked absentmindedly, as she tried to picture herself somewhere completely different.

"Sunday. They took her to the airport Sunday," Nora replied.

Hallie frowned, and stopped picturing herself bundled up in a sweater and raincoat, looking at Buckingham Palace. "Sunday?"

Nora looked at her. "Yeah, Sunday. Why?"

"I had the newspaper, but they took it from my bag. It was Wednesday's paper," Hallie said. "The front-page story was about a girl they found."

Nora shrugged her shoulders. "So?"

"The article said the body was recovered Monday morning; she was unidentified," Hallie said carefully, recalling the words. "All they knew was she'd likely gone in the water Sunday night, and she was a dark-skinned young girl of Hispanic descent."

They both looked at each other, and Hallie could see the same look of fear she felt, reflected in those bright blue Scandinavian eyes.

47

SATURDAY

Cristal sat at her desk and drummed four digits on the glass top as she exhaled a long plume of cigarette smoke. Her uneasy feeling this morning had been right, as usual, but what bothered her now was that it hadn't gone away. That damn detective; she kept coming back to him. His questions came across like idle interest, but she knew they were pinpoint targeted like a sniper's bullet. He didn't ask anything without a reason. And then there was the issue of the Caymanian girl. She'd let Raposa talk her into it because the kid had the perfect look. Young, ability to look even younger, stunningly pretty in an innocent way, petite, and of course she had those ridiculous eyes. The members would fall all over themselves for her. But she failed on one of the unbreakable rules, and Cristal herself had allowed that rule to be broken. Well, she decided, short of girls or not, that kid's gotta go. She stubbed her cigarette out and was about to pick up her mobile, when her desk phone rang. The phones in the resort were only connected internally; there were no external lines. She used her mobile for outside calls, so the staff and girls had no access to an outside connection. She could tell by the light flashing on the phone that the call was coming from the front gate. If she didn't answer it, one of the seven women she had working as cleaners and chefs would get it. She'd never hired a receptionist. Every extra person was a salary, and a further security risk. With a sinking feeling in her stomach, she picked up the receiver.

"International Fellowship of Lions, how may I help you?"

As she spoke, she clicked her laptop to the security feed, and sat bolt upright in her chair. From the camera at the gate she could see the detective standing by the entry pad. Next to him was a tow truck sporting an industrial-looking front bumper. Behind that was the detective's Ford Explorer, followed down the driveway by a series of police cars.

"Miss Sombrio, we have a warrant to search the premises, including both boats. Please open the gate immediately, and have your staff and students assemble out front." The detective was holding a piece of paper in his hand, showing it to the gate camera. Cristal had no doubt it was a legal warrant. She grabbed her mobile.

"Miss Sombrio, I strongly urge you to open the gate immediately, or I will have this truck knock your lovely entrance way open."

Cristal hit her speed-dial for Raposa on her mobile phone keypad, and punched the mute button on the desk phone. It rang for what felt like an agonisingly long time, as she watched the tow truck ease up to the front gate, lining up to break it open. She was wondering how well those incredibly expensive steel gates would hold up, when Raposa finally answered.

"Hey, what's up," he said, chuckling, obviously in the middle of sharing something humorous on his end.

"They're here!" she bellowed into the mobile.

"Who's here?" he replied, oblivious.

"Damn it Raposa, the detective! He's out front!" Cristal yelled, exasperated as she watched her curiosity being resolved: the tow truck easily pushed the gate open in a shower of broken masonry and dust.

"Maybe he just wants to ask some more questions, no reason to panic," Raposa replied calmly.

"He has a warrant, you idiot! And the whole damn Cayman police force is with him! You have to leave, now, right now! Take the Hatteras to international waters, and Raposa?"

"Yes?" he responded with appropriate urgency now in his voice.

"Get rid of that bloody girl!"

"Okay, shit," she heard him say as he hung up.

48

SATURDAY

Hallie and Nora had moved downstairs to Nora's new stateroom at the bow. They figured they couldn't be heard tucked away in there, but they still spoke in hushed tones. Nora had opened up about the real reason she was bruised, and they'd compared notes on what they'd been told when they were recruited. Hallie was getting more paranoid and scared as they talked. Then the boat moved. They looked at each other, scrambled out of the berth and ran down the hallway. Bursting into the master stateroom they peered out the only portholes on the lower deck. They were pulling away from the sea wall.

"Where the hell are we going?" Nora asked. "I haven't heard Marguerite come back aboard, have you?"

Hallie shook her head. They ran out of the stateroom and up the curved stairwell to the salon. They could now hear a raised voice coming from outside, and saw Raposa on the aft deck, throwing the mooring line away behind the boat, as the big diesel motors roared from below. He was shouting up top, presumably to Van Heerden, and they watched him run up the outside stairs to the enclosed fly-bridge above them.

"Oh shit," Nora exclaimed, looking out the port side windows, "that looks like the marine police."

Hallie joined her and, sure enough, sitting at the exit of Salt Creek, where the narrow channel led away past a series of homes on the water, sat a Joint Marine Police boat. On deck, in full tactical gear, with semi-automatics strung across their shoulders, were two officers, looking right at the Cova do Leão. The big boat turned towards the police with the props thrashing, then throttled back to idle, but kept moving towards the channel. The girls ran out the salon door to the aft deck and looked up at the fly-bridge.

"We shouldn't go up there," Nora said and ran back into the salon. Hallie looked behind at the resort and saw several policemen and women swarm onto the dock. She quickly figured out where Nora was heading and followed her back through the salon. Beyond the galley was a breakfast room that stretched full beam, with a sloped window facing the bow. A large, curved cushioned couch resided under the windows, and the girls knelt on the couch and stared at the drama unfolding in the bay. The Hatteras was a hundred yards from the police boat, and the officers now had their guns raised and pointed, at what felt to Hallie like her forehead. She ducked down a little and couldn't believe they were still motoring towards the police.

In a whirl of motion, the police boat started to rock, and the two jet-skis they'd seen earlier raced by the outside of the vessel and into the creek, throwing up huge rooster tails of water. The two armed officers spun around and aimed at the jet-skis, then back at the Hatteras, clearly taken by surprise and trying to stay balanced as the wake rolled them around.

"Is that the man? The scrawny looking one?" Hallie shouted and pointed at the skinny guy on the second jet-ski as he slowed to an idle off their starboard bow and floated by on their right.

"That's the bastard," Nora growled, and leapt off the couch, sprinting out the starboard doorway, and onto the narrow walkway outside. When Hallie caught up to her, Nora was glaring at the man as the Hatteras kept moving past him. But the man didn't notice her. He was staring at the police standing on the resort's dock, as they waved for him to come over. A high-pitched scream could be heard from the other side of Salt Creek, where the second jet-ski pilot was seemingly unaware, or uncaring, of the police presence. The shrill of the motor rose as the craft's engine was pegged to its max, before the note changed again when the jet-ski left the water, launching off the wake of the Hatteras and flying through the air behind the big yacht's stern. The girls were still staring at Symanski when Al Jacobs landed his jet-ski across the seat of his unsuspecting friend. Hallie couldn't process what happened exactly as it was over so quickly. One second, the arsehole that had hurt her new friend was sitting on a fancy jet-ski in front of them, and the next, there was a deafening collision with an eruption of parts and a shower of water. Now there was silence, beyond the idling diesels, and nothing but broken parts floating on the surface.

"What happened?" Hallie managed to say, turning to Nora.

"Screw you, shithead," Nora said quietly, and held up two middle fingers at the debris field.

A clunk came from below decks as the props were taken out of drive and the Hatteras slowed. A man's voice resonated from a crackly speaker on the police boat.

"Stop where you are. This is the Royal Cayman Islands Police Service, Joint Marine Unit. We have a warrant to search the vessel. We will be boarding your boat shortly. Stay where you are, while we attend to the jet-ski incident."

Van Heerden and Raposa appeared to be complying. Hallie heard another clunk with the props going into reverse, dragging the boat to a complete stop, and then one more as they selected neutral. The police boat pulled alongside, and to Hallie the guns in the officers' hands looked even scarier close up. Several other officers came to the bow and helped scour amongst the carnage in the water, searching for signs of life. The police boat had four outboard engines hung off the back and looked capable of ridiculous speed. Hallie could see one body floating, face down, fifty feet from where they'd collided, but couldn't make out the other man.

Hallie and Nora almost fell backwards down the walkway, barely hanging on to the railing, as the Hatteras lurched back to life, accelerating for the channel. Hallie thought about jumping over and taking her chances, swimming for the mangroves, but her instincts took over and wouldn't let her run to the police. She'd spent too much time doing the opposite. Nora must have had the same thought because she went to duck under the railing. The Hatteras started a hard turn to starboard at the channel entry, dipping the walkway down towards the water. If they jumped now, they'd be dragged down the side of the hull and possibly into the props. Nora stood back up.

"Shit, we should have bailed out before it took off," she said, frustrated. "I think I'd rather deal with the police than these two." She nodded up towards the bridge.

"What can we do?" Hallie asked, looking at the wake from the big boat throwing a powerful wave against the mangroves on one side, and the sea walls of the large, waterfront homes on the other.

"Ride it out I guess, Nora replied. "They'll either escape to open water, or the police will catch them before they get there. They have to make it twelve nautical miles offshore to be in international waters. Puts them out of Cayman police jurisdiction."

Hallie looked at her. "Where did you learn all that?"

"I've sailed a bit," Nora replied with a shrug.

The Hatteras cleared the channel into the North Sound, and from the tone of the engines was running as hard as she could. The girls made their way down the walkway to the stern, and looked at the roiling waters behind the boat. The motor yacht had a maximum speed of 24 knots, or almost 28 mph, but speed across turbulent water always appears a lot faster than on land. Hallie didn't know any of that, she just looked at the sea being torn up behind the boat and instantly decided she wasn't jumping. They went back through the door to the salon and sat down on the couch. Neither had any great ideas that immediately sprang to mind.

49

____

SATURDAY

Detective Whittaker stood on the dock of what had been the resort known as the International Fellowship of Lions. He was pretty sure after today it would be seized by the Cayman authorities, and no longer be in business. But right now he had his hands full, as complete carnage had broken out when he'd tried to serve the warrant. It had taken him hours of persuading and personal guarantees to get the judge to issue it, and now he'd be explaining this mess for weeks. He watched the one marine unit he'd brought along haul one of the bodies from the creek. The officer at the helm had made the right call and prioritised the jet-ski incident over holding the boat. But now he wished they'd hurry up so they could take chase, before the Hatteras made the twelve-mile mark. All the other marine units were on the west or south coasts. They put the police helicopter in the air but what they could do to stop a boat, he had no idea. On streets you could put up roadblocks, use spikes in the road, there were options, but boats were a different story. Only way to stop a boat is outgun them. Right now, his big gun, and very fast boat, sat stationary in Salt Creek, searching for the body of the second idiot from New York. As Whittaker watched one of the officers starting to don scuba gear, he heard a yell from the boat as they spotted the second body bob to the surface.

Whittaker walked back inside the building to a throng of people. His officers had separated the so-called students on one side, the resort staff, who all appeared to be Hispanic women, on another, and guests took up only two seats. According to Cristal, there were currently four guests staying; two were being retrieved from the creek and put in body bags, and two sat on the couch. One was the New York friend of the jet-ski stunt riders. The other guy apparently had the misfortune to arrive earlier that morning. The detective had asked to see everybody's passports and work papers. So far, the only identification he could confirm were the two guests, who both held US passports with legitimate visitor stamps from immigration, and Cristal Sombrio's Brazilian passport. She handed him a stack of business paperwork, claiming it all to be legit of course, and he'd given it to an officer to bag and label for later examination, by someone other than him.

Officers were searching the villas and he had Rasha start her inspection with the centre console, still moored to the sea wall. He walked over to the area where they'd corralled the young girls. Not one of them claimed to be Caymanian, which worried Whittaker further. Maybe young Thomas Bodden was mistaken, and one of these girls before him was aboard the Hatteras. It's possible he'd mistakenly confused one of them for his cousin. He didn't see the blonde girl with the bruises either.

"Were any of you aboard the motor yacht in the last few days?" he asked the group. They all looked so young and terrified, he felt bad for them. Two girls looked at each other, then down at the dining tables they were seated around. Whittaker walked away and spoke briefly to a female officer, before departing the main room and walking into the front reception lounge. He took a seat and waited. After a few minutes the female officer led the two girls who had caught his eye into the room, and Whittaker stood while he offered them a seat. The curvy-figured, darker-skinned girl was clearly scared to death. The other girl, he guessed of mixed race by her features and skin tone, seemed more confident, and somewhat defiant.

"I need you two to help me with something," he started, his voice pleasant and, he hoped, encouraging. "I believe a Caymanian girl may have been on the motor yacht in the last few days. You've both been on the boat, did you happen to see her?" He figured asking them again would get him a denial, even separated from the others, so he let them think he knew more than he did. Neither girl responded. One looked off out the window, feigning disinterest, the other looked at the coffee table and fidgeted.

"What's your name?" he asked the one looking down. She peeked up to see if it was her being addressed, and her shoulders tightened when she realised it was.

"Abigay," she said quietly and looked back down.

"Well, Abigay, did the Caymanian girl tell you her name?"

The girl fidgeted some more and breathed in deeply.

"Hallie. Her name's Hallie," the second girl said abruptly. "Leave Abigay alone, can't you see she's terrified, she's been through enough."

"Okay, thank you...?" Whittaker asked.

"Zoe," the second girl said and returned her gaze out the window.

"Where is Hallie now?" Whittaker asked, more urgently.

"She's still on the boat." Abigay said, apparently finding courage from her friend. "Her and Nora are still on there."

"Is Nora the blonde girl, blue eyes?"

They both nodded. Whittaker stood up and pulled the VHF radio from his hip.

"All units, all units, this is Whittaker. Be aware, two potential hostages on the craft under pursuit, two potential innocents on board."

50

SATURDAY

AJ watched Sully line up his one millionth shot of a sea fan waving in the gentle surge over the reef. They were on their third shallow dive of the afternoon, and even though Thomas and AJ had been alternating dives all day, she still felt like she'd spent the day underwater. Usually, she didn't mind that, but hanging in one spot for thirty minutes at a time got old after a while. A ringing metallic sound resounded through the water, and they both stopped and instinctively looked around. AJ quickly realised what it was, and signalled for Sully to head to the boat. They were only in twenty feet of water and with the gin-clear visibility they could see the hull of the Newton, less than fifty yards away. AJ finned hard and, as she got closer, she could see Thomas's hand reaching underwater and bashing the side of the aluminium ladder with a dive weight. He was rapping it three times, then pausing for fifteen seconds before making three more strikes. She had no clue what the emergency could be, but both divers knew the recall signal when they heard it.

AJ climbed the ladder behind Sully, who was struggling to board the boat carrying his camera rig in one hand and his fins in the other. Thomas would normally take them from him, to help him aboard, but she couldn't see him. Once on deck they both dropped onto the benches lining the gunwales and aligned their tanks with the holder to drop them in place. AJ then caught a glimpse of Thomas at the bow, releasing the mooring line. She slipped out of her BCD, leaving it attached to the tank, and hauled the hinged, aluminium ladder up, tying it in place. She then scurried up the steps to the fly-bridge and started the diesel motor. Thomas had finished stowing the mooring line and looked up as he quickly made his way back around the side of the cabin. AJ still didn't know what the emergency was, but by Thomas's actions she'd realised they needed to get moving as soon as possible. His hand pointing to the north gave her the answer. She saw the big Hatteras, up on plane, heading straight out towards deep water, having come through the North Sound reef via Stingray Deep Channel cut. Hazel's Odyssey had been moored on Bear's Paw, east of the cut.

She dropped the Newton in drive and swung the boat around.

"Hold on Sully!" she yelled down, and Sully tossed his lime green weight belt into the crate they stored them in, and quit trying to wriggle out of his wetsuit. Instead he sat down and grabbed the rail behind the bench. Shoving the throttle forward, the revs quickly climbed, and the prop spun furiously in search of purchase in the water. The bow of Hazel's Odyssey rose rapidly and as she gathered speed AJ was able to level her out on plane and start the chase. Thomas clambered up the steps and joined AJ.

"So, what's the deal?" she asked, water flying from her wet hair and dripping wetsuit.

"I was listening to the VHF, heard the call from Whittaker himself. He said there's two possible hostages on the boat they were pursuing," Thomas said, out of breath.

"And that's the boat they're pursuing?" AJ asked, making sure.

"It's the Hatteras from the resort place, and he just ran the cut at wide-open throttle," Thomas replied, as a helicopter swept low over their heads in a direct line towards the boat they were chasing. They could easily read the word 'Police' emblazoned on the side of the copter. AJ looked at Thomas.

"Yeah, I think it's that boat."

She had the throttle pegged, and as they cleared the drop-off, the waves picked up a little more to a rolling swell. She glanced at the speed gauge; 26 knots. She had no idea what the Hatteras was capable of, but time would tell.

"Here, take the wheel," she said to Thomas, and let him move over to the pilot's chair. Dialling her mobile, she covered the microphone with her hand, protecting it from the wind rushing through the open fly-bridge.

"AJ, I'm afraid I'm rather in the thick of it right now, can I call you back?" Whittaker's voice said, sounding weary.

"Yeah, I just wanted to let you know we're chasing that Hatteras you're looking for. He's heading three degrees off north, heading for deep water, my guess would be the twelve-mile mark," AJ answered, shouting over the wind noise.

"You're chasing them?" Whittaker responded, sounding surprised. "How far behind them are you?"

"About four or five hundred yards I'd say, hard to tell if we're gaining or not but we're running wide open. Your chopper is just ahead of us tailing him too."

"AJ, don't try and engage those guys in any way, we have no idea what we're dealing with. From what we've learnt here, there's two men on board, and they should be considered dangerous. They may even be armed, we don't know. There's two girls on there too," Whittaker trailed off, sounding like he regretted adding that last part.

"Hallie one of them?" AJ immediately asked.

There was a pause. "I believe so, and the girl the men you heard discussing – I met her this morning. We believe they're both on board. I need to tell you to back off chasing them AJ, you know I have to tell you that."

"I know you do, sir, and I respect that. But you know I can't. If it makes you feel better, there's nothing we can do if we did catch them anyway, except follow them to the twelve-mile point," AJ replied.

"Okay, call me back if anything changes. Our Joint Marine Unit just left here, but they're ten minutes behind you. Of course, that boat will run over 50 knots, so it'll catch you at some point. The chopper is trying to raise the Hatteras on the radio, with no luck yet. By the way, the chopper pilot says you're slowly gaining on them. Please be careful," Whittaker finished, with genuine care in his voice.

"You know me, Roy, I won't do anything crazy," AJ replied and heard the man laugh as she hung up the phone.

Thomas looked at AJ as she tucked her mobile into a holder on the dash. "Hallie?"

AJ nodded. "They think she's on there."

Thomas turned back ahead; laser locked on the boat they were pursuing. He pushed on the throttle again, verifying for the umpteenth time it was wide open.

Sully climbed the steps to the fly-bridge. He'd managed to shed his wetsuit, and hung on to the framework as the Newton bounced and rocked in the open ocean. He carefully made his way to the front, next to Thomas and AJ.

"So, what exactly are we doing here?" he asked, a little out of breath, and sounding somewhat concerned. "I see we're heading towards Cuba at a great rate of knots. And there appears to be another boat ahead." He looked to the sky and shaded his eyes with a hand against the bright, late afternoon sun. "And a police helicopter involved."

AJ tried to smile, as though a smile would make the situation somehow seem better. "Yeah, so we're chasing that boat, which we believe is heading for international waters. We're pretty sure Thomas's cousin is aboard, and apparently another girl too."

"The girls are driving that big yacht?" Sully asked.

"No, no, there are two guys piloting the boat, from what we've been told," she corrected, and then realised that didn't help make anything sound better.

"Oh my," Sully said, looking a bit pale. "I assume these two gentlemen are unsavoury types?"

AJ looked at Sully and raised her eyebrows. "They're running from the police, not usually a thing innocent blokes do."

"No." He frowned and shook his head. "I don't suppose they do."

AJ reached past Thomas and put a hand on Sully's shoulder as the boat jolted and bounced through the waves. "Likely we'll just chase them out to international waters; there's really nothing we can do if we did catch up to them anyway. They've got size on their side."

Sully smiled but a frown still creased his forehead. "I write about this stuff all the time," he said quietly, "but I wasn't planning on getting in the middle of it actually happening, you understand?"

51

———————

SATURDAY

"We can't just sit here," Nora finally said, as the Hatteras continued to travel farther away from the island. She stood up and walked to the back of the salon, using her arms to steady herself against the rocking boat.

"Shit, you gotta see this, there's a helicopter chasing us!"

Hallie jumped up and stepped around several bottles rolling around the floor to join her at the rear door. Nothing had been secured before leaving the dock, and they'd heard all kinds of things crashing and banging around, as the Hatteras ploughed through the swells. She looked out the back and saw the helicopter about a hundred feet off the water, following them. Beyond that she saw another boat, which also appeared to be giving chase. Looked just like the dive boat she saw the other day, the one with the tattooed, purple-streaked-hair woman. Neither vessel seemed to be doing anything other than following.

"That doesn't look like a police boat, does it?" Nora asked, hanging on to the side of the bar as they ploughed along.

"I don't think so, I think they work with the resort somehow," Hallie replied tentatively.

"Really? Maybe we should just jump," Nora said and peered at the churned-up water behind them. "Or maybe we'd be killed in that mess and they'd run over our bodies."

"I think we should jump, and chance it," Hallie blurted out. "I have a bad feeling what's gonna happen if we stay on here."

Nora looked at her and scoffed. "I have no doubt what will happen if we stay here," she said with resignation. "Think about it. We're just baggage now. Their whole resort plan has fallen apart and these two are running for international waters. Last thing they need is us. We're dead as soon as they get the chance."

Hallie hadn't reached that conclusion as assuredly as Nora, so the words hit home, hard. Hallie felt a wave of fear surge through her; they really were in deep trouble. She watched the helicopter close on the boat. She had a sudden thought that SAS or SBS soldiers were about to lower down on cables from the helicopter, board the boat, and save them. But the copter flew right over them for some reason, and went ahead of the Hatteras. They watched its shadow go by through the starboard windows. When Hallie turned back, she froze in absolute terror. Raposa was outside the salon door, pulling rope and other stuff from the storage locker on the aft deck.

Nora grabbed her arm. "We gotta hide," she hissed through gritted teeth. They both turned and Hallie frantically tried to think where to go. It was a big boat, but not that big. She looked at the stairwell down to the staterooms and took off in that direction. Nora had apparently thought the same, as she was already heading that way. As Hallie struck out, she immediately trod on something smoothly rounded and her planted foot rolled straight out from underneath her. With her arms flailing for balance she crashed to the carpeted floor as a rush of cool, air-conditioned air swept over her towards the rear door. She bounced and landed roughly but quickly scrambled, pushing herself back to her feet. She gathered both feet under her and shoved hard with her right hand, ready to take off again, when she caught a glimpse of Nora. Her new friend turned from the top of the stairwell and glanced back with a look of horror on her face. A strong hand took Hallie's arm and spun her around. She looked straight into the eyes of the man she'd fanta-sised over for the past three days. The man she'd believed would take her from being a girl, to a woman. She watched his fist swiftly bear down on her delicate face, and felt the searing sting of the blow to her left cheek.

Knocked senseless and disorientated, she fought to stay conscious as he dragged her across the salon by her feet. As she bounced violently over the door frame to the aft deck, she saw the upside-down image of Nora hesitating at the top of the stairs across the salon. The door swung closed and she was left alone with her face burning and aching. She fought the nauseous feeling in her stomach. Raposa roughly held her legs, binding them with some-thing coarse and painfully tight. Her head cleared as the salty air rushed over her, and she tried to sit up. As she did Raposa's strong arms lifted her up like a bag of rice, and threw her over his shoul-der. She could tell they were going down the steps to the narrow swim platform at the stern, and her head bounced against his torso. She felt the firmness of his muscular back and powerful shoulders as the sweet smell of his perspiration filled her senses. What she'd yearned for now felt so hateful. She reached out to grab anything she could find, but her hands slid down the slick, wet fibreglass of the boat and found no purchase. She'd survived for so long on her physical speed and quick thinking, but the past few moments had happened so fast, and with such decisive force, she felt overwhelm-ingly helpless.

She wanted to fight, but she had no strength. She wanted to run, but there was no way to escape. She knew the end was close, and could only hope it was swift and painless. She prayed Nora had found a good hiding place.

52

SATURDAY

The helicopter had already flown ahead of the Cova do Leão and dropped even lower, trying to persuade the boat to slow, AJ presumed. The three had watched from the Newton as a man descended from the enclosed fly-bridge of the Hatteras to the aft deck. He'd rummaged through a storage cabinet on the port side, but they couldn't see what he'd taken out. He'd flung the door to the salon open and a few moments later reappeared, struggling with something, but again their view was obscured by the low wall across the back of the aft deck. With horror, they'd realised what he'd been doing, as he slung what appeared to be a girl over his shoulder and started down the rear steps to the swim platform.

"Spot the entry point Thomas!" AJ yelled and ran to the ladder, sliding down the rails instead of using the steps. She looked around the bouncing boat for what she needed, starting long inhalations of breath. She grabbed her mask that was hooked over her BCD, and her fins from under the bench below that, sliding them over her right wrist. She put her mask on as she snagged the first weight belt she found in the crate. It happened to be bright green, with weights for a larger man. Feeling Hazel's Odyssey suddenly slow, she knew she had only moments to gather what she might need. Strapping the belt around her waist she heard Thomas yell from above.

"Now!"

AJ took two steps across the deck, jumped to the bench, pulled her dive knife from its sheath on her BCD still hanging on a tank, and continued in a singular motion over the side. She hit the water hard, with the boat still moving pretty fast, tumbling down below the surface, one hand holding her mask in place and the other gripping the knife. Sea water leaked through her mask seal as the force of the impact and turbulent water tried to wrench it from her face. Her fins pulled and swirled from her wrist, hitting her in the head, then her side, and yanking on her arm. Every instinct screamed at her to reach back for the surface as the violence of the entry tried to pound the air from her lungs. AJ willed her mind to stay calm, let the turmoil happen around her, and her muscles relaxed. As the rolling slowed, she orientated herself and slid her fins on her feet. She spotted the girl, maybe thirty feet below her and some way ahead; she'd have to swim down diagonally to reach her. It was hard to focus as the salt water in her mask swirled around and stung her eyes. Instinctively, she wanted to clear the mask by exhaling through her nose and letting the air push the water out, but she remembered in time; she wasn't on a scuba tank, she needed every molecule of air in her lungs. She aimed below the girl's position and swept her legs in long, even strokes, making the fins do all the work.

She could see the girl was clawing at the water with her arms, trying to swim up, but a rope around her ankles pulled her down with some kind of weight tied to it. She knew the girl would quickly run out of breath working that hard, but fighting the descent was the only way she could get to her. AJ continued her long sweeping kicks, but the closing rate was agonisingly slow, and her lungs began to burn as the oxygen was used up from her own efforts. She saw the girl look her way, and recognised Hallie from seeing her the previous day. She knew the kid wouldn't be able to focus without a mask; she just hoped she could make out help on its way, and not think it was a further threat. By Hallie's determined strokes for the surface, she still had some fight left. AJ stole a glance at her dive watch and saw she was passing sixty feet. She'd done a fair amount of freediving for fun, but she was by no means skilled at it, and fifty feet was usually her comfortable limit. The most she'd been down to on breath hold was sixty-five feet, which she now passed through, and was still more than ten feet from the descending girl. As the water pressure increased and lessened the effective buoyancy of the air in their lungs, their rate of descent increased so it felt like she was chasing an accelerating train.

AJ was close enough to see Hallie's face, and could tell she was losing her. The girl's efforts were slowing and her eyes losing lucidity. She was sure she'd get to her, but was now doubting if either of them could make the surface alive. AJ saw the image of the poor girl they'd found, floating face down. She saw her face as they'd rolled her over. She saw the grey hue to her beautiful skin. With gritted teeth, AJ kicked with all her might. She reached Hallie and kept going until she could grab the girl's legs. With a sweep of the short, serrated blade of her dive knife she severed the rope and released the weight. Immediately Hallie's body slowed its descent, and the taut pull on her torso was relieved. AJ ripped the catch open on her own weight belt and let it go, feeling her own descent come to a halt. Hallie's legs feebly kicked as she tried to swim up. AJ took the girl's hand and used her fins to start the long haul back to the precious air eighty feet above them. Her lungs were on fire, but she knew the more they ascended the more the water pressure lessened its clamp on their lungs, and it would feel like they had gained some air back. She just hoped Hallie could hang on that long. She hoped *she* could hang on that long. The saltwater stung the hell out of her eyes, but the light above them was a beautiful sight, and she could make out the silhouette of the Newton.

AJ's mind began to lose focus and her vision started to fog. She looked down at Hallie, who was no longer kicking, a dead weight dragging behind her. Thoughts wouldn't stay clearly in her consciousness, and the idea of letting go tried to take hold. AJ had been here before; she had enough clarity of mind to keep telling herself to fight. To kick, to make the surface. It seemed like it was right there, another kick away, but with each new kick she still didn't get there. She felt her strength draining away and her legs weren't doing what she asked. A tiny part of her oxygen-starved brain still yelled for her to keep pushing, but it couldn't make her muscles respond. She felt herself slipping away. She looked up and the boat seemed so close. She saw what appeared to be a hand reaching down, deep into the water towards her, and she stretched out to touch it. But it wasn't a hand.

AJ shoved the regulator into her mouth and took a long, deep breath while hitting the purge valve to flush the water from the mouthpiece. She quickly took two more breaths, before pushing the reg into Hallie's mouth and purging again. Hallie hung from AJ's arm, limp and frail, with the regulator resting in her mouth, but no sign of movement. And then the girl's throat heaved, and a thin stream of bubbles escaped the reg. AJ couldn't believe it. Breathe girl, breathe, she urged. Hallie's body convulsed and her eyes twitched. She let her keep trying to suck in breath and kicked hard with her fins, dragging the regulator hose with them for the last fifteen feet to the top.

They broke the surface behind Hazel's Odyssey with two pairs of arms reaching down to grab them. Thomas and Sully dragged them both aboard and AJ coughed and choked and sucked in the glorious, hot, humid air. Hallie pulled the regulator from her mouth, rolled on her side and coughed up a stream of sea water. She spluttered and croaked, trying to speak.

"Take it easy Hallie," Thomas said soothingly. "You're safe now, just give it a minute, you gotta catch your breath back."

Hallie reached for Thomas's arm and looked up at him, her voice barely audible. "Nora. Nora's still on their boat."

53

SATURDAY

Nora had spent six weeks in training on the Cova do Leão, and several nights aboard as a host after that. She'd explored every inch of the eighty-foot vessel. If there was a nook or cranny, she knew where it was. When Raposa had grabbed Hallie, her instinct had been to run back across the salon and help her. But she knew it would be tackling Raposa in his element; she wouldn't stand a chance. She'd also explored every inch of the man, and he was built to scrap. She, on the other hand, was 110 pounds, soaking wet. There was nothing she could do for Hallie, except hope the girl would find a way to stay alive. Nora decided her only chance was to remain out of reach until help arrived, and for help to arrive she had to slow this boat down. Hoping he'd seen her going down the stairwell to the staterooms, she'd come back up while he was busy at the stern and hidden in the storage below the curved, cushioned couch in the breakfast room. It was a snug fit, but she was able to wriggle down and pulled the cushioned board back over her, praying nothing looked out of place from above.

It felt like forever, just laying still and waiting, as the boat droned on as fast as it would go. Sound was muffled by her wood and cushioned surroundings, so she felt the diesels' throb through the hull, more than heard them. What she was waiting for was foot-steps, and she had no idea if she'd hear, feel or sense them in any way. But she did. She guessed Raposa must be figuring she's trapped downstairs with only one way out, so why be quiet. The subtle patter of feet vibrated through the boat's flooring, and it seemed to lessen as it went, so she gambled he was going down and away from her. If she'd missed him descending the stairs, and he was in fact on his way back up, she was a dead rabbit. Pushing the cushion carefully aside, Nora climbed from the under the couch storage, and stepped softly across the small room to the galley. Stairs led up from her left, curving around to the fly-bridge above, and the sound of radio chatter echoed down the stairwell. She care-fully continued, listening for any sounds giving a clue to Raposa's whereabouts. Peeking into the salon she didn't see him, but heard a door close firmly downstairs. He was likely searching room by room. It wouldn't take him long and he'd be back up. She scurried across the salon and silently opened the door to the aft deck, slip-ping through and closing it tightly behind her. Nora had held an unrealistic hope she'd find Hallie, trussed up on the aft deck, but she was nowhere to be seen. Nor was the boat that had been following them. The helicopter was now off to the side and higher up, but swept lower as she descended the steps to the stern. Damn it, she thought, don't give me away.

She opened the hatch in the stern that led down to the crew quarters and the engine room. Stepping down through the small doorway, she turned and dogged the security ring for the water-tight hatch behind her. She knew once she was in the engine room she'd be trapped. There was only one door, and the noise of the diesels would prevent her hearing anyone approaching, unless she could shut them down. She didn't have a choice. Moving down the narrow hallway, she passed the cross hall to the crew's tiny state-rooms, and kept going forward. Ahead was a soundproof door with a small, double-glazed window, allowing her to peer in at the big motors. She went through the door and closed it behind her.

The room had low-voltage lights running at all times, and she figured that ought to be enough for her to see by so she didn't search for the main light switch. Nora had no clue what made the diesels run or, more specifically, how to stop them, but she looked around for any kind of switch or lever. She walked down the gap between the engines, which vibrated and droned a deafeningly loud, guttural roar, and she wished she'd grabbed a pair of earmuffs she'd seen on hooks when she came in. Behind the port side engine, she saw a red tool chest under a bench, with numerous drawers. Behind the starboard engine were two large metal machines marked 'Onan'. Lines, conduits and bunches of wires ran everywhere in the room, all neatly secured to the walls and ceiling. She had no idea what any of it did. Against the wall ahead was a large white box with more clusters of wires and to the right another dark grey, plastic control box of some sort. Printed on the front were the words 'Engine Room Module'. Big wires or cables plugged into the sides of that box in about ten places. Nora decided it looked really important and, reaching over, she tried pulling one of the plugs out. It didn't budge. She yanked, pulled and wrenched on the plug, to no avail. Cussing to herself, she took a firm grip and threw her bodyweight at the stubborn connection. It resisted again, but her effort made her lose her footing, and she slipped on the metal floor. Hanging on to the plug to stop her fall, she inadvertently twisted the connection, and off it came, sending the cable loose and her sprawling to the deck. She yelped as she skinned her knee and bashed her already bruised arm on a pipe. She thought she heard a change in the sound of one of the engines. Re-energised, she leapt up and started twisting more connections loose. A couple changed the engines' note some more, and the fourth one shut them both down.

The Cova do Leão rapidly slowed as the big boat dropped deeper into the water and picked up more drag from the hull. The sound slowly lowered in the engine room and the lights blinked a couple of times. One of the big boxes marked 'Onan' whirred and kicked into life, making her jump, and sounding like a new engine starting up. The boat didn't accelerate again, but the lights stopped blinking. Generator, Nora decided. She didn't have much time now, she needed to get out; they'd be down to the engine room to see what the problem was. She ran to the door and pulled it open. As she did, she saw the wheel spin on the exit hatch. She had less time than she'd imagined. Racing back inside the engine room she wriggled by the back of the port engine and started pulling drawers open on the tool chest. She found screwdrivers, pliers and all kinds of smaller hand tools but it took until the last drawer to see anything useful: a large adjustable spanner. She turned and dropped to her knees. Machinery in the back of the room hid her from the window in the door, but she needed to get closer to the entryway. Her goal was to slip out the door, after whoever it was came in, hoping they'd leave the hatch open so she could bolt straight outside. She crept along the floor, but stopped when she heard the metal hinges creak as the door opened. She carefully shuffled up to sit on her haunches, and waited. A sandalled foot appeared, and she glanced up, straight into the face of Raposa, looking right back at her. Nora exploded upwards, and swung the wrench with all her might, feeling the hard steel contact something soft that gave way with her blow. She heard a low groan and pushed past the falling man to slip through the door into the hallway. She dared not look at what she'd done, she simply ran. Looking ahead she was relieved to see the hatch hung open. Clambering up the steps, she ducked through the opening and stood on the swim platform with the rear railing before her. She looked at the spanner still in her hand. Blood covered the end of the metal, dripping to the deck. A sound from above made her turn and she looked up to the aft deck. Van Heerden looked down at her with hatred in his eyes.

"You little bitch," he growled and started down the steps towards her. She launched the spanner in his direction and dove off the side of the swim platform, into the water, and kicked as hard as she could. She stayed under, swimming for all she was worth until her lungs could take it no more. When she finally surfaced, she was fifteen yards from the boat, and the sound of sirens filled the air.

She spun around to see the Joint Marine Police boat coasting towards the Hatteras, officers on the bow with guns pointed at Van Heerden, who was clutching his shoulder with his opposite hand. The dive boat they'd seen earlier pulled up next to her. Initially she was unsure whether they were friendly, until she spotted Hallie leaning over the railing.

A cool-looking woman with purple streaks in her blonde hair and tattoos down each arm reached over the side and guided Nora to the ladder at the back of the boat. She wearily climbed aboard and threw her arms around Hallie.

"Thank God you're alive," Nora whispered.

Hallie squeezed her so tight she could barely breathe.

54

TWO WEEKS LATER

AJ watched Jen walk over to the table for two in the back corner, where she sat with Detective Whittaker. Jen placed two coffees down.

"Are you sure that's all you want? I've got some lovely muffins, fresh out the oven."

"I'm good thanks Jen," AJ replied and Whittaker politely smiled and shook his head.

"Alright then. The internet's down I'm afraid," she said loudly, then leaned in and whispered, "Add an exclamation mark to the password: it's working. I just have a group of eight that, so far, have ordered one coffee to share, but they're all trying to get their phones on to my Wi-Fi."

AJ chuckled as Jen went back to the counter.

"So, tell me how young Hallie Bodden is doing?" Whittaker asked.

AJ smiled. "Really well I believe. Thomas's parents have filed for custody as guardians, and she's been living with them. She went back to school to finish her final year. Apparently it's as though she never missed any classes at all, she's more advanced than most of the other kids."

"Good to hear," the detective replied warmly.

"What's happening with the case? Do you have what you need to lock them up?" AJ asked more seriously.

Whittaker slowly nodded. "I believe we will. Please keep all the details to yourself, but we found a fishing priest. It's like a billy club for smacking a fish once it's on the boat. Anyway, we found one on the small boat at the resort. It has traces of blood and hair we matched to the girl you found. Carlina Arias was her name, by the way; she was Dominican. The club also had fingerprints from the man they called Raposa. There was rope on the boat too: it matched the fibres we found in the girl's ankle wounds. That evidence, plus the attempted murder on Hallie, and we have plenty on him. Of course, he'll be in the hospital for a while yet, I'm told it'll be a few more surgeries until they get his jaw pieced back together. That fella will be drinking through a straw for some time to come."

AJ couldn't help a smirk. "What about Sombrio?"

Whittaker sipped his coffee and took a moment. "We have her on human trafficking as well as human smuggling, which are two different things. She was bringing the girls, and the other staff, here to the island illegally, which is the smuggling part. With the statements from the girls, and Bill Russo – he was one of the members at the resort when we raided it – we can prove human trafficking. She was having the girls work under false pretences and guarantees of money. Of course, there's the prostitution angle as well, but the girls never actually got paid, so we're focusing on the trafficking angle."

"It seems incredible, all this was going on right there, tucked away in Salt Creek," AJ said, shaking her head.

"Well, Sombrio was clever," Whittaker replied. "She set everything up legally as a resort. It was the personnel side that crossed lines. And the whole intention of the place, of course. The US Federal authorities have taken quite an interest in the membership list – appears most of them were US citizens."

"And what happens with the girls, Roy? I feel so bad for them.

Seems like they were tricked into believing there'd be a better life at the end of this."

"No doubt," he agreed. "Very unfortunate. But sadly, we have to return them to their native countries, the staff too. Those ladies were all from Venezuela. They were getting paid, or rather their families were. A pathetic amount, but a little goes a long way in rural Venezuela." The detective went to take another sip of coffee, but paused and continued speaking. "The other two employees had quite the pasts as well. The boat captain Van Heerden, whose real name is Van Meerden, is wanted in South Africa on under-age pornography charges. We'll extradite him and he can take up a jail cell back home. The woman the girls knew as Marguerite is actually Helena Grossman, a German national, who also came up on Interpol's radar. She ran a shelter for runaway girls, but fled Germany eleven years ago, when several former residents came forward claiming they'd been coerced into sexual relations with the woman. We're looking into extraditing her too."

AJ was dumbfounded. "That's insane, how on earth did these people get on the island, without being flagged in immigration?"

"Really good false papers, it appears. They also brought all the girls and maids in by boat; they never passed through immigration," Whittaker replied.

"But the girls, Roy? Some of them will go back to some horrible situations, from what Hallie told us. She only met three of them, but they all had troubled backgrounds," AJ urged sympathetically.

"I agree, but it's in the hands of our immigration department I'm afraid." He took another sip of his coffee before continuing. "I did want to ask you something, actually."

"Sure," AJ replied. "What's on your mind?"

"You haven't seen, or heard from Nora, have you?" Whittaker asked, his face blank and hard to read.

"Nora? No, I haven't seen her since the day on the boat. Hallie and I asked a few days after if we could visit her, wherever the girls were being held, and we were told we couldn't at that time," AJ answered, curious about the question.

"Yes, well, we weren't really set up to detain the girls while immigration sorted out what to do with them, so we kept them in the dorms at the resort, and placed a couple of officers with them. It was not an arrangement that was made to accommodate visitors, I'm afraid."

"I see," AJ said, still curious. "Why do you ask about Nora?"

Whittaker frowned. "It appears young Nora didn't care for those arrangements. She slipped away, and we can't find her."

"Oh, wow, well she didn't contact me, but I'll let you know if she does," AJ replied, wondering what the girl was up to.

Whittaker sat back in his chair. "Funny thing, we got back a hit from her fingerprints. Turns out they matched a missing person from Norway. Girl took off on a little sailboat with a gentleman and they both went missing, presumed dead. Supposedly the girl was a very competent sailor. Happened over a year ago. They found wreckage of the sailboat but no bodies. I went over to Salt Creek to ask her about it, and she'd gone."

AJ tapped her finger on the table. "Wait a second, didn't a really nice sailboat just go missing from Crystal Harbour?"

Whittaker nodded. "Indeed it did, day after Nora disappeared the boat was noticed missing. I don't know a thing about sailing boats, but I was told it was a very nice 32' Jeanneau, worth a lot of money by all accounts."

"I'm no expert either," AJ added thoughtfully. "I've never really sailed much, but some of those nice sailboats you can sail single-handed, I believe?"

Whittaker nodded again. "So I'm told. Has to have all the right computerised equipment and controls, apparently."

"This boat have all that?" AJ asked, pretty sure she already knew the answer.

"This particular Jeanneau Sun Fast 3200 was equipped with every piece of gear needed to sail the Caribbean, alone, according to what the owner told me."

They looked at each other, and neither could hold back a slight smile.

ACKNOWLEDGMENTS

My biggest supporters are my amazing wife Cheryl and my great friend James Guthrie, who both offer their honest and incredibly supportive feedback. I'm blessed with love and encouragement from my wonderful Mum and my brother Michael, along with his family.

I've come to rely on and place enormous trust in my editor, Andrew Chapman; the final touch to my books is in his caring and capable hands. He can be found at PrepareToPublish.

Thanks to the incorrigible Jen Skrinska of Greenhouse Café and our lovely friend Casey Keller for their input and permissions. A big thank you to my friend and fellow author Nick Sullivan for allowing me to have some fun with his character. You'll love his series, available on Amazon.

Along with Nick, a couple more fantastic authors have offered their help, guidance and friendship. Wayne Stinnett and Cap Daniels; Gentlemen, you have my respect and everlasting gratitude.

I'm proud to have Drew McArthur's stunning photography gracing the cover of this book, and hopefully more to come. Thanks to Sigrid Menschaart for her perfect silhouette!

Thank you so much to my growing ARC group whose input and feedback is invaluable, and improves the final product.

Above all I thank you, the readers: it is your kind words that have opened the door to more adventures for AJ Bailey and myself.

LET'S STAY IN TOUCH!

To buy merchandise, find more info or join my Newsletter, visit my
website at
www.HarveyBooks.com

If you enjoyed this novel I'd be incredibly grateful if you'd consider
leaving a review on Amazon.com
Find eBook deals and follow me on BookBub.com

Visit Amazon.com for more books in the
AJ Bailey Adventure Series,
Nora Sommer Caribbean Suspense Series,
and collaborative works;
The Greene Wolfe Thriller Series
Tropical Authors Adventure Series

ABOUT THE AUTHOR

A *USA Today* Bestselling author, Nicholas Harvey's life has been anything but ordinary. Race car driver, adventurer, divemaster, and since 2020, a full-time novelist. Raised in England, Nick has dual US and British citizenship and now lives wherever he and his amazing wife, Cheryl, park their motorhome, or an aeroplane takes them. Warm oceans and tall mountains are their favourite places.

For more information, visit his website at HarveyBooks.com.